D0922246

THE PIONEER
A Journey to the Pacific

An American Journeys Novel

Richard Alan Schwartz

Village Drummer Fiction
www.villagedrummerfiction.com

Previously published under the titles *American Journeys: From Ireland to the Pacific Northwest Book2, American Journeys: The Pacific Northwest and the Oregon Trail,* and *American Journeys: From Ireland to the Pacific Northwest (1847 - 1900)*. Content has not changed. Title change and Author name change (from pen name of Richard Alan to legal name of Richard Alan Schwartz) necessitated a new ISBN number.

ISBN: 978-1-970070-27-9 (print)
ISBN: 978-1-970070-28-6 (Kindle)

Previous ISBN:
ISBN: 978-0-9974546-7-3 (print) ISBN: 978-0-9974546-1-1 (Kindle)
ISBN: 978-1-970070-18-7 (print) ISBN: 978-1-970070-19-4 (Kindle)

Dedication

This book is dedicated to my grandson Zane. May your life be filled with good health, scholarship, Jewish values and life-long learning. It is also dedicated to my wife and partner Carolynn.

Notice

In this volume, faithful readers will notice the name of Myra and David's daughter has been changed from Ciaran to Ciara. The former is the masculine form of the name so required a change. My thanks to an eagle-eyed reader who noticed and advised me of the correct spelling.

Contents

THE PIONEER

A Journey to the Pacific

PART ONE

Prologue

From enclaves in the east, Americans, a people with wanderlust in their veins, became emigrants. Their perilous journeys across the continent and sea voyages through Panama and on to the west coast, hardened most but destroyed others. They suffered the loss of family and friends due to buffalo stampedes, torrential storms, and tempests at sea. The emotional and physical battering shaped those who survived as metal is hardened and formed in a forge.

Chapter One: Families Reunite in Seattle

Kathleen Kaufman, a black-haired, short, slim, woman in her mid-twenties, walked along the dock next to her sister. "It's such a relief now that you're here."

Similar size and similar appearance but for her bright red hair, Myra Kaplan, her husband, four children and sister-in-law had disembarked from their sailing ship. They had endured a sea voyage from New Orleans to Panama, a rail journey across that isthmus, and up the West Coast of Central America and the States to Portland Oregon.

Myra's sister-in-law Sarah said, "Believe me. We're glad to be here as well."

Kathleen nodded at Sarah's swollen belly.

"Due in a three months," Sarah said. "You?"

"A few weeks."

Sarah said, "We heard about Jack when we were transiting Panama. I'm so sorry."

The corners of Kathleen's mouth turned down briefly. She replaced her frown with a forced smile. "Let's enjoy your arrival. We'll talk about him later."

"Are those scars on your cheek?" Myra asked.

"Later," Kathleen said.

Myra's ten-year-old daughter Abbey stated, "Hey, after so many weeks at sea, it feels funny to walk on ground."

Five-year-old William giggled. "It's not moving."

Seven-year-old Nathan shifted from one foot to the other and laughed. "I don't need sea legs anymore."

"No more sea-sickness," Celeste said, clapping her hands in celebration.

"Kathleen, I want you to meet Celeste. She's five and lost her family during a tornado. She's part of our family now."

"Welcome," Kathleen said and turned to Myra's husband. "David," she said, as a man of medium build approached them. "I'd like you to meet Mr. Breuer. Mr. Breuer, this is my business partner, David Kaplan."

"A pleasure to meet you sir."

"I as well."

Mr. Breuer made a sweeping gesture at the building and wharf space behind him. "This is your storage company, sir. Over there, the woodshop and ironworks. Twenty-six men on staff right now. Sorry about Mr. Kaufman. I'd never actually met him as he died so soon after he arrived."

David's head spun to Kathleen. "What woodshop and ironworks?"

She shrugged. "Apparently it was part of the deal that Jack purchase all of it."

"You've been running the place alone?" David asked.

Suddenly grim faced, her body stiffened, Kathleen nodded. "It wasn't easy but you taught me well. Plus Mr. Breuer and the others stood by me."

"Mr. Kaplan, if you'll show me your goods, I'll get them on wagons for you and young Jamison will go with you to help unload."

"We don't have much," David said.

Kathleen regarded Myra with a questioning expression.

"Two weeks before we left Independence, a tornado came through and destroyed our home along with the majority of our belongings. We have clothing and a few other items." Myra sighed deeply. "Thank the good Lord, we all survived and the store was still intact so we lived in the apartment above it until we sailed out here."

"Aunt Kathleen, we found our Sabbath candleholder almost a block away," William said. "And I held Ciara while Dad, me, and Nathan were in the storm cellar."

"My mom, dad, and brother died," five-year-old Celeste said. "The tornado killed them. These are my mom and dad now. The tornado put a big hole in my leg. William stopped it from bleeding and Abbey sewed up the hole."

"Abbey sewed?" Kathleen said.

Myra nodded. "Remember all the time she and Nathan practiced on animal skin? Dr. Beckham injured his hands.

He asked Abbey to close Celeste's and many other's wounds."

"My niece the future doctor." Kathleen grinned. She turned to Nathan. "Did you sew up anyone?"

He nodded. "I didn't put in as many stitches as Abbey but I must have put a million bandages and splints on lots of bloody injuries."

***

Their wagons stopped in front of two similar two-story homes south of Portland.

"The one on the left is mine, Kathleen said, "and the similar one twenty-yards past it is yours. Frame houses with lots of room. Four bedrooms upstairs and a lovely kitchen. Each of our lots contains forty-acres but Jack wanted the houses near each other. I've started adjoining gardens for each of us."

"They're lovely," Myra said as she admired the two buildings, each with porch wrapping around the front and sides.

"I met a Turkish man just after I arrived. He sells fruit trees. I had him plant an orchard for each of us. They meet at the property line so we can work on them together."

"An orchard. How thoughtful," Myra said.

"What type of fruit?" Sarah asked.

"Apples, peaches, pears, and apricots."

"Apri-whats?" Nathan asked.

"Apricot. A small fruit but honey sweet," Kathleen said. "I've also planted a vegetable garden. A man from California has been tending the garden and orchard for us. In payment, he gets half the crop."

"The children can help with that now."

"We haven't even seen the inside of our new house and Mom is lining up chores for us," Abbey said to much laughter.

Myra and the children hurried into their new home.

Kathleen hung back. As David and the helper unloaded their possessions, she walked up to him and threw her arms around him. He embraced her and noticed her tears.

"What's wrong?"

"It's been the worst time of my life; trying to run things without you or Jack."

Chapter Two: Kimimela's Struggle

"I will go there alone and die surrounded by the mountains' beauty."

Early one morning while the other's slept, Kimimela took a bow and arrows, a knife, and a tiny amount of dry tinder to be used as fire starter. With a sorrowful glance over her shoulder and final heart-wrenching glimpses of her parents, brother, and young sister, she set out on the four-week journey. Kimimela shivered as the damp and dreary late winter air whipped around her. She'd left her warmest clothes behind in the hope someone who wasn't heading out with the intention of ending their life could use them.

It was a cold, late March day in 1854. The previous year, summer was brief and produced little food. The cold, damp fall dealt the Native Americans a second blow as few salmon swam up the streams from Puget Sound. They depended on smoked fish for surviving the winter months. Even the usually plentiful fruits and berries were scarce so there was little to dry and store. Many of the tribe's children became sick and died as the tribe rationed their meager food stocks.

Kimimela considered her empty womb which, in three years of marriage, hadn't produced a child.

She shook her head and thought, *"A woman who can't produce children is a burden on the others. And now that I am gone, there will be one less mouth to feed."*

***

Kimimela traveled for three days without food. The movement of a rabbit caught her eye. Kimimela moved across the leaf-strewn terrain with as much stealth as her shivering body could muster and put an arrow through the rabbit. After roasting on a fire and saving half for the next day, she thanked the rabbit for giving her a few days strength to continue her journey. It removed the hunger pangs; if only temporarily.

On the morning of the seventh day, she awoke and found a whitetail deer silently grazing ten yards away. It wasn't aware of her presence. While moving at a snail's pace, she gradually put an arrow in her bow and from a sitting position, sent the arrow in the deer's direction. The moment the arrow struck, just behind the Deer's front shoulder blade, it leaped up, all four legs off the ground, and ran. She grabbed her few belongings and pursued it. She followed a blood trail all morning. Her lack of food was catching up to her. Kimimela's body was tired and her thighs and calves ached. They wanted to stop but her mind knew she must keep going despite the pain or a predator might steal her kill.

After a grueling six-hour chase, she located the deer where it collapsed next to a stream. She took a moment to thank the deer for giving up its life so she could eat, quickly hung it from a tree, and used her knife to gut the animal. Kimimela struggled to remove a hind quarter. With a twist of her knife at the hip joint the leg fell free.

A low growl echoed through the woods. She shuddered. A bear, likely just ending his winter hibernation and ravenously hungry, must have scented her kill. Kimimela hoisted the leg onto her shoulder, and moved as quickly as possible away from the area; leaving the balance of the kill for the bear so it would, hopefully, occupy itself with the remaining carcass and not pursue her.

Her calves and thighs seemed to be on fire while the sweat pouring down her face felt cool. Kimimela pushed herself for the next four-hours. Not an easy task with her tiny frame carrying an additional forty-pound-weight which she alternated from one shoulder to the other. The longer she hiked, the heavier her burden seemed.

Late in the afternoon, Kimimela traveled underneath darkening skies while an icy cold wind chafed her cheeks and exposed lower legs. Her skilled hands lit a fire which began as tiny glowing embers but which she coaxed into a crackling warm blaze. She sliced the venison into strips which she hung beside the fire on a hastily constructed rack made of small branches. Being desperately hungry, the first two strips were eaten before they were heated through. She kept the flames going all night, drying the meat, plus enjoying the fire's warmth and protection. Even the mighty bear feared flame.

The following morning's sky was covered with leaden grey clouds. She thanked the gods for watching over her and giving man the ability to control fire.

Her cache of dried venison was consumed sparingly during the next few weeks and was occasionally supplemented by meager handfuls of berries and roots.

She'd run out of food a few days before she arrived at the lake the Salish tribe called *Tsi Laan.* Kimimela spent one night sleeping next to the lake. Using the last of her strength, she walked into the mountains north of the lake to the picturesque place she remembered visiting the previous summer. When she arrived, she sat down at the base of a large tree and admired the view of the distant lake, the huge heavily wooded valley to her east bordered by far away mountains, as well as the long range of jagged mountains to the north. She looked at the row of raspberry bushes which were lifeless now but would burst forth in the summer's sun with deep-red, juicy berries.

A tear came to her eye as her mind flooded with warm memories of her family. She put her hands to her face and cried. Pain in Kimimela's empty belly reminded her life would be over soon but the knowledge the others in her tribe would be better off warmed her.

The western sky was dark with clouds. She deeply inhaled the crisp mountain air and thought, "*Snow will be here shortly. I will die adorned in white vestment. This is a good place to end my life's journey. Please gods, take me now so I can forever be a part of your beautiful mountains.*"

Chapter Three: Kathleen's Story

Following evening meal, Kathleen removed apricots from her apron. They were gathered around the kitchen table in the Kaplan's home.

"Be careful," she said. "There's a seed in the middle that you don't eat."

"The juice exploded in my mouth when I bit it," Nathan said, wiping his chin.

"Honey-sweet, indeed," Myra said.

"Mmm, we need lots of these," Celeste said.

"We can put them in jars for the winter but folk out here also dry them and eat them like candy or bake with them."

"Kathleen," Myra said. "Have you heard from your family?"

"The wanted to come out here but need more money."

"Your sister Daire?"

"Believe she's around sixteen now. Mom wrote that she's a strong and tough young lady."

"Like her big sister," David said with a laugh.

Kathleen looked around the table at the smiling faces. "Let me tell you about Jack and my arrival." She took a deep breath, noted her listeners rapt attention, and leaned forward in her chair with her hands clasped and elbows on the table. "Our ship docked mid-day Saturday. We moved into the house next door. On Sunday morning, we decided to take a buckboard ride on a trail that paralleled the Columbia River. After an hour, we discovered a broad meadow which was blanketed with wildflowers so we ate a meal there. The weather was cool and damp but we loved being off the ship."

"I know that feeling," Sarah said.

"On the way home Jack pulled the buckboard to a stop when we saw two bear cubs playing next to the river. They were only a handful of yards away. They noticed us, started bawling, and shinnied up a tree." Kathleen appeared lost in thought for a moment then continued, "I remember our horse seemed anxious when we stopped. He kept tossing his head and wanted to continue but Jack held him back. We should have heeded his warning." Kathleen looked at the anxious faces surrounding the table. "We were laughing at their antics when the cubs' mother attacked us."

Myra gasped, putting her hand over her mouth.

"She sunk her teeth into Jack's shoulder and flipped her head, throwing him to the ground. He landed like a rag doll. The bear slugged my face with a huge paw, knocking me unconscious. The blow tossed me onto the back of the buckboard—fortunately as it turned out."

The children's faces were horror struck.

"I have no memory of it, but the commotion must have spooked our horse. A farmer and his wife who live just outside town, noticed a buckboard without a driver. They brought it to a halt. I was barely conscious and not coherent. They brought me in their house and found a doctor to check on me and dress my wounds. The scars on my cheek are from the bear's claws."

"What happened to Uncle Jack?" Abbey asked.

With tears welling up in her eyes, she still attempted to smile. Kathleen sat up straight, looked at each of them, and said, "A number of men went to look for his body but couldn't find it."

"Did the bear drag him away?" William asked.

"We don't know for sure but...probably."

"Poor Uncle Jack," Nathan said, shaking his head.

"Too bad you didn't have a gun or a rifle," William said.

"Everything happened so fast, I don't know if it would have made a difference. If we'd known better, we'd have avoided the cubs."

"It's getting late. Bedtime children," Myra said. "We have lots to do tomorrow. Say goodnight to Aunt Kathleen."

"I'll tuck them in," Sarah said.

Abbey walked up to Kathleen and gave her a hug. "I'm going to miss Uncle Jack."

"He told us such funny stories," Nathan said, wiping a tear off his cheek.

"Uncle Jack taught me how to be a scout," William said.

Kathleen nodded. The children hugged her and ran upstairs with their Aunt Sarah.

David asked, "The bear grabbed his shoulder?"

"Not really. I said that for the children's benefit."

David hesitated for a moment, then asked. "What happened?"

"It ripped his throat out and grabbed the back of his neck in its jaws."

"Oh no." Myra said.

"I heard bone breaking. According to the doctor who treated me, Jack was likely dead before he was tossed off the buckboard."

Myra wrapped her arms around her sister. The two held each other and wept.

Ten minutes later, David asked, "Why has it been hell running the business?"

Kathleen crossed her arms. She replied in an angry tone. "You mean besides men yelling and cursing at me because they don't want to do business with a woman or the fact that I haven't slept much as I've had to do all the accounting myself; even with a degreed accountant working as a laborer for us and not being able to use his ability?"

"Why not?" David said as Sarah rejoined them.

"He's negro. I've been advised a negro and a single white woman working in the same office could cause problems."

"Disgusting," Sarah said shaking her head. "My dad hired negro men at the ironworks. They worked hard like anyone else; but I understand your predicament."

"He'll be working in the office tomorrow." David said.

Kathleen folded her arms as if hugging herself. "I felt so alone. Only this baby and the knowledge you would be out here gave me the energy to keep working."

Myra put a hand on her sister's shoulder. "You're not alone now."

Kathleen relaxed her posture and smiled. "I know. They'll be no more yelling with David and Sarah around."

"How big is the Jewish community?"

"About fifteen families plus six or eight single men."

"Are you enjoying Portland?"

"It's more pleasant now than in the winter."

"Because of the weather?" David asked.

"Not the weather so much," Kathleen said. She sighed, folded her arms across her chest before continuing. According to the eighteen-fifty census, Portland has two-hundred woman and eight-hundred men. The majority of the men are lumberjacks and spend the warm months logging in the mountains. In the winter they descend on the town for boozing and whoring. You avoid the area around the docks in the winter because of the drunks and ruffians. Half the two-hundred women earn a living by servicing the lumberjacks."

"The police?" Myra asked.

"Barely effective and decidedly crooked. Currently, there exists one bar for every forty men, women, and children. Most of the women work at the bars which are mostly owned by politicians. There are rumors of men being Shanghaied to work on ships. In fact, the word Shanghaied was invented here. Mr. Breuer thinks we've lost a few men who got drunk and ended up forced onto ships. This is more of a frontier town than we expected."

Chapter Four: Andre

A light snow fell as Andre Gaultier de Varennes de la Verendrye, a stocky Frenchman in his mid-thirties, arrived at a clearing in the mountains north of a lake which, years later, would be named Chelan. Andre found the remnants of the lean-to he used on previous stays. His worn leather and fur clothing blended well with the forest environment which contrasted with his ruddy complexion. The trapper's face and hands evidenced more wear than age. He cut and crafted branches for repair and pine boughs for bedding. A buffalo hide was unrolled which he stretched over a frame to create a roof. The trapper squinted at the sky which remained leaden grey as a light snow fell. He shrugged knowing the snowfall would likely continue into the night.

Andre knelt to start a fire. In the distance he noticed the outline of someone, lightly dusted in snow, sitting back against a tree. Rocking back on his feet, he approached. Andre discovered a squaw having weak shivers every few seconds and apparently little life left. Dusting the snow from her face, he picked her up and carried her to his lean-to, placed her on the pine boughs, and wrapped her in a bear hide. The trapper noted her lack of proper clothing for cold weather; thin moccasins, no head covering, or decent jacket.

"Why did you come out here by yourself?" he asked.

She didn't appear to understand him. Kimimela studied his face and gave him the tiniest of smiles.

He returned her smile. "Yes, your clan visits here in the summer. Good people. I believe I've seen you, but what are you doing by yourself?"

She closed her eyes and made no attempt to reply.

Andre hastily built a fire and heated water. Pieces of pemmican, made from dried meat and berries went into the water. As soon as it was warm, Andre patiently fed her spoonsful of the stew interspersed with sips of water.

Kimimela put up a hand, indicating she'd eaten enough, weakly smiled at him, pulled the fur up to her neck, and closed her eyes. She no longer shivered, he noted.

***

Late the following morning, Kimimela awoke with a fright. Someone had removed one of her moccasins. She hurriedly pulled her feet under the bear hide. The trapper held up the fur-lined leather boots he'd crafted. She allowed him to slip them on. They were immediately cold but soft. Lined with fur and extending up to her knees, they quickly warmed.

Andre held up a deer hide and pantomimed putting on a jacket then pointed to her..

Using a knife and needles made of bone, they sat on pine boughs by the warmth of his fire and together crafted a hooded jacket with a long waist. Kimimela thought, "*A kind and generous man to give up his precious furs to clothe me.*"

While her nimble fingers sewed the edge of the coat, Andre edged the shearling lined hood with a wolverine fur ruff. The ruff would provide a warm breathing chamber on the coldest of days.

Kimimela pointed to his worn, ragged hat.

Andre laughed. He handed her a raccoon skin. She skillfully crafted it into a warm hat. It took the balance of the day to complete the clothing but with another meal, her young body was quickly recovering.

"*Quel est votre nom?*" the trapper asked.

Not understanding French, Kimimela simply shrugged.

He pointed to himself. "Andre."

She pointed to herself. "Kimimela."

"Kimimela," he slowly repeated.

Putting her hands together and hooking her thumbs, she flapped her hands, imitating a butterfly's wings.

"*Papillon,*" he said, slowly nodding at her. "Kimimela… *papillon.*" He stared into her dark brown eyes and smiled. "*Sedsuisant*…yes, a beautiful little *papillon* you are."

"I speak some English," she said.

"Good. English it is."

The sky cleared as darkness enveloped them. She listened to the crackling fire. Gazing skyward, she noted a canopy of crystalline stars. They bundled themselves in fur and slept.

In the middle of the night, Kimimela startled awake by the rasping sound of a two-man saw like the Europeans used to fell trees.

She raised herself on one elbow and listened. It wasn't a saw. Kimimela giggled and thought, "*Having a snoring man next to me is annoying but less annoying than the silence of not having a man next to me.*"

She gently huddled against him, enjoying his warmth.

***

At first light, they packed his furs and camping gear. Without words, Kimimela's actions indicated her desire to accompany him.

"I'm traveling west on this lake below us to hunt in the mountains."

She nodded.

He rolled his remaining furs together, gathered his camping gear, and secured lashings to tie the gear to a backboard. She touched his arm and pantomimed; she wanted to carry part of the load.

"I could use help," Andre said after a sigh. "My joints ache. I may be getting too old for this type of life." He smiled at her. "And someone to accompany me would warm my soul." Combining branches and leather strips, the trapper constructed a backboard for Kimimela. He gave her roughly one-third of the load. She easily hoisted it to her shoulders.

Andre raised his eyebrows and smiled. "And a strong *papillon* you are."

She smiled. "Strong, yes thank you."

By late afternoon, they trudged out of the mountains and onto the eastern end of Lake *Tsi Laan.* In the distance, Andre spotted a deer. He pointed to it. They quietly lowered their loads. Andre loaded powder and a ball in his rifle. In slow motion, they began stalking. When fifty-yards away, Andre gradually shouldered his rifle. Kimimela noticed the deer's lovely antlers, now partially hidden by a tree. She took one more step for a better view; in the process stepping on a small branch. It split with a sharp report. The deer bounded away. Kimimela blushed and hung her head, knowing the noise startled the deer.

"Not every hunt is successful, *Cherie*," Andre said.

Chapter Five: Kimimela and Andre's Journey

Andre uncovered the canoe he'd carefully hidden.

Kimimela looked away and shivered. She relived her one and only canoe ride. On a cool and windy fall day, her much older brother invited her into his canoe. Halfway across the same lake she and Andre were about to traverse, the canoe tipped and pitched her into the freezing cold deep lake. She had no knowledge of swimming and didn't know where the surface was. Her brother rescued her but she coughed and sputtered lake water for hours and it took the rest of the day to warm up.

"My canoe needs some work. We'll stay here a day or so."

She left the edge of the lake and gathered firewood. With her arms loaded, she spied movement off to her right.

Rabbits! Quietly but rapidly leaving the firewood at the beach, she retrieved her bow and arrows. Within five minutes she returned to the beach holding two fat rabbits.

"So," Andre said in his booming voice, hands on hips and chest thrust out. "My new partner is an excellent hunter."

She started a fire and cleaned the rabbits. After they ate she would preserve their fur.

The following day, bright sunshine greeted them.

Kimimela thought, *"At last a warm day to enjoy. A good day to bathe."*

Using her prized sliver of soap which she'd purchased from a settler earlier that year, she wet her body then soaped all over. The frigid water was uncomfortable, made her nipples hard, and turned her skin light blue. She glanced at Andre. He kept his eyes averted.

After she dressed, Andre walked to the water's edge, and removed his clothing. He dove into the water and disappeared.

Kimimela sucked in her breath and held it until he resurfaced. His arms reached ahead of him and his feet splashed at the surface.

"You travel like a fish," she shouted.

He left the water, picked up a bar of soap and covered himself in white lather.

***

They paddled his canoe up the long, dark-blue lake. Kimimela enjoyed the terrain. A mixture of gentle hills and mountains reached the water's edge while snow covered, jagged peaks filled the sky to the north. A harsh avian cry caught her attention. Peering into a wetland populated with tall reeds, she listened to the raucous call of the yellow-headed-blackbird.

"Welcome to your summer home," she called out after spotting him.

"What?" Andre asked.

She pointed into the wetlands. "Bird with yellow head."

Many herons and egrets were stealthily fishing along marshy areas at the lake's edge. As travel by canoe was almost silent, they were able to closely observe them.

Kimimela and Andre stopped for the night at the water's edge just as the sun reached the horizon. A full moon was visible in the darkening sky. They camped on a grassy knoll.

"The days are getting longer," she said while starting a fire.

"A few weeks travel in the mountains and we'll return to my cabin."

"Cabin?"

"A tiny place but dry when the spring rains come. A friend and I constructed it some years ago."

"I saw a deer on the mountain side. May I borrow your rifle?"

"Take careful aim. I'll give you one ball and the powder horn. Don't go far. No moon tonight. Easy for a bear or wolf to sneak up on you."

She entered the woods behind the grassy area. Kimimela's legs were tiring as she plodded up the steep wooded mountainside. Spotting the deer, she carefully loaded the rifle. Moving to get a closer shot, she heard Andre shouting. Hurrying back to their campsite, she stopped at the edge of the woods. Two men stood over a prostrate and unmoving Andre.

The taller of the two men said, "He's unconscious but he'll remember our faces. Best to kill him. Let's take his furs, and get out of here."

Kimimela's heart began pounding as she put powder in the rifle's pan. She held the rifle barrel against the side of a tree to steady it. The second man aimed a pistol at Andre's unmoving head. Kimimela moved the hammer to full cock, took careful aim, and squeezed the trigger. The rifle's report echoed through the woods. Bird calls rang out as they flapped away from the sound. A cloud of smoke from the rifle's barrel briefly obscured her view. The shooter was on the ground as his partner rapidly disappeared into the woods. Kimimela dropped the rifle and ran to Andre. She slapped his face a few times. He moaned. She tried to get him to his feet but he collapsed while trying to stand.

She heard a raven's cry and its wings flapping. Kimimela thought, *"The other man is returning."*

She ran into the woods and dropped to her knees. Scanning the woods she strained to see where he was. The tall fir trees filtered out any light. Kimimela closed her eyes and gradually rotated her head from side to side. The insects to the front and right made their usual sounds but those to her left were quieting. Turning toward the silence, her hand slid down her side to grasp her knife. When the sound of a leaf being crushed twenty-steps-distant reached her ears, she threw the knife with all her might. A gun fired and it's bullet ripped across her heel. Kimimela retrieved the rifle and grasped it with both hands near the end of the barrel.

She approached her antagonist; who she sensed more than saw. He'd pull the knife out of his upper chest and swung blindly. Kimimela retreated out of the wood. Each time she put pressure on her right heel sharp pain raced up her leg. The minute the man appeared she swung the rifle, striking him in the head. He staggered back a step and lost his grip on the knife. They both dove for it but Kimimela reached it first. He landed on top of her, coughed and gagged on his own blood but still tried to wrestle the knife out of her grip. She sunk her teeth into his throat. While he gagged, he used one hand to pull on her braids, the other to restrain her hands. She freed the wrist holding the knife and sliced across his throat. The robber's body quaked a few times and became motionless. She rolled his body off. Kimimela repeatedly spit his out blood as she limped to the lake. Kneeling at its edge, she rinsed her mouth numerous times. She returned to Andre who had managed to lift himself on one elbow. He shook his head to clear it. "You're injured."

"I will wrap this and be fine."

He displayed a weak smile. "My *papillon* is a fighter."

"They were going to kill you."

"Help me up. I'll bury them."

"Bury them?" Kimimela spat in their direction. "Leave them for the wolves."

"I will dig a grave for these retched men; they don't deserve one but I was raised a Catholic."

"Those men had Indian jewelry," Kimimela said. "Not my clan but I recognize it."

"How did they get it?" Andre asked.

"Those devils most likely stole it. Probably killed for it."

"I'll fill in their graves and we'll see if we can track in the direction they came from."

The pair followed a trail for five hours. Eventually the trail climbed a hill, bisected a small wood and opened into a large meadow. Kimimela turned her head into the wind and took a deep breath. "Do you smell that?"

"Something's been butchered."

They walked in the direction of the scent. Kimimela grabbed Andre's arm, whispering, "Quiet."

They remained motionless, then heard a child's brief whimper.

"This way," Kimimela whispered.

The instant the child saw them, the little one jumped up and started running.

"Do not fear," Kimimela yelled as she dropped her things. Despite the pain in her injured foot, she leaped over a few small bushes and ran zigzag between a number of trees. Wrapping her left arm around the girl's waist, Kimimela lifted her off the ground. The girl screamed, flailed her arms and legs, then tried to push out of her grasp. "I am not here to hurt you." The girl screamed again and fought harder. "*I am not here to hurt you,*" Kimimela said, this time in Salish.

The girl froze. Kimimela slowly lowered her to the ground. The little one turned to face her. Wide eyed and terrified, her body trembled.

In Salish, she asked the girl, "What happened?"

"Two bad men were chasing us. My brother shot at one and they killed him. Mother told me to hide in the woods. I heard more shooting then my mother and sister screaming."

Kimimela held out her hand. *"What's your name?"*

"Nekota."

"Come with me."

At the edge of the wood, Kimimela saw Andre waving them away.

"*We'll move over here, Nekota.*"

"Does she speak English?" Andre asked as he approached.

"*Do you speak English*?" Kimimela asked in Salish.

The girl shook her head.

Andre took a deep breath. "Those bastards killed her family. Abused the women then gutted all of them; most likely to attract animals to dispose of the remains. I'll bury them as is the Chelan custom."

"We'll take her with us."

Andre nodded.

"*My family*?" the girl asked.

"*Gone.*" Kimimela picked her up and continued walking toward the lake. Nekota was wracked with sobs.

Arriving at the western end of *Tsi Laan* lake, they followed a trail next to a rapid stream which took them high into the mountains to a narrow pass through the craggy peaks. Kimimela walked behind Nekota. She delighted in seeing the young one regularly stop to examine the season's early flowers plus turn in the direction of bird calls. Occasionally, she became motionless, then would begin crying. Kimimela would pick her up and carry her until the little one's anguish subsided.

The following morning, Kimimela woke with a start when a rifle shot echoed through the woods. Within minutes, Andre returned with a large mountain goat. Nekota ran her hand down its neck.

"A beautiful animal," she said. "How sad it died."

"We'll thank it for giving up its life so we can eat and use its fur to warm us."

Nekota turned away while the adults skinned and butchered the animal.

A band of Cayuse entered their camp. Two of the men warmly greeted Andre.

An old woman approached Kimimela. "Your child is beautiful."

"Thank you but she's not mine. We found Nekota after her family was murdered."

"Whites?"

Kimimela nodded, then motioned toward Nekota. "I was thinking of having her call me big sister."

The old woman eyed Nekota who was picking wildflowers and arranging them in her hair. She rapidly shook her head. "Nekota is young. She needs a mother's guidance; not a sister."

With a handful of wildflowers, Nekota ran to them and presented a few to each. The old woman patted her shoulder. Andre traded some of the goat meat for dried clams and fish.

The old woman took Kimimela aside. "Be careful. The whites are spreading a disease. Your skin becomes hot and itching then red dots appear. It was the death of many of our people."

"Thank you for telling me."

"Your man?"

"He is good to me and the child."

"May the gods protect you."

The Cayuse headed further into the mountains.

"The men told me furs sell for little money. We should head down the Columbia and sell them before others arrive which will depress the prices. We'll be warm in my cabin."

"Large enough for all of us?"

He laughed. "Yes but set up for one person. I've passed many winters there." Gazing at the distant mountains, he added, "I may have to change my way of life."

"I as well," Kimimela lamented.

Chapter Six: New Way of Life

Nekota bundled herself in a deer hide in the middle of the canoe and slept as the they followed the Columbia river to an area west of Walla Walla, Washington.

"We call it trapper town," he said. "This is my winter…," he laughed, "but now summer home."

The interior of the fourteen-by-ten-foot cabin was devoid of furniture.

"After I sell my furs, I'll check the roof," Andre said. "From the condition of the floor, it must leak."

"More windows would be nice," Kimimela said.

Andre nodded then brought in logs and kindling for the fireplace while she stored their gear.

"I'll begin cleaning," she said. Kimimela bundled sticks together and smiled as Nekota imitated her. They began at the back of the cabin and swept the floor.

Andre returned and handed her a few gold coins. "In case you wish to buy something."

Kimimela thought, *"Again his warm soul demonstrates his generous nature.* She thanked him with a warm smile and a gentle squeeze on his arm.

He used a stone to sharpen his ax. Within a few hours the roof was repaired and he crafted a table which could be used for eating and sleeping. He paid a man who delivered three chairs.

"Women need privacy when they…"

"I'll see to it," Andre said.

By the end of the following day, Andre was exhausted from digging a pit and constructing an outhouse over it.

***

On a Saturday morning, a group of trappers gathered in a clearing which was rimmed by trees. They each put a gold dollar in a leather bag and engaged in a knife throwing competition.

Kimimela watched them briefly, then approached the man with the coins. She handed him a dollar.

"New competitor," he announced. "Best-of-three throws."

The crowd of trappers parted. One of them motioned her to the throwing line. She placed one foot just behind it and pulled her knife out of its sheath. The men were throwing at an eighteen-inch tree about twenty-paces-distant.

Kimimela studied her target. She reared back and threw. The spinning knife created a silvery flash on its way to the tree. It landed with a solid "thunk." But in the wrong tree. Some of the men laughed as the blade sat in an eight inch diameter tree to the larger tree's left.

She smiled and held out her hand to a trapper for another knife. Nekota's caretaker silenced the laughter by placing the second blade six-inches above the first. A second trapper handed her his knife. As a third silvery flash reflected in the sun light, it embedded itself just below the first.

"Anyone think they can better her throws?"

Two tried but were unsuccessful. A leather bag with twelve gold coins was handed to Kimimela. She eyed the now sullen trappers. She counted out five coins and handed back the balance while announcing, "For the next best and the next best." A number of the men smiled. The winner turned to leave. She smiled and thought, "*Best not to be greedy.*"

The coins made a pleasant jingle as she proceeded on her way.

***

"I have friends who've invited me to…visit," Andre said.

Kimimela put her hands on her hips and shouted. "You are going out to drink that vile liquid which turns men's minds into mush. Why? You have a family here."

He avoided her angry gaze. “I’m going to meet my friends,” he said and walked out the door.

The moment he returned, it was obvious he had trouble standing straight.

Kimimela shouted. “Look at you. Barely able to stand. You stink. Go sleep outside. You don’t deserve to be in the presence of this fine child.”

Andre held up his hands in a gesture of surrender. Still wobbling, he strained to focus his eyes. “You are correct. As my blessed wife predicted, my head has turned to mush. Please forgive me…but…it’s raining outside.”

“You sleep on the floor tonight,” Kimimela raged with hands still on her hips.

He sheepishly nodded and stretched out in one of the cabin’s front corner. Immediately, the sound of his rasping snoring filled the cabin.

“You are angry with him?” Nekota asked.

“Yes, but he also filled my heart with rainbows.”

“Rainbows? How?”

Kimimela’s expression now radiant, she said, “He called me his blessed wife.”

***

A thoroughly inebriated stranger entered their cabin late on a Monday afternoon while Andre was away. Kimimela warmed food in the fire place. Initially, Kimimela thought it was her husband. The drunk spun her around and yelled, “I want them gold coins.” She kicked his shin hard enough that he yelled and slapped her. He grasped her by the shoulders. Nekota ran out the door screaming for Andre. Kimimela twisted out of his grasp and grabbed a fire poker. She gripped the end of the three foot metal rod with both hands and swung it with a motion which put all her body weight into it. The bar struck the man on the side of his head, knocking him off his feet. He shook his head to clear it, gathered his feet under him and stepped toward her. She swung again, this time catching him across the belly.

The assailant staggered backward three steps, gasped for air then screamed, "You fucking Indian bitch. I'll kill you."

Wide-eyed and snarling, Andre exploded through the front door with Nekota following. He knocked the man to the ground, got on top of the him and used his fist like a jack hammer to repeatedly beat the man's face. Kimimela screamed, "Hold him still and I'll burn his thing off."

The man screamed, "No! Mercy! No!"

Andre dragged him out of the cabin and threw him into the street. The would-be-assailant landed like a rag-doll but quickly struggled to his feet, ran three steps and tripped; flopping to the ground. He glanced back, a look of terror in his expression as Andre started toward him. Scrambling to his feet a second time, he took off down the road.

Out of breath Andre turned to Kimimela. "Are you all right?"

"I'm fine."

Andre embraced her.

Taking a minute to catch his breath, he then asked, "Would you have burned..."

"No. But he doesn't know that. Let him warn his friends that I am crazy. They will leave us alone."

"You fought like a mother bear."

She nodded at Nekota. "I am."

He laughed and gave her another warm embrace.

***

Andre brought home a feather-filled-sleeping-cushion for them and a small one for Nekota.

"My pretty, hard-working *papillon* and our daughter should not have to sleep on a hard table or floor."

Kimimela thought, "*Such a kind and thoughtful man. After Nekota sleeps, I must make him mine.*"

He sighed. "I spoke to the fur buyer. The fur trade is ending."

"What will you do?"

"For the next couple months, there is carpentry work I can do around town."

Kimimela nodded.

Andre's body, even though worn from years of trekking in the wilderness, still responded to Kimimela's touch. She pulled up her dress and he rolled on top of her.

She giggled to herself and thought, "*Perhaps his arrows are stronger than my husband's.*"

***

Four-weeks-later on a cool morning, Andre and a few friends were warming themselves around a potbellied stove at the general store.

Andre said, "We've lived in peace with the Cayuse, all the years we've lived here. Among them, as well as the Salish, I have true friends."

"The Cayuse murdered the Whitman family and other white folk. The fact that your wife is Indian may not help you," an Army officer said. "They're still riled up from losing so many of their number to disease. They blame us for that."

A man stated emphatically, "Disease happens. We didn't give it to them."

"They never experienced the diseases before we came here," Andre said.

"There's going to be a war in this valley. I strongly urge you to leave," the officer said. "Soon enough, Captain McClellan may ban all whites from this area."

***

Back in their cabin, Kimimela put food on the table and asked, "If we leave, how will we live?"

"Furs no longer sell for enough money to make a living and I fear a war is coming. Time to find new work and a new place to live." Tears filled Andre's eyes. "I have a friend who is a foreman at a warehouse near a city called Portland. I went hunting with him a few times. Named Breuer. He might help us." He ate a few bites. "I haven't lived in a white settlement since I was a child."

"I never have."

"It will take some adjustment."

"I fear they will hate Nekota and me because we're not white."

"We shouldn't be caught in the middle of a war." He nodded at Nekota. "We have to do that for her."

Kimimela nodded. "We'll head to Portland, and find this Breuer man."

***

"Look at them Indians," Timothy shouted. He rubbed his neck and reached for an ax. Another worker at the woodshop pulled a large lever which stopped his steam operated machine. He picked up a length of wood.

"Turn around and get out of here." Timothy seethed and rubbed his neck again.

"I wish to talk to Mr. Breuer," Andre said.

"He don't want to talk to no damn Indians."

A tall burley man approached. "I'll decide who I talk to. Get back to work."

Timothy lowered the ax but glared at the newcomers with unadulterated hate.

"Andre my friend. Good to see you," Mr. Breuer said.

They shook hands as Andre introduced his family.

"Mr. Breuer, I need work. The fur trade no longer provides an adequate income and I have a family to feed."

"I don't know. We have enough laborers." He glanced around the property. "I need someone to learn to sharpen the drills and blades in the woodshop."

"I can learn. I am good with my hands."

"It takes huge patience." Mr. Breuer grinned and slapped Andre's shoulder. "Like the patience you taught me when we sat for hours waiting for deer to approach."

"Thank you, Sir," he said shaking hands.

Kathleen approached.

"We have a man with skilled hands to learn sharpening tools in the woodshop, Ma'am. This here's Andre and his family. Andre, this is one of the owners."

Andre introduced Kimimela and Nekota.

Kathleen shook hands with them. Kimimela noted her warm smile and greeting. This was in stark contrast with the unadulterated hatred she saw in the eyes of many of the woman's employees.

"Where are you living?" Kathleen asked.

"Don't have a place yet."

"I have a small worker's cabin in an orchard on my property. No one lives there now. It's yours if you want until you find your own place. It'll take some fixing up but the roof is good and the stove is practically new."

"We'll manage," Andre said.

"Andre you can start immediately."

"I'll walk home with Kimimela and Nekota to show them the cabin," Kathleen said.

Before walking into the orchard, Kathleen entered her home and returned with apples for her new acquaintances.

"Let's put your things in the cabin."

"Some of the men were angry with us. Why?" Nekota asked in Salish after finishing an apple..

"Some people just hate," Kathleen said after Kimimela translated. "I was born a Catholic in Ireland. The looks of hatred you received from my workers is little different from the looks we received from some Protestants."

Kathleen put a hand on the little one's cheek and said, "You have beautiful eyes."

Nekota smiled. "Thank you."

Kimimela looked around the cabin, "We need to clean this place."

Kathleen said, "I'll get some things from the house and I'll help."

She returned to the cabin with rags, a floor brush, soap and a bucket, plus a handful of clothing.

"Hello inside," Kathleen called out.

"Please come in," Kimimela replied and wiped sweat from her brow while she set aside the bundle of sticks she'd been using to sweep the wood floor.

"Kimimela, you and I are about the same size. I suggest you change into these clothes and I have a dress one of my nieces has outgrown. You and Nekota won't look like Indians. Maybe folks can forget who you are."

Kimimela shuddered while remembering the hate-filled-stares and unkind words she'd experienced when they arrived. She nodded.

"I think we should call you Kim from now on for the same reason."

Kimimela nodded. "I understand."

"Your long braids need to go."

"What?"

Kathleen used her hands to pantomime a cutting motion on Kimimela's waist-length-braids.

Nekota's caretaker gazed at the floor and shook her head. "Many of these people would kill me as easily as they kill a rabbit." She looked at Kathleen. "If it will be safer for my child and me then I'll cut them."

"Nekota needs an English name as well."

Kim called Nekota to her side. "She wants to give you an English name."

Nekota shrugged.

"How about Monica," Kathleen said.

"Monica," Nekota repeated slowly as if trying to savor the sound of each syllable. "I like."

Kathleen turned to Kim. "What was your full Indian name; in English words."

"You would say, Butterfly of the Woods."

"How about a last name of Holt. It means small woods."

***

After a day of cleaning, Kim examined the dress she'd been given. It had a pocket on each side.

She pulled the threads that closed the seam on the bottom of the right hand pocket, then pulled the dress over her head. Kim modified her knife sheaf so it would strap to her thigh; now hidden by the skirt but accessible through the pocket.

Her waist length braids flopped in front of her as she bent forward. She cut each to shoulder length. A bittersweet memory ran through her mind; her mother singing while braiding her raven black hair.

"Beautiful Kimimela of the woods. Her splendor radiates like the summer sun; She brings beauty to all who see her."

Kim thought, *"Oh how I would love to see her once more."*

She wrapped her braids in a deerskin jacket, carefully storing them with the balance of her clothing.

Using a carved clam shell, she combed out the remaining braid. Kim combed and trimmed Nekota's hair as well.

"Your eyes have water," Monica said.

She pulled the five-year-old onto her lap and put an arm around her. "Precious girl, the way of life I was raised with is being torn from my heart; but I know of no other path for us." Kim ran her fingers through Monica's hair. "The white's customs are being forced on us. We must learn to live with them. I fear it will be a struggle, but we must."

Monica toyed with the collar on Kim's dress. "Must we look like them?"

"We will look like the whites so they leave us alone," she explained.

Andre entered the cabin and stared at the twosome.

Kim explained, "The Kathleen woman suggested we change our names. For the safety of our child, I believe it is a good idea. Our last name will be Holt. They will call me Kim and she will be Monica."

He shook his head. "My full name is Andre Gaultier de Varennes de la Verendrye. None of those English speakers can pronounce it. Therefore I will also take the name Holt."

Kim, Monica, and Kathleen proceeded to town and entered the dry goods store.

"Mrs. Ginsberg, this is Kim and her daughter Monica. Her husband works for me."

"Pleased to meet you," Mrs. Ginsberg said.

Kim inspected bags of lentils, dark beans, and barley. She purchased a pound of each plus requested a few lengths of cloth.

As Mrs. Ginsberg cut the final length of cloth from a large bolt, Kim leaned toward her and sniffed.

"Your skin. It smells like flowers."

"It's the soap. My mother taught me to make it."

"May I buy one?"

Mrs. Ginsberg eyed her. "I don't have time to make soap to sell; what with the store and lessons for my children."

"Oh," Kim said with obvious disappointment.

"Mrs. Holt, I'll give you one bar but you agree to let me teach you how to make it and I'll buy all you make."

***

"Doctor," Kim said in Doctor Trent's office. "Where a bullet struck my foot, it doesn't seem to be healing."

"Your infection could progress to a point where it may kill you. I can treat this but it will be painful."

Dr. Trent turned to his wife. "Boil water and prepare my instruments."

"Lay down over here, Mrs. Holt. You must remain absolutely still. Andre will help keep your leg still. I know this will be painful but please remember, pain has no memory."

She trembled. "Please begin."

At the first incision, Kim gritted her teeth for a bit then screamed. The scent of rotted flesh and pus filled the air. The doctor's wife turned her head to the side and tried to hold her breath to avoid inhaling the putrid odor.

"I'm sorry to cause so much pain," the doctor said.

When Kim dared look again, the doctor was using needle and thread to close the wound.

While applying bandages, the doctor said, "You have to keep pressure off this foot and keep it as clean as possible for a few weeks."

"Thank you, Doctor" Kim said. Still trembling from the pain, she sat up and wiped tears from her cheeks.

***

Four-weeks-later carrying fresh soap to the general store, Kim saw Dr. Trent. She hurried to walk at his side.

"Doctor, I may have sickness."

"Your foot?"

"No. My foot is improving every day. This is different. Every morning my stomach wants to come up and I have to make water many times."

"You're pregnant."

"No. I had a husband three-years before Andre. Tried many times but never pregnant."

"I'd say your first husband's bullets couldn't find their mark but Andre's did."

"Um…" She stared at the wooden walkway while her footsteps slowed. Kimimela rubbed her chin with her fingers. "Husband's bullets couldn't find…Andre's did." She covered her mouth as laughter burst forth.

Kim caught up with Dr. Trent. She grabbed his arm. "Bullets. You mean baby?"

"Yes, baby."

Kim smiled so wide her cheeks hurt. She giggled. "I must tell Andre."

After her delivery of the fragrant soap bars to Mrs. Ginsberg, she hurried to the cabin and prepared evening meal. When Andre arrived she shouted, "Your bullets work."

Confusion written in his expression, he asked, "What? My bullets?".

"Yes," she said pointing at the front of his pants.

"You're?"

She pantomimed a swollen belly. "With baby."

The proud mother-to-be stood on her toes and put little kisses all over his face.

Chapter Seven: Kathleen vs the Bank

Kathleen sighed. "There's more to the story about our arrival. Let me start from a few days after I lost Jack. I was at the bank with the papers to take ownership of the business."

***

A bank employee directed Kathleen to a seat opposite Mr. Alton, the bank's owner. The grey-haired, short, and thin man sat behind a large desk in a huge leather chair which made him appear smaller still. "What brings you to the bank this morning?"

"Getting our business signed over. Here are all the papers to take ownership of the warehouse," Kathleen said.

"These are all in Jack Kaufman's name," Mr. Alton said peering at Kathleen over the tops of his reading glasses.

"I'm his wife."

"Where is he?"

"A bear killed him a couple of days ago."

"Do you have his death certificate?"

"We can't find his body, therefore one can't be issued."

"I can't sign this over to you. How do I know you're actually his wife?"

"I have our marriage certificate."

He shook his head. "That's not a legal document and I'd need a death certificate before turning anything over to you."

"His body was likely dragged away so there won't be one."

"I'm sorry about your loss. There's little that I can do. The bank will maintain its interest in the business until Mr. Kaufman presents himself or you can provide proof of his death. There will be charges."

She shook her head. Her voice quivered. "No… Wait…No you're not. You're not taking over anything. Jack paid for this and I'm his wife so it's mine."

"Again, you don't have the necessary paperwork. You needn't worry your pretty head. The bank will take care of everything for a nominal fee."

Kathleen stood and slowly shook her head with her mouth agape. She stammered, "You…can't…do this."

***

"You mean we don't own the business?" David asked.

"We're making money despite all the bank charges. I talked to an attorney and he told me there was nothing I could do."

"David, calm down," Myra said.

Kathleen noticed his dark expression and furrowed brow.

"We'll go to the bank on Monday and clear this up," David said.

"On a happier note," Kathleen said, "The local Jewish Community is having a get-together at my home. I could use some help setting up."

"We'll all be there," Myra said. "Should be a great opportunity to start making friends."

"Let's attend Sabbath services tonight," David said.

***

The Jewish community gathered for Friday-night services at a private home.

Dov Rifkin led. "Let's begin our Kabbalat service with Psalm ninety-seven to get our minds cleared of the concerns of the week and into the proper frame of mind to welcome the Sabbath." During the service, he kept glancing at Nathan.

After the evening's final prayer, Dov approached him.

"Your voice…it sounds like my brother…and you appear similar to him."

David said, "Nathan was his family's only survivor after a steamboat explosion. We've been raising him since he was two."

Nathan added, "I had a brother named Eric. That's all I remember about my birth family."

Dov's eye's widened and his jaw dropped. He took a step back and became so unsteady he appeared to be losing his balance. David and Kathleen each grabbed an arm and guided him to a chair. He covered his face with his hands and sobbed.

Regaining control, he placed a hand on Nathan's shoulder. "Your father's name was Aaron. He was my brother. We called him Ari." Dov took a deep breath, exhaled slowly and steadied himself. "Your mother's name was Dora. My father, your Zadie, is a famous rabbi and comes from a long line of learned rabbis. He lives in Philadelphia. When he learns you are alive, Baruch Hashem - Bless the Lord" Dov paused to wipe a tear off his cheek, "we'll see the light from the joy in his heart all the way out here."

***

"I work for the Northwest Territory on various legal matters," Andrew Khasina said, shaking David's hand at Kathleen's home on Sunday.

"Pleasure to meet you. I could use some legal help."

David related his headache with the bank.

Andrew said, "Crooked bankers seem to spread like wildflowers out here. A wedding certificate is certainly a legal document. I'll go back to town with you, look over your documents, and if needed, file for a court date."

"Much anti-Semitism out here?" David asked.

"Not too bad," Robert said. "Everyone has to work long hours to make a living which doesn't leave time for much else."

Andrew said, "Dov Rifkin, he also works for the Northwest Territory, got knocked around one time. I took a pistol barrel to the back of my head once from someone who didn't want a Jewish lawyer in his town."

"I met Dov at services yesterday," David said. "Great discussion of the week's Parsha."

"His father is a famous Rabbi and Dov leads our services when he's in town."

Everyone was called to the table. A tall lanky man pulled out a chair for Sarah.

"I'm Fred Levin."

"Sarah Levin. Pleased to meet you. I saw you at the ironworks."

"I'm here for a few months to improve the equipment. I'm a mechanical engineer and specialize in steam-powered equipment."

"Where will you go afterward?"

"Seattle. A company will be designing a new locomotive engine and wants my help."

The children in attendance sat at one end of the table. Kathleen watched as five-year-old Celeste noticed a girl her age who seemed quite shy.

"Sit next to me," she said. "I'm Celeste."

Monica looked at her mother who nodded.

"I'm Monica."

"Are you Jewish?"

"No. Salish."

Celeste became pensive. "Hmmm. A different kind of Jewish, I suppose." She eyed a large platter mounded with dark orange strips. "Hey, look at those."

"My favorite," Monica said.

"That's salmon," Kim said. "We smoked it over alder wood."

William tried a piece and his eyes went wide. "Nathan," he said, picking up the platter and passing it to his brother. "You gotta try the…smoked salmon stuff."

"Wow. This is fish?" Nathan said.

"Big fish." Monica held her hands wide apart.

Nathan's eyes grew large. "How do you catch such a big fish?"

"With a net," Andre said.

"Will you teach us?" William asked.

"If your parents agree."

In a cheery voice, Kim said to the bright eyed children. "Some salmon are arriving now but many more will be coming from the sea. In a good year, as many as there are stars in the sky."

"We gotta see that," Nathan said.

"As many as stars in the sky? Wow. Just wow," Abbey said.

Following dinner, Myra announced that all were invited to her home the following Sunday.

"Mom," Abbey said. "Mister Holt wants to teach us fishing for salmon. Is that okay?"

"Certainly," Myra responded.

"Can Monica come next Sunday?" Celeste asked.

"Who?"

"My new friend. She's a different kind of Jewish. Salish, she told me."

"Yes. Make sure her parents know they're invited for next Sunday as well."

"Remember Kathleen. We're meeting tomorrow at the court house," Andrew said.

"I've got my fingers crossed," Kathleen replied.

***

Attorney Andrew Khasina, with Kathleen Kaufman and David Kaplan at his side, strode into the Portland courtroom wearing a tailored suit. He motioned them to take a gallery seat. Two unsmiling men wearing Territorial Marshall's badges, entered behind them but remained standing on either side of the entrance. Andrew and a taller man, also dressed in a fine suit, approached the judge, speaking in low tones. The longer they talked, the less color remained in the judge's cheeks. His brow furrowed and he sunk lower in his tall-backed, black leather chair.

Andrew proceeded to Mr. Alton. He leaned forward, resting his hands on the table where the banker sat with his attorney. He said in a pleasant voice, "Do you know who I am?"

The banker was also leaning forward, his elbows on the table while resting his chin on interlaced fingers. He smirked at the young man. "I don't give a damn who you are, sonny. Get away from me."

Andrew brought his six-foot frame upright and gripped his lapels. "I have a friend at your bank right now. His name is Dov Rifkin."

The banker gave him a dismissive shrug and looked away.

"Behind his back, crooked bankers on the west coast call him the damned Jew accountant."

The banker slowly sat up straight; his arms moving to cross his chest. His smirk evaporated and his complexion became ashen as the wiry-grey-beard on his lower lip began to quiver. He moved as far back in his chair as he could.

Kathleen couldn't help but smile.

Andrew continued, "So, you've heard of him. I'll bet your accountant doesn't want to go to jail so I suspect he's been singing a pretty song to Mr. Rifkin's inspectors. I presume you've been cheating the folks in this town. Mr. Rifkin's associates and I will be analyzing every jot and tittle of your books and contracts with particular enthusiasm."

A young man entered. He searched for Andrew. Upon seeing him he held up two fingers.

Andrew saw him, nodded and said to the banker, "That's Mr. Rifkin's assistant. He's just let me know they found two sets of books at your bank, Mr. Alton." In a voice dripping with sarcasm he added, "A terrible thing to do, sir."

Turning in the direction of the other nattily dressed man, Andrew announced in a firm voice, "Double set of books at this bank, Prosecutor Kent."

"Marshall," Kent said. "Arrest Mr. Alton."

The stern faced prosecutor turned and nodded to the judge who said, "Court is adjourned in this matter and will reconvene for adjudication in seven days." The sound of his gavel echoed around the room.

Andrew leaned toward Kathleen and David, "Dov will have your papers ready shortly."

"So you're not just a lawyer," Kathleen said.

"I work in the territorial prosecutor's office."

"Thank you for all this," David said.

"My pleasure."

"I'm so relived. Where will you go next?" Kathleen asked.

"After we finish here, I have to travel to a small town with a funny name – Walla something or other – near the Columbia river and near one of the most beautiful forests I've ever seen. Then on to a town up north called Seattle."

Andrew's confident demeanor waivered momentarily,, he cleared his throat and said, "Mrs. Kaufman, I'll be back in a month or so. May I call on you then?"

She shook her head. "I've recently lost my husband. It wouldn't be right."

David interjected, "Jack wouldn't have wanted you to be alone."

Kathleen hesitated then smiled at Andrew. "You know where I live. When you return, please stop by."

Myra and Kathleen walked home. They were in front of their homes when Kathleen stopped, bent at the waist, grabbed Myra's arm, and said, "Wait.".

"What's wrong?"

"The baby. My water broke."

Jack Kaufman was born 11 hours later.

"We'll gather the Jewish community up here," Myra said, as radiant, but tired, Kathleen cuddled her newborn. "There's going to be a circumcision."

Kathleen nodded, sighed, and said, "If only his father could be here to see him."

Chapter Eight: Kathleen Assists Again

Two months later on a Sunday morning, members of the Jewish community gathered at the Kaplan's home for a picnic. While admiring the blooms on the trees in her orchard with David and Kathleen, Myra said, "The apple blossoms are particularly fragrant."

"Wouldn't these have been a blessing to our families during the Potato Famine," Kathleen said, as she nursed Jack She turned to David, noting his constant grim expression. "You seem preoccupied."

"As the fall weather approaches, there's less shipping so the warehouse is barely making money. I'm going to lay-off some of the workers."

"The woodshop and ironworks?" she asked.

"Making money hand-over-fist."

Myra said, "With the children's help around the house, I need more to do."

"With myself, our accountant, and the foremen we have everything covered at the business."

"Which is what allows me," said Kathleen, "to stay home with Jack." She glanced at Myra. "How about we start up your dress business again."

Myra said, "I'll make up flyers to distribute and create another book of designs for potential clients to view."

David nodded. "There's a small, single story building for sale, not far from here. It has a wide store front and a small apartment in the rear of the building."

Kathleen asked, "We haven't started and you want to buy a building?"

"It's dirt cheap," David replied. "We earned good coin with Myra's business. It paid for my college and our living expenses. With Kathleen's knowledge of accounting, you can run it without my help."

"There's still something bothering you," Kathleen said.

"I stopped by the bank today. Mr. Alton was out of jail and back running the place."

"How can that be?" Kathleen asked.

"Most likely he paid someone. I talked to him and he pointed out his nephew works for us and said we were nice people so as long as we take care of his nephew and the local sheriff's men, he won't try and get even for the trouble we put him through."

"Take care of the sheriff's men?" Myra asked.

Kathleen explained, "They get money to keep the peace around our building. This also prevents it from going up in flames."

"What kind of place is this?" Myra said.

Chapter Nine: Myra and Kathleen's Business

Word went out to the community about the birth of Sarah's son, Michael. Friends and family gathered in the Kaplan's home for a ceremony on a Sunday on his eighth day. Following his circumcision, most were gathered in the parlor and a few women in the kitchen.

"I know you're occupied with Michael but since arriving, Fred Levin's only had eye's for you," Myra said.

Sarah held up her nose. "There's never been a man in my life. Don't think I need one."

Kathleen said, "I had a man in my life and it was the best days of my existence."

"I'm doing fine."

"If Andrew Khasina is still interested, I'll let him court me next time he's in town."

Myra said, "Sarah. If you two get together you wouldn't have to change your last name again."

Sarah giggled then became serious. "That's enough, please." She eyed Fred. "Mr. Levin, dinner's ready."

***

At the dress shop, Kathleen measured lengths of cloth while infant Jack slept in a cradle.

"So this is your dress making business." A busty, middle-aged woman in a gaudy dress said after she entered the store front. She brushed a lock of hair out of her overly made up face and approached Kathleen.

"I'll get my tape," Kathleen said, "and take your measurements but the cloth samples won't be here until tomorrow. Myra, let me present my friend."

"Britta Regenbogen," the women said, shaking Myra's hand. "A local dress shop should do well. My fellow workers pay big money to have dresses sent from San Francisco." She looked at the floor. "Others may not purchase from a store that has us type for clients."

Kathleen glanced at Myra. "She may be right."

Myra pursed her lips while considering a response. "If you think it's a bad idea that they visit the store, we could visit them. I'll show them my design book and cloth samples then take their measurements."

Myra's four older children burst through the front door.

"Hi Mom," Abbey yelled. "Hi Aunt Kathleen."

Myra said, "This is Miss Regenbogen."

"I think that means rainbow," Nathan said as he shook her hand.

"Miss Rainbow. Nice name," Celeste said taking a turn shaking hands.

Ciara began fussing.

Celeste ran to her crib and picked her up.

"Maybe she's hungry?" Celeste said.

"Probably," Myra said. "I need you girls to head home and bring back the left over corned beef, sauerkraut, boiled beets, and bread plus dishes so we can have dinner over here. Nathan, walk over to the supply store and buy a kettle, a sauce pan, and a fry pan. Remind Mr. Koenig who your mother is so he doesn't jack up the price."

"What should I do?" William asked.

"Bring stove polish and rags."

"Mom, please. Not that."

Myra turned to Britta and Kathleen. "One of my boys used most unkind language during a disagreement with his sister last night."

"Words can hurt," Kathleen said, sending a disapproving visage toward William.

He hung his head. "Stove polish and rags. Yes, Mom."

Myra noticed Celeste gloating.

"His sister responded in similar language so she's going to help him."

"Mom, he started..."

Myra peered over the tops of her glasses and put one hand on her hip. "Keep talking young lady. The outhouse over here needs a good scrubbing."

Celeste clamped her mouth shut and dropped her eyes.

"Everyone has something to do so get busy."

They headed out the door.

"Miss Regenbogen, will you join us for a meal," Kathleen said and pulled out a chair for their first customer.

"Yes, thank you." She turned to Myra. "You have lovely children."

"They're behavior is usually tolerable but the two six-year-olds seem to pick at each other." Myra began nursing Ciara. "But let someone else go after them and they support each other like barrel-staves."

***

The following day Britta returned to select cloth. Myra brewed tea.

"Britta, pardon my ignorance but I'd like to know how you ended up doing…you know."

"Well…"

"If you're uncomfortable telling me, I understand. It's certainly none of my business."

"You won't think the less of me?"

"Certainly not."

"I started life in an orphanage. Never knew my parents. When I was twelve, a year-older friend told me she found work cleaning. Turned out to be a cat-house. The owner was strict but fair. We cleaned bedding, swept and mopped the floors, and performed kitchen chores. Also did little favors for the woman who serviced the lumberjacks and sailors."

Kathleen asked, "How old were you when you realized what the woman were doing?"

"Maybe fourteen or fifteen." She giggled. "Looked through a crack in a wall when I wondered what all the grunting was."

Myra and Kathleen laughed.

"Thought it was disgusting and I'd have nothing to do with it. A couple years later these" she waved her hand in front of her substantial bust, "grew in. A man offered me a dollar-gold-coin to reach in my shirt." She regarded the floor for a while. "It wasn't long before the other girls my age were doing it so I thought I would as well."

Myra asked, "Weren't you embarrassed?"

"At first but after a while it was just work. I didn't have any other skills to make a living. I didn't know about the diseases then."

Kathleen asked, "But you decided to quit."

"Some of the girls got terrible and painful sicknesses which killed them or birthed babies with deformities and such. Others took heroin which ended up killing them. After I lost my best friend, I found I was pregnant. I decided to try for a new life. Praise the lord, my baby is healthy. I'm good with numbers and do bookkeeping for a few bars."

Myra said, "We're not so different. When I was a teen in Ireland during the Potato Famine, I used my body to get food for my family."

"Does your husband know?"

"He does."

"Has it ever been a problem?"

"No. Not once. In fact, it brought us closer."

***

A freight wagon came to a halt in front of the dress shop. A short, rather rotund man left a woman and four children on the wagon. He entered the store and removed his hat.

"The owner please," he said.

"I'm one of the owners," Kathleen said.

"I am Victor Anchote. I make men and woman's boots and shoes. I was hoping I might rent space to set up a business."

Kathleen called Myra over.

"Your products would complement the dress shop," Myra said. "Let's sit down and discuss this. Where are you staying?"

"Just arrived in town with my family. No place yet."

Myra said, "If we can come to an agreement, you can stay in the small apartment behind the store front until you find your own place."

Chapter Ten: More Family

Myra helped Kathleen slip her wedding gown over her head.

"Your big day," Myra said.

"Yes."

"Andrew is a good man."

"Yes."

"And yet not one smile this morning."

"Before wedding nerves."

"It's more than that." Myra stepped back and looked over the dress. She regarded Kathleen's blank expression then grabbed her friend by the shoulders. "What's wrong?"

"Andrew is a wonderful man. He loves me and adores Jack."

"Do you love him?"

"His career pays well. We don't lack for anything."

"Do you love him?"

"Please, Myra. Help me finish getting dressed and don't ask about love."

***

The Kaplans plus Andrew and Kathleen, who held her infant son Jack, just finished an evening meal of homemade noodles and meat sauce.

There was a loud knock on their front door and a voice shouted, "Hello Kaplans!"

William ran to open the door, swung it open and yelled to those inside, "It's Doctor Beckham and Mrs. Beckham plus a lady and some kids."

They met in the parlor.

Kathleen screamed when she recognized her sister. "Daire, I had no idea you were coming out." Two teens and a young girl followed Daire into the house.

"Mom sent me with Dr. Beckham and his wife. She and Myra's parents didn't have enough money to come west so they stayed behind to work. Is this?"

"Your nephew, Jack." Kathleen handed him to Daire who gently took him in her arms.

Daire asked, "Where's your husband?"

"This is Andrew."

Daire shook his hand. "Thought your name was Jack."

Kathleen told her, "Long story. I'll tell you later."

With a wave of her arm, Daire motioned the children to her side. "Kathleen, I want to introduce you to…more family. Their parents died on the trip and I've been taking care of them. This is Gavin, Theresa and Angela."

Kathleen smiled at the trio. "I live next door and we have room. You stay with us."

"Have you eaten dinner?" David asked.

"We have," Dr. Beckham said.

"Please have a seat," David said.

"Myra, you look well," Mrs. Beckham said.

"Thank you. It's so good to see you again," she said with a brief embrace.

"Mrs. Beckham," Abbey said. "You're expecting?"

"In three months," the doctor's wife said with pride.

"Dad," William said. "Can I show Dr. Beckham how I can sew noodles?"

David nodded.

"William's been practicing and practicing," Abbey said. "His hands can sew little bitty stitches and he doesn't tear the noodles."

The six-year-old returned with two flat noodles on a plate and a small curved needle with thread.

"Who made the little needle for you?" Dr. Beckham asked.

"Dad did. I couldn't use the big needle you gave us to sew little stitches."

William proceeded to sew evenly spaced and consistent sized stitches which precisely joined the pasta.

"You have incredible hands, young man," Dr. Beckham said.

"I have an engineer's hands to build things," William said.

Dr. Beckham ran a finger across the stitches. "This is more like a doctor's handy work."

Chapter Eleven: Oregon Trail

"How was your journey on the Oregon Trail?" Kathleen asked during Sunday dinner at the Kaplan's home..

Dr. Beckham's expression brightened. "At times, we found ourselves submerged in the Lord's unending beauty. We travelled amidst oceans of wildflowers, majestic mountains and forests; enough splendor to make an atheist a believer." His brow furrowed. "But also enduring the devil's heel on our necks for weeks-at-a-time."

***

After two days of rain, their prairie wagon was mired in the sticky mud of the Kansas section of the Oregon Trail.

Sixteen-year-old Daire bent her knees, and wedged her shoulder against a spoke on the rear wheel. Dr. Gunter Beckham yelled; entreating six oxen to strain against their yokes.

Rain drops the size of acorns thumped Daire head. They slapped the earth and struck percussive notes on the canvas canopy of the prairie wagon. She heard Mrs. Rivka Beckham groan as she strained against the opposite wheel. The wagon creaked at the contrary forces; the mud gripping it's wheels like anchors versus the animate forces trying to liberate it.

The wheel groaned as it started to rotate. Daire repositioned her shoulder under the next spoke…and grinned briefly, reliving the moment she declared to Mrs. Beckham after one dry and dusty week on the Oregon trail, "This journey seems to be made up of nothing but long periods of tedium interrupted by longer periods of tedium."

Daire jammed her shoulder against the next spoke and strained against it. The wheel continued to move. The young woman tried to take a step but her foot was mired. She fell forward, extending her arms in a futile effort to stem her fall. The sixteen-year-old felt wet clay oozing between her fingers while mud splashed onto her face. Daire wrenched her hands out of the muck, sitting on her knees. She repeatedly coughed and spit out the gritty soil which also stung her eyes. Looking for a relatively mud-free area of her skirt to wipe her hands, she wiped the mud and grit off her face as best she could. Daire closed her eyes and held her face up to the punishing torrent; hoping it would clear more of the mud. She wiped her eyes on her shoulders. The wagon was getting bogged down again. With eyes still stinging, she slogged back to the wheel, and renewed her effort at keeping it turning.

***

"Mr. Anderson just died," Dr. Gunter Beckham said. "He was out getting water and keeled over at the stream's edge."

They heard a woman scream.

"Sounds like Mrs. Kelsey just told his wife."

"I'll see if I can do anything to console her," Rivka said.

"Tell Preacher Straus. We'll need him for a burial."

***

Daire shook her head to help clear the sleep from her brain. A few birds sang; which meant the rain stopped. The early hour provided sparse illumination in the tent. "At least it's not raining," she said to the empty tent.

Sitting up, she rotated her sore shoulders, still stiff and uncomfortable from wedging them against the wagon wheels the day before. Two weeks sleeping on the cot made her other muscles sore but cots and tents were customary for travelers on the Oregon trail.

She heard Rivka calling her. "Be right there, Mrs. Beckham." Daire pulled on clothing and examined the hem of her dress. It was stained by the mud and dust it continually dragged through. Tilting her head, she listened to a woman crying.

"What's wrong?" She asked the doctor's wife as she left their tent.

"Mr. Anderson died this morning. Mrs. Kelsey is with his wife. She's been a widow since her husband passed during the tornado that came through Independence last spring. She'll help Mrs. Anderson manage as will the rest of us. There'll be a burial as soon as they get a grave dug." The doctor's wife slowly shook her head. "Sad. He wasn't that old." She took a brief rapid breath then said, "Daire, I need a few slices of bacon, please."

"Yes, Mrs. Beckham." She hurried to the bran-filled barrel which held the pork belly.

"Breakfast in thirty-minutes," Rivka called to her husband while mixing pancake batter.

"Mrs. Beckham, you always put on a clean apron every day. It seems extra work when everything else gets so filthy on the trail."

"I realize we don't have time for regular washing so we have to re-use clothing day after day. It may be frivolous but I'm determined to start every day with a clean apron."

***

Captain Burgess, a tall, wide shouldered man, and the elected leader of their wagon train, approached while they ate. He squinted at the cloudless sky. "It's cool but sunny now. Should warm up later on."

"Cup of coffee, Captain?" Rivka Beckham asked.

"Ah'd appreciate that, Ma'am."

He surrounded the tin mug with both hands to remove the chill from his stiff digits. Captain Burgess took a noisy sip of the dark liquid. "We'll take a day to empty the wagons and dry everything out." He turned to Dr. Beckham. "I suggest you check your axles and grease them if needed."

"That'll be good," Dr. Beckham said. "After all the strain on the oxen, they could use a day of rest and eating."

"I could use a day of dry," Daire said. "We had storms in Ireland but I've never experienced such large drops of rain. They pelted my head like acorns."

"Sometimes these storms are accompanied by terrible winds. We were lucky on that account," Captain Burgess said.

"We survived the tornado that came through Independence," Rivka said with a shiver. "A nightmare to experience."

"These plains hold immense beauty which can quickly turn into ugly tragedy," Dr. Beckham said.

"You speaking from personal experience?" Captain. Burgess asked.

"Lost my first wife and two children to a prairie fire up in the Dakotas. They tried to outrun it."

"Dr. Beckham, I'm so sorry," Daire said.

"I don't mention it often," he said with a sigh. "That fire did bring me to Rivka."

She smiled.

"Rivka's not only been a fine wife but taught herself enough medicine to be my nurse. Should have seen her running around bandaging and caring for people after the tornado."

"Gunter," Mrs. Beckham said, "remember the children who helped us? Warmed my heart the way they assisted with so many injuries."

"Children?" Daire asked.

"Three of them from the same family, two boys who were five and seven, and a sister around ten."

Dr. Beckham grinned at the memory. "I hurt my hands and little Abbey sewed up a young girl's leg wound. I let her brother, a seven-year-old put a few stitches in as well."

"Did you say she was ten?" Burgess asked.

Dr. Beckham nodded. "I did. Lots of backbone in those three. Like their parents. The five-year-old knew to use his hand to close a puncture wound to stop a similarly aged girl's bleeding. Probably saved the child's life."

Mrs. Beckham said, "The older boy stayed at my side and helped me care for the ugliest of injuries. Afterward, he and his sister spoke of becoming doctors. Family name was Kaplan."

"I believe Kaplan was the name of the family my sister lived with before she traveled west," Daire said. She addressed Capt. Burgess. "My family got us to Independence where we'd planned to meet my sister Kathleen but she'd moved on to Portland, Oregon as did the Kaplans. The Beckhams agreed to take me with them. My folks stayed behind to work."

***

"Daire," Rivka said. "Let's get things out of the wagon and into the sun."

The evening prior, the wagons were pulled into a tight circle, nose to tail, with little space between them. The oxen were left to roam the inside of the circle and enjoyed the lush Kansas grass.

The two women emptied the wagon and placed damp items in the sun.

Daire said, "Many women have gorgeous quilts. They are not only pretty but I imagine, warm."

Rivka told her. "They're more treasured keepsakes than used for warmth."

"Keepsakes?"

"Most of them were made by family and friends who didn't expect they'd meet the emigrants again. The quilts are full of the names and symbols of the folks left behind. They were a going away present; a remembrance so to speak."

***

The oxen-pulled-wagons traveled at a leisurely three-miles-an-hour. A week of bright sunshine turned the formerly muddy trail into fine dust which billowed into the air with each impact of humans, horses, oxen, and wagon wheels. Daire, usually in the company of similarly aged and energetic teens, walked faster than the cattle and would circle their wagon train a few times each morning.

When passing Mrs. Kelsey's wagon for the third time, she slowed down to talk while the middle aged woman maintained a slower pace at the side of her oxen.

"How's Mrs. Anderson taking the loss of her husband?" Daire asked.

"She's busy with her chores and children. It may seem cruel to say but in time she'll be so busy he'll be forgotten. I know. It happened to me."

"I heard you lost your husband in the tornado. Sorry about that."

"Thank you, dear."

"I lost brothers and sisters in the Irish Potato Famine. It tore me apart."

"You were a child then. You're a grown woman now and don't let any man fool you, we woman are tougher than they are. There isn't a man who ever lived could stand the pain of childbirth but we women get through it numerous times."

They walked in silence for a few miles, the only sounds being the oxen's footsteps, the wagon's creaking, and the rumble of the wheels as they bumped over occasional rocks.

Mrs. Kelsey used her switch to swat one of her oxen. "When I first married, I believed I'd need a husband to take care of me and provide an income as well as give me children. Not being married, you don't know what it's like to have a man rooting about and grunting when he's between our legs." She shook her head. "Back breaking labor during the day with children on our teats; men thumping our bodies at night. It's amazing we live as long as we do."

"Mrs. Kelsey, aren't you…"

"Embarrassed? Certainly not. Men talk about it. Why not us?" She laughed and leaned closer to whisper, "It's between our legs they're always wanting to stick their willies. Why shouldn't we talk about it?"

Daire blushed.

"I've watched you. You're a tough young lady. The match of any man. Don't let anyone tell you otherwise."

"Get up there Gip," Mrs. Kelsey swatted the same oxen on its rump. "He tries to let Tyler do most of the work but I watch the yoke and don't let him get away with it."

"I've helped Dr. Beckham with his oxen. They're peaceful creatures."

"Less excitable and stronger, but slower than horses. By the way, there are ruffians among the cattle drovers. You keep an eye out young lady."

"Yes, Ma'am."

"Do you have anything for personal protection? A pretty woman like yourself should."

"Never thought about it."

"I have a Bowie knife strapped to my thigh. It hides nicely under my skirt. I have an extra which I'll let you borrow while we travel."

"Thank you."

"Mrs. Kelsey," Mrs. Anderson yelled from the following wagon, "I'm having trouble with the oxen,"

"Poor thing. She's afraid to use the switch. I'll help her if you'll walk next to mine and keep them moving."

***

They were crossing a wide, flat plain with few trees and widely scattered scrub bushes. Dr. Beckham turned toward a faint rumbling sound and saw a distant cloud emanated from the horizon.

"No flame visible at its base." Dr. Beckham said to Capt. Burgess as he put a hand up to shade his eyes and squinted slightly to get a better view. "There's brown below it."

Capt. Burgess yelled in his loudest voice, "Buffalo stampede! Get the women and children in the wagons!"

As the animals neared, the ground began shaking. Screams now mixed with the thunder of thousands of hooves.

Dr. Beckham repositioned his wagon so its tail was facing the rumbling herd.

He told Daire, "According to Captain Burgess, a buffalo cow can weigh eleven-hundred-pounds and a bull two-thousand-pounds and those monsters can run forty-miles-per-hour."

Some folks fired guns in the air to frighten the herd but to little affect.

Screams emanated from a wagon which was knocked on its side. An old man and his son, in front of their overturned wagon, were trampled trying to keep the animals from crashing into it. Any cattle not in a yoke, started running. The cloud of dust filled the air. Those who knew, put a cloth over their face. The rest gagged, coughed and choked on the fine particulate.

In the lee of her family's overturned wagon, a four-year-old girl screamed for her parents while she held tightly to her screaming two-year-old brother. Many wagons hitched to horses, were uncontrollable as the equines panicked.

Out picking wildflowers, Mrs. Anderson's three youngest children huddled by a four-foot-tall and similarly wide rock. She saw the youngest trying to run back to their wagon but he was trampled under the thundering hooves.

Unable to control her instinct to protect her children, Mrs. Anderson ran to their rescue but suffered a similar fate.

***

Over an hour later, the balance of the herd passed. Mrs. Anderson's three remaining children approached Mrs. Beckham.

The oldest, fourteen-year-old Gavin, said, "Mom's gone. No trace of her or Tom. And our wagon's on its side."

"I'm sad for you kids but we have to get ready to move again," Mrs. Beckham said. "Let's inspect your wagon and, if it's in good enough shape, we'll right it."

"Daire," Dr. Beckham said while splinting a broken leg, "Why don't you plan on staying with them for the rest of the journey. You slip their wagon behind ours when we start moving again."

"Let's plan on having meals together," Mrs. Beckham said. "That should give you a chance to set up a routine with them."

***

Daire stood with hands on hips after the wagon had been righted. "Front-right-wheel's broken."

"I'll search for a replacement," Gavin said.

With a bit of effort and help from friends, Daire and Gavin replaced the broken wheel.

"Walk around and gather as many of your possessions as you can find," Daire told them. "We'll be leaving soon."

Four-year-old Angela wept. "I want my mom."

Daire picked her up. "She's gone to live with the angels, sweet girl." She told Gavin and twelve-year-old Theresa, "I'm going to be depending on the two of you. You need to watch out for your little sister. Gavin, are you old enough to walk next to the oxen and keep them moving?"

He stood tall. "Yes, Ma'am."

"Theresa, we need to organize and repack the wagon. I need your help but we also have to keep Angela close."

"You children pay attention to Daire," Mrs. Beckham said. "You mind her and you'll be fine."

They heard angry male voices.

"Mr. Goshen again," Rivka Beckham said, glancing in the direction of the sounds.

Daire said, "He seems to yell at anyone who comes near him."

"Gunter tried to give him advise about the fittings on his wagon. They nearly came to fisticuffs."

"Same happened to Captain Burgess."

Rivka shook her head. "If you've heard the expression, there's no fool like an old fool, Mr. Goshen is a perfect example."

***

"Mrs. Beckham," Daire said, while carrying the four-year-old, "Angela's been lethargic the last few days and wants to sleep a lot. Her eyes have been red and watery. She's had a sore throat plus cough for the last few days. Now she has these red areas on her face which seem to be spreading to her chest and arms."

Rivka took one look and yelled for her husband.

He examined the little one and shook his head. "Measles. Damn. We're in for it now."

"I had it as a child," Daire said.

"You won't get it again but any adults who get the sickness will be in rough shape. I'd better tell Capt. Burgess and help him spread the word."

"I read that two-thirds of the native population of Cuba died from a measles outbreak during the fifteen-hundreds," Daire said.

"Fifteen-twenty-nine, if I remember correctly," Rivka said. "The native populations in this country have little ability to fight the disease. If it spreads it may devastate them as well."

"What should I do for my three?"

Dr. Beckham said, "Make sure they get plenty of rest and they need to eat. If, after they get the redness, they become quite hot, complain of extreme headache or begin convulsing, find me immediately. Those may be symptoms of a disease which can kill them."

Arriving back at the Anderson's wagon, Theresa approached Daire. "I'm coughing and my face is getting red."

"Dr. Beckham said to rest and be sure to eat."

"Gavin's eyes are red and he's been coughing too."

"All of you are sick. You rest in the wagon."

***

"How are your patients?" Rivka Beckham asked Daire that evening.

"Angela mostly sleeps. Theresa is helping me with chores. Threatening a severe thrashing was needed to get Gavin to ride in the wagon and rest. I think he was in there all of two seconds and he fell asleep."

Rivka shook her head. "Typical man. Doesn't know when he needs to rest. Gunter hasn't slept more than an hour since we discovered the sickness." She shook her head. "We'll stop for a few days. Capt. Burgess is worried because we'll be behind schedule if we do."

"Then why stop?"

"Quite a number of adults are sick. If they don't rest, the disease can kill them. Gunter explained they need all their strength to fight the sickness."

***

Two weeks later, Theresa told Daire, "A good day to be on the trail after all the illness. It looks like we're traveling through a carpet of wildflowers with an azure blue sky over our heads."

"Azure – good vocabulary."

"Back in Indiana, I was the best reader and speller in my class."

"We seem to be slowing. Capt. Burgess said there would be a river crossing today."

"Will we have to unload the wagon?" Theresa asked.

"I doubt it. Our wagon's light and this river's only a-couple-feet-deep plus the water is slow moving."

***

"A good day despite the rocky trail," Captain Burgess said one evening the following week. "Covered at least twenty miles."

"Mrs. Beckham put milk in our butter churn this morning and I strapped it to the side of our wagon," Daire said. "The constant bumping and banging from the trail caused a nice roll of butter to form."

They both laughed.

Captain Burgess said, "Those wagons do ride rough. Lots of folks supposed they'd ride 'em to Oregon but they mostly end up walking. Only the tiny ones and the sick manage to stay inside when moving."

That evening, a violin player and guitarist entertained the crowd. A few danced to the lively tunes.

A skinny teen approached Daire. His pock-marked face evidenced as many bumps on it as the rock-strewn trail they traveled that day.

"Will you favor me with a dance?" Timothy, the preacher's son asked. She blushed and nodded. They twirled to the sound of a lively tune.

An outrider approached Daire and asked for a dance. She agreed but didn't like the look in his eyes.

***

The wagon train stopped just before a river crossing. Four Indians waited at the water's edge. Captain Burgess conversed with them and returned to a group of men. Many emigrants craned their necks to gain sight of the first Plains Indians they'd run into.

"They want five-cents-per-wagon. They say we're crossing their land."

"Five cents?" A short, wide man said, pulling a hat off his bald head and throwing it to the ground. "There's at least three-hundred wagons behind us."

"If there's four Indians standing here, there could be hundreds hidden nearby. We pay and they'll leave us alone."

"Tarnation," Preacher Straus said.

Waiting for their turn to cross the river, Daire asked Rivka, "I've heard that word tarnation out here. Wonder how it came about."

"Polite society doesn't swear. Since the Puritans arrived, people have been inventing words to use as epithets that aren't swear words or contain religious connotation. Tarnation is a combination of eternal and damnation."

Daire wrinkled her brow. "Damnation I can understand but eternal?"

"Eternal isn't polite to some as it may be used as the Lord's name like the Eternal One. Colloquial speech changed it to tarnal."

The teen laughed. "And I thought I knew English."

***

The same outrider she'd danced with, slowed his horse to walk next to Daire.

"July fourth, in two days, Miss Devlin. Independence Rock is nearly in sight. Should be a right fine celebration."

"That's what I've heard."

"Save a dance for me?"

"Maybe."

"Maybe's good enough for me." He spurred his horse and galloped away.

"I don't like the way he looks at me," she told Mrs. Kelsey and Mrs. Beckham while they walked to a stream to fetch water.

"What do you mean?" Mrs. Kelsey asked.

Daire splashed water on her face, then grinned. "His stares at me the same as Captain Burgess when he was drooling over the pork belly you were smoking."

The threesome laughed.

Mrs. Beckham said. "The celebration will be a public affair. Stay where people can see you and you'll be fine."

***

"Independence Rock means we're half way," Captain Burgess announced.

"It looks like a loaf of bread that needs to be punched down," Daire said. Mrs. Beckham laughed.

The youngsters gathered near violin and squeeze-box players whose melodies inspired foot tapping initially and dancing eventually.

A group of roughly twenty Indians wearing an odd mixture of traditional and European clothing, watched the Independence Day celebration from a distance.

Dr. Beckham nodded toward them and told Rivka plus a neighbor, "No celebration in those faces."

"I'd bet our carrying on appears as celebrating the end of their way of life," Mrs. Kelsey said.

Rivka nodded agreement. "New versus old has caused wars and hatred throughout the history of mankind." She sighed. "And hunger. The children's eyes are sunken in those gaunt faces. Their bodies are nothing but skin and bone. I'm taking some of our beef and bread over to them."

"I'll help," the doctor said.

Two smiling women came forward and were handed the food. With children following, they moved behind the row of otherwise sullen Indians. The Beckhams hurried back to their wagon.

"You won't get your pans back," Mrs. Kelsey said.

"I'll manage," Mrs. Beckham said. "Maybe they can sell them to secure more food."

The neighbor added, "They're a thieving people. We think four horses were stolen last night. Best keep an eye out. With those hate filled looks, there's no telling what they might do next."

***

Daire noticed Preacher Strauss and Capt. Burgess talking.

"How's our pace?" Preacher Strauss asked him.

"We're on schedule but the Rockies up ahead are unpredictable. We may have to travel some Sundays."

Preacher Straus stood stiffly and declared, "I'll not be putting a yoke on my oxen on any Sunday. Both man and beast need a day of rest."

Captain Burgess said, "As long as we stay on schedule. We get behind and many will die trying to get through freezing weather and snow covered trails. I'm sure the Lord wouldn't be in favor of that."

"By keeping His day holy, I'm sure he'll allow us the time and good fortune to maintain our schedule."

***

One week after the July fourth celebration, the wagon train stopped to rest near a wide stream.

"We're almost to the mountains," Captain Burgess said. "We've got good water and grass here so we'll stay for a couple days to rebuild wagons and let the cattle eat."

Daire, with similarly aged teenagers Jessa and Timothy crossed the stream to search for berries.

"Where are the Anderson children?" Jessa asked.

"Spending the day with Mrs. Beckham."

After two hours, Jessa said, "I'm hot and there doesn't seem to be anything out here but more heat." She glanced around. "Let's climb to the top of that rise. If we don't see anything, we'll go back."

"Down there in that little valley." Timothy pointed from the hillock. "Junipers. Might have berries."

"That's a couple miles. We're getting far from the wagons," Daire said.

"I've got my pistol."

"I'm not sure…" Daire said.

"If we see anything," Jessa said, "We'll run back to the wagons. At least we won't have come out her for nothing."

As they arrived at the Juniper trees, five Indians appeared around them. Timothy took out his pistol and fired. The tallest grabbed at his chest and collapsed. The percussion cap of the next round jammed the cylinder so he couldn't fire a second time. Two of the Indians were on him in a flash, taking the gun and holding him down while they tied his hands behind his back plus a leather neck strap. The girls were secured similarly. Jessa screamed and was rewarded with a kick to her belly. She doubled over and fell to her knees.

Daire yelled, "Leave her alone."

An Indian, about her age, approached. He twisted his upper body away from her then backhanded her across the face. She too, fell to her knees. Despite her dizziness, she managed to remain standing after being jerked to her feet by the leather neck strap.

The three captives were hauled away in the opposite direction of the wagon train.

***

Daire estimated they were at least seven miles from the wagon train. She and Jessa were tied together, back to back, with leather neck and wrist straps. When the Indians dragged Timothy some distance away, Daire struggled for a number of hours to free her wrists and recover her knife. She quickly cut through her and Jessa's bonds. They heard Timothy's repeated screams.

"We'll send back help for Timothy," Daire said as she began running.

"How will we find the wagon train?" Jessa said, as they ran.

Daire glanced skyward. "The stars will tell us."

After four miles of running, Jessa collapsed. "I can't run any further. I'll hide and wait for someone to find me."

Daire tugged at her arm. "Don't quit now. We keep going and we'll be back with the others."

"I can't. You go."

Alone now, Daire ran another mile.

Too late, she heard footsteps. He grabbed a handful of hair and threw her to the ground. Hands on hips, he stood over her in triumph; his sweat covered upper body glistening in the moonlight. When she tried to stand he brought an open hand from as far back as he could reach to slap her across the face. A blinding flash was accompanied by momentary dizziness. He struck her again and again, alternating hands. His face now covered in fury, he shoved her onto her back and forced her legs apart. One sweaty hand grasped her throat and the other pushed his pants down. She did her best to ignore the pain when he entered her. Daire shoved her hand between his legs; violently crushing his sack with all her might. He screamed and rolled off, curling himself into a ball. Daire retrieved her Bowie knife. With both hands, she jammed it into his neck. He clawed at her face, trying to gouge her eyes. She felt his nails digging into her lower lids then scraping across her face and neck. His body quaked three times and stopped moving. Daire leapt to her feet, ran three steps and stopped. Returning to the body, she pulled out her knife which made a sucking sound, wiped it on her skirt and returned the blade to its sheath. She took a deep breath, looked around and continued running.

After another mile running at a torrid pace, the adrenaline from the fight wore off. The pain from her torn and blistered feet was sending pain up her legs. Daire briefly considered stopping to check them.

She thought, "*If I see how bad they are, I might want to quit.*"

Every footfall was now accompanied by sharp pain. Each foot print was accented with drops of blood. She looked to the east. Day light was approaching.

Her body developed an economy of effort which balanced her breathing with the motion of her legs and arms. Her cheek felt damp.

Putting a hand on it, she realized it was bleeding.

"*His clawing at my face and neck*," she thought.

She came to a small stream. Splashing water on her face and a handful into her mouth she looked over her shoulder and noted the bloody footprints. Her body involuntarily shivered but she resumed her torrid pace.

Daire heard voices ahead of her. She dove into the tall grass which lined the trail. She turned an ear toward the sound.

"English. Thank God."

She ran onto a river bank.

"Over here. Help me," she yelled while waving her arms.

On the other side, men were calling to each other and three of them splashed across. The moment the first man reached her, she collapsed into his arms.

***

Daire awoke on a cot in the Beckham's tent with Rivka at her side and Mrs. Kelsey standing over her.

"Did you see how bad her feet are?" She heard Mrs. Kelsey say.

"Good Morning," Rivka said. "How are you feeling?"

"Glad to be alive."

"You have nasty cuts. Dr. Beckham said to stay off your feet for a few days."

"How long was I asleep?"

"Nearly twelve hours."

"Jessa and Timothy?"

"Both alive. Timothy barely."

"They found Jessa tied to a tree," Mrs. Beckham said.

"She'd been repeatedly abused," Mrs. Kelsey said.

"And Timothy?"

"Has burns all over his body. He may not live," Mrs. Beckham said.

"I tried to get Jessa to run with me but she quit after a few miles."

"I'm sure you did your best," Mrs. Beckham said.

"Only the strong survive out here," Mrs. Kelsey said.

"I killed one of them."

"The Bowie knife?" Mrs. Kelsey asked.

Daire nodded.

Mrs. Kelsey smiled.

"That's also how I cut our bonds."

"I'm proud of you," Mrs. Kelsey said putting a hand on Daire's cheek.

***

Six weeks later, an old Indian slowly walked to the edge of the circled wagons. He removed his hat and pantomimed eating.

"He's starving," Daire said.

The instant Timothy saw the old man, his pulse increased, he panted and trembled. Timothy kept rubbing his neck as if he wanted to be sure there was no longer a leather strap around it.

A shot rang out. The old man crumpled to the ground.

"There was no call for that," Dr. Beckham screamed at a middle-aged-man.

"He could have been one of the Indians that burned Timothy and did you-know-what to Jessa," the shooter said.

"He was a hungry old man. That's all. Was no reason to kill him."

"Tell that to Timothy."

Timothy continued trembling while staring at the collapsed form.

Mrs. Beckham grabbed his face with both hands and turned it to look at her.

"Timothy, you calm down," Mrs. Beckham said. "You're safe now."

His nodding could barely be discerned from his trembling as he walked away.

"There's big fights at the Hendricks," Dr. Beckham said.

"About Jessa?" Daire asked.

"Her family is humiliated she's carrying an Indian's child."

"It wasn't her fault."

"I tried to tell them," Mrs. Beckham said, "but they're ashamed. The way they carry on, you'd think she did it on purpose."

Chapter Twelve: Jessa's Story/Oregon Trail

Jessa and Daire stood and looked over the gently-lowing-cattle which grazed fifty-yards from the wagon train's evening encampment. A drover approached on horseback.

"Howdy Ladies." He slid off his saddle and removed his hat. "I'm Charles Wagoner."

She gave him a curt nod of her head. "Jessa Hendricks."

"Daire Devlin."

"Miss Hendricks, I hear tell there's been some friction twixt you and your family."

"They won't even talk to me." She returned her gaze to the cattle. "Not that it's any of your business."

"Sorry. I shouldn't have commented on family matters."

She folded her arms across her chest.

The drover fidgeted with the brim of his hat. Daire walked a few steps away from the two but remained in earshot. "Miss Hendricks, I own six-hundred-sixty-acres north of Ft. Boise. Fifty of these cattle are mine. I'm adding them to the herd I own up there. I done asked around and everyone says you're a right fine lady. There's a decent cabin on my land and I have enough money to build you a proper house."

"What are you talking about?"

"I'm talking about a future."

Jessa spoke in an anger tinged voice. "Are you touched or something? I'm with child. An Indian's child."

He ground the toe of his boot into the dirt. "We're all God's children, Miss Hendricks. I's born in Texas and that's what those what raised me taught me."

"You're a fool. Get away from me."

"Sorry to have troubled you." He mounted his horse and trotted away.

"He seems a nice man," Daire said.

"Did seem sincere," Jessa said with a shrug.

"If things don't improve with your family, maybe you should consider his offer."

***

A week later and after suffering another week of contempt from her family, Jessa in the company of Daire, appeared at a campsite where four drovers sat on the ground next to a fire.

"I wish to speak with Mr. Wagoner, please."

He stood and they walked away from the others.

Jessa cleared her throat and said, "I might never see my family again if I leave with you."

"Seems like they ain't real anxious to have you around."

Jessa glared at him. "They're still my family."

Charles did his best to smile. "I'm an orphan ma'am. Our children would be our family."

She shook her head, turned slightly away from him but remained where she was.

The drover looked at Daire who nodded in Jessa's direction

He cleared his throat. "It's beautiful country up there. Good clean air to raise children. None of that stink like the cities."

She remained motionless.

"Miss Hendricks, why did you come out here?"

"I was giving thought to a possible future."

"And…"

After a pause, she continued, "I have lots of anger in me since I was attacked. I may not be the most pleasant person to have around."

"Miss Daire says you're one of the nicest folks she knows. Coming from her, that's good enough for me."

Jessa spun her head in Daire's direction.

Daire nodded. "It's true…no matter what your folks are saying. There's lots to do on a ranch. You might find some peace in that."

The pregnant girl took a deep breath. "When will we be in Ft. Boise?"

Charles smiled. "Sometime tomorrow."

"Is there a preacher in Ft. Boise?"

His expression brightened. "Yes Ma'am. Nice Church as well."

"If anything you've told me is a lie…"

"I wouldn't. If anything ain't like I'm tellin' it, I'll bring you back to the wagon train. Y'all got my word on that."

"If anything you've told me is a lie," Jessa said with hands on hips. "I'll flatten you like a buffalo stampede."

***

A sudden snowfall dumped eight inches of snow on the trail, and was accompanied by below freezing temperatures and brutal winds. A group gathered around a fire, trying to keep warm.

"It may remain cool as we head into the Blue Mountains," Captain Burgess said, holding his hands out toward the flames. "Our progress has slowed considerably. May not have made five miles today. I'm going to talk to Preacher Straus about traveling on Sunday."

"He'll pitch a fit over that," Mrs. Beckham said.

"Daire," Dr. Beckham asked, "is that blood on your skirt?"

"My cuts," Daire said as she lifted her skirt a few inches to show cuts around her ankles. "It's the ice you know."

"What ice?" Dr. Beckham asked.

"It forms on the bottom of our dresses as they drag on the snow."

Dr. Beckham looked at his wife. She raised her skirt to reveal her left ankle with a similar injury. Mrs. Kelsey did the same.

"No one told me this was going on," he said.

Mrs. Beckham said, "Most woman suffer in silence from this."

Mrs. Kelsey laughed. "As we do about most things."

His brow furrowed. "If these injuries become diseased, I may be removing feet."

"We've been discussing the problem. Time to begin wearing bloomers," Mrs. Beckham said.

"I agree," Mrs. Kelsey said.

"They'll likely be some resistance to that," Dr. Beckham said.

"Daire, Mrs. Kelsey, and I will wear them beginning tomorrow."

Mrs. Kelsey chortled. "Wonder what Preacher Straus will think about that?"

***

"Women shouldn't dress like men," Preacher Straus implored the following morning.

"That's why we're wearing bloomers—not britches," Mrs. Beckham said.

"It's wrong, I tell you."

"Come talk to me away from these folks," his wife said.

Daire watched as Preacher Straus's eyes widened as his wife raised the front of her dress to show the bloody damage the ice had caused.

"Is there no other way?" he asked.

By the next day, roughly one-third of the woman wore bloomers. The balance of the women would leave a trail of blood stains and tears going into the mountains and a number would lose their feet as the doctor had predicted.

***

On Sunday morning, a crowd gathered for church service.

"I've done some hard, hard praying about this," Preacher Straus said. Tears welled up in his eyes. "We're going to have a brief service this morning and" he looked skyward, "Lord, please pardon us…we begin traveling as on any other day."

Murmurs went through the crowd.

"It's a matter of safety. More delay and we might become trapped in snowstorms which could result in many deaths. "

They sang three hymns and retired to their wagons.

"Thank you, Preacher." Capt. Burgess said while shaking his hand. "I know it was a painful decision. We'll be at the Dalles soon enough and then it's just a brief boat ride to Portland."

Chapter Thirteen: Outdoor Lessons

Myra, William, Nathan, and Celeste, greeted Kim and Monica at the general store. The boys approached Kim while Celeste, Monica and Myra discussed cooking

"Mrs. Holt," eight-year-old William asked, "Nathan and I were wondering, what was it like living outside all the time?"

She smiled and said, "You learn to work with nature instead of fighting it."

"Like what?" William asked.

"When cold weather occurs, you put on appropriate clothing."

Nathan carefully considered her words. "But what happens when there's snow everywhere? How can you work with snow?"

"Ask your parents if they'll let me take you outdoors this weekend. Andre and I can teach you many skills."

The duo ran to Myra.

"Mrs. Holt wants to take us to live outside this weekend," Nathan said.

Myra replied, "You may but I expect nothing but excellent behavior."

"What about Celeste?" William said.

"I'd like to go," she said.

With delight in their eyes, the children ran back to Kim. She told them, "We'll meet Saturday morning at our cabin. Dress warm."

***

"When the boys asked about the two day trip, William asked if Celeste could go as well." Myra smiled as she David, and Kathleen were busy canning the last of the garden's produce. "William and Celeste are such a wonderful brother and sister."

David became pensive then shook his head. "No. No they're not. Watch closely. They're more like close friends. If they were older, I'd say boyfriend and girlfriend."

"They're little more than children," Myra said.

Kathleen mentioned a few of their interactions she'd observed, thought for a while and said, "I believe David is right."

***

"First we need shelter," Andre said after they hiked four-miles from home and into the snow-covered foothills of the Cascades. "The boys and I will make a lean-to and I will teach them how to start a fire."

"The girls and I will dig a snow cave," Kimimela said.

After a number of hours of activity, each group demonstrated the results of their efforts.

"The snow cave was pretty neat," William said as he and the others sat on pine branches around the fire.

"It was a lot of work but in an emergency at least you'd be out of the weather," Celeste said.

"The boys will sleep in the lean-to tonight and the girls in the snow cave," Kimimela said.

William wrinkled his face after he bit off a piece of pemmican. "Kinda chewy," he said.

"But delicious when you're hungry and don't have anything else to eat," Andre said.

"Who has cold feet?" Kimimela asked.

"Mine aren't exactly warm," Celeste said.

Andre unrolled a piece of deer hide. "How about making yourself a pair of boots?"

The children watched in fascination as Kimimela's dexterous fingers used a knife and bone needle to fashion one boot and then guided the children as they completed the second.

"My feet are warm as a sunny day," Celeste declared after trying out the knee-high boots.

They hadn't gone far on the hike back home, when a dog growled at them.

"He has the dog sickness. See the foam around his mouth?" Andre said.

"What should we do?" Nathan asked.

"Stay still." He removed a pistol from his waist.

He pointed it at the dog and pulled the trigger. It only clicked.

The dog ran at them.

A silvery flash left Kimimela's hand and struck the dog who yelped once and collapsed.

"My Mom's pretty good throwing a knife," Monica said wearing a huge grin.

"Good? I'd say that was great," Celeste said.

"Look over there!" William pointed as two skiers slid into view and came to a halt next to the amazed children.

"What are those? Snow sliders?" William asked.

The duo laughed. In a thickly accented voice, the man replied, "They're called skis. We're from Norway and this is how we get around in winter."

"How do you go uphill?" Monica asked.

The woman said, "We attach skins which allows us to ascend."

"Keep an eye out," the man said. "We heard wolves last night."

They watched in fascination as the skier's schussed down the balance of the trail.

"I gotta learn to do that," William said. The others nodded agreement.

"When we travel outside of town, we are surrounded by wild animals," Andre said. "An important rule, perhaps the most important one when hunting, is to watch for animals that may be hunting you!"

They continued walking back to town. William noted Monica walking last.

"You walk in front of me. I can watch behind us so no wolves sneak up on us."

"I can do that."

"My Uncle Jack taught me how to be a scout so it should be me. You can help if you want but I need to be the last one."

Kimimela glanced over her shoulder at the procession. She smiled when she saw Monica and William stop and carefully survey the scene behind them before continuing.

Back at the cabin, the Kaplan children thanked the Holts and hurried to their own home bursting with stories to tell their parents.

***

Two weeks later, Dr. Beckham arrived at the Kaplan home. Myra and Kathleen greeted him.

"I have some sad news to relate. A hunter encountered the remains of a wolf ravaged body. He found it just into the foothills at the top of a steep trail," Dr. Beckham said to Myra and Kathleen. "It's Andre."

The trio walked out to Kimimela's cabin. She was bringing an arm load of kindling into the cabin when she saw the long-faced-trio approach.

"No," she screamed, putting up her hands as if that would stop the awful news.

"Kim, I'm so sorry."

She and Kathleen helped her into the cabin.

***

After the funeral at the Catholic cemetery, Kathleen asked Kim where she would live.

"Not sure. We lived here because Andre worked for you."

"You can stay there," Myra said.

"Thank you but I need to find work and should get a smaller place."

"Mr. Anchote and his family lived at the back of our dress shop until he found his own place," Myra said. "We can rent that space to you cheaper than the cabin."

"Why don't you begin sewing leather jackets," Kathleen said. "You design them and I'll assign you a helper. We can discuss how to price them when you feel up to it. Personally, I'd love a shearling lined jacket and I know my family would as well."

Kim smiled at her friends. "Thank you for your kindness." She stopped walking and put a hand on her nine-month swollen belly. She turned to her friends. "My water. My baby is coming."

That evening, Kim delivered fraternal twins, Andre and Alex.

Chapter Fourteen: Kathleen's Dismay

"It certainly has been warm," Kathleen said the following summer while sipping iced tea in her kitchen along with Myra.

Her sister said, "Even the children sleep with their windows open."

Without looking up from her tea, Kathleen said, "They heard us shouting again?"

Myra nodded. "Want to tell me what's going on?"

"I know the children are in school but is Ciara awake?"

"Taking a nap."

Kathleen stirred more sugar into her tea, then twisted on her chair. "He left for Salem today."

"You don't like him traveling?"

"I look forward to it."

"Why?"

Kathleen sighed and said, "When he returns, he'll find separate beds in our room. I told him last night."

"Kathleen…"

"Andrew is every woman's dream. Good income. Amazing father to Jack. Great husband."

"But?"

Kathleen shivered. "My skin crawls when he touches me."

"You've been married for nearly a year."

"And everything's great except the bed part."

They sipped their teas in silence until Myra asked, "How long has it been?"

"The last time was at least four months ago."

"Doesn't your body…"

Kathleen interrupted. "Yes, it wants a man."

"Why not Andrew?"

Kathleen squirmed on her chair then banged the table with her fist. "My God Myra, I've been wracking my brain trying to figure it out. What the hell's wrong with me?"

"Was there a problem with you and Jack?"

She smiled at the memory. "When we sailed out here after our wedding, I hardly saw the ocean for all the times we retired to our cabin."

"Do other men still attract you?"

"Well…" Kathleen again twisted on her chair. "Two weeks ago, that muscular carpenter who worked on our houses making changes to the interior…"

Myra's eyes went wide. She said in a remonstrating voice, "Kathleen, you didn't…"

Kathleen shrugged. "Andrew was out of town for the week. I carried a pitcher of water up to my bedroom. He was wearing work overalls but no shirt. One glance and my body was on fire. I slipped out of my shoes, undid the fasteners on the back of my dress and pulled it over my head. I walked up to him and unsnapped the overall's shoulder straps."

"Did Andrew find out?"

"No." She leaned back in her chair, closed her eyes and grinned. "But, heaven forgive me, it was great."

"He's not your husband."

Kathleen shook her head and said, "I didn't care. After we finished, I let him rest then made him want me again."

"This is so wrong."

"Of course it is but the damn carpenter satisfied me for the first time since Jack senior died."

"What's Andrew supposed to do?"

"Truth be told, I don't care where he gets it…and I told him that...he was furious."

"Will your relationship survive?"

"We're staying together for now. Besides, I think he has someone in town to do it with."

"A street walker?"

"No. A middle aged, single woman who's barren. That's all I know about her. They use each other and he comes home."

"And you?"

Kathleen shrugged her shoulders. "Don't know what the hell I'm going to do."

PART TWO

Chapter Fifteen: Monica is Educated

Three boys blocked Celeste and Monica's path to the school yard.

"I haven't punched an Indian today," the largest of the three said.

"You must be new around here. Leave us alone or I'll scream," Celeste said.

"Who cares?"

Celeste smiled. "You will."

The bully smirked, shoved Monica and laughed as she fell and her books scattered across the ground.

Celeste screamed.

William came running at full speed to his sister's side with Nathan close behind.

"There's still three of us, punk," the bully said looking down at William who was a head shorter.

William uncoiled like a snake and buried a fist into the boy's belly. The bully doubled over, and dropped to his knees, gasping for air. Nathan and William eyed his friends with fury in their eyes such that the others didn't move.

Celeste put her books down and helped Monica to her feet.

"Now you're out numbered," William said as nearly six-foot-tall Abbey arrived.

The bully said, "She's just a dumb Indian."

"Behind my back I've heard you refer to me as one of those evil Jews," Celeste said.

"At least you're white," one of the bully's friends said.

"What's that damn Indian to you?" the bully said after catching his breath but still on his knees.

"She's…our cousin," Nathan said.

In an anger filled voice and displaying body language which promised further mayhem if needed, William said, "You lay a hand on her and I'll beat the hell out of you."

"No," Abbey growled in a deep voice. "We'll all beat the hell out of you."

"If anything happens to my cousin," Celeste said in a sweet voice, "I'm going to tell my brothers and sister it was your fault."

"What?" the bully said in a shocked voice.

Celeste smiled and said in a sweet voice, "Please be certain your friends leave her alone."

***

"Mom, you need to talk to Mrs. Holt," Celeste said as she entered their parlor at the end of the school day. "Monica is way behind at school. Miss Pringle doesn't help her and is always making fun of her."

"Making fun of her?"

"Because she's an Indian."

Myra seethed. Through clenched teeth she said, "Thank you for letting me know. Kim and I will meet with Miss Pringle."

***

"Did you talk to Miss Pringle," Celeste asked during evening meal the following day.

Myra nodded.

"What happened," David asked.

"I advised Miss Pringle her current behavior with regards to Monica was unacceptable and that I would be monitoring Monica's progress."

"And…" David said.

"That I would be advising the school board as to Monica's progress at contract renewal time."

"Thanks Mom," Celeste said.

"It's not that simple. Monica is far behind the other students her age."

"Monica should come home with us every day so we can study together," Celeste said.

Myra stopped eating and stared at Celeste.

"What?" the eight-year-old said.

"My precious Celeste. Of course she should. I'll discuss your idea with Kim."

***

William, studying in the kitchen with his brothers and sisters, noticed Monica struggling to decipher a simple reader. After a glance at his mother and Celeste, who were occupied preparing evening meal, he invited her to study with him in the dining room.

They sat in adjacent chairs. Monica struggled to read a simple sentence. She sat up straight and folded her arms across her chest. "I'm stupid. Everyone reads better than me."

William shrugged his shoulders and said, "I don't care. Anyone can work hard. Keep reading. When you encounter an unfamiliar word, please write it down along with its definition."

"I won't."

William slammed his fist on the table. A booming sound echoed across the room.

She jumped.

Monica's eyes filled with tears. "That was mean."

In a pleasant voice he said, "Please start reading."

She hesitantly read a few lines. "Mary's dad made a … bench for her." She looked at William. "Excuse me. I'm not sure what a bench is."

William explained. He helped her pronounce and decipher new words plus patiently helped her write them in her notebook.

"You have beautiful printing," William said.

"It's kind of like drawing so it's fun."

After completing an entire chapter in her reader, they reviewed her new vocabulary.

"I think I know that stuff now," she said.

"Arithmetic next," William said.

"We're doing multiply. I don't like it."

"Watch." He wrote basic multiplication facts on a foot-square chalk board again and again. Finally, he just asked the problem. With sufficient repetition, they were committed to memory.

"Oh!" Monica's face brightened. "I can do this."

Myra entered the room, sat in the corner and picked up her knitting.

"I can do multiply, Mrs. Kaplan. William teached me."

"Excellent. Work hard, dear."

Nathan entered. "William, I have a math word problem I don't know how to approach."

His brother replied, "Write down the facts and I'll be there in a minute."

Nathan walked away mumbling, "Write down the facts…" A minute later he yelled, "I GOT IT!"

"You help your big brother," Monica said.

William nodded. "Just with math. He helps me with geography and language."

"I wish I had family to help me."

In a pleasant tone and putting a hand on her arm he said, "You do. I'm your cousin, remember?"

Monica smiled; her eyes radiant as she addressed William. "I remember." She abruptly sat up straight.

"Please, ask me the multiplication facts again. I don't want to forget them."

"Mom," Celeste called. "Your stew is boiling."

"Move it to the side and I'll be right there." Myra set her knitting aside. As she left the room she raised her eyebrows and mouthed to William, "Good teaching."

Monica tore a blank page out of her notebook. Using a handful of rapid strokes, she completed a sketch and handed it to William.

His jaw dropped.

"What is it?" she asked.

"A Great Blue Heron fishing in reeds." He looked up at her. "This is great."

"It's yours because you helped me."

Chapter Sixteen: Family Coming and Going

The late-summer festival was in full swing. A banjo, squeeze-box, and guitar enticed dancers.

After completing a number of dances with Celeste, twelve-year-old William said, "Monica hasn't danced yet. I'll ask her."

He approached her and said, "Hi Monica. You look great."

Her eyes sparkled. "Thank you. You too."

The music started again. "Dance?"

Monica nodded. They proceeded to spin around the dance floor.

"William and Monica. Cute couple," David said, standing at Celeste's side and nodding at the twosome.

"They're laughing. Look how they gaze at each other," Celeste said. She turned to David. "My ankle hurts. I'm going home."

***

Family and friends gathered at the Kaplan's to say goodbye to Abbey, who was leaving for Medical College.

"Write to me big sister," Celeste said while giving her a hug.

Dr. Beckham addressed Abbey. "One thing to consider when you've finished your college medical studies. There's going to be a war over slavery. The attack on Fort Sumter may be the beginning. If you doctor the wounded soldiers, you'll learn more about surgery and doctoring than any single person could possibly teach you."

"I'm not going to be a soldier."

"That's fine," the doctor said. "The medical units are away from the fighting. I'm certain they'll employ civilian doctors."

***

At the following Friday-night-services, grim-faced Robert Khasina, standing next to his teary-eyed-wife Esther and their four-year-old daughter Shifra, asked for the group's attention. "I've just received a letter from my brother in Odessa. Some months ago a cruel pogrom occurred. The Jewish community suffered many deaths."

"Russians?" David asked.

"No. Greek sailors and local Greeks attacked the Jewish section of town. My brother wrote that a number of my family members were killed as well as his teenage son. His wife was severely injured. I'm sending as much money as I can to help them and would appreciate any other assistance to bring them to America."

David, Mr. Goodman and Mr. Goldenberg huddled for a quick meeting. The three men headed the local Jewish Benevolent Society.

"Dad," Celeste asked, "didn't you tell us relatives in America sent money to Ireland to bring your family to Philadelphia or you'd still be in Ireland?"

"That's what happened," David replied.

"Family and their friends in American brought my brother Colin and me over," Myra said. "We were starving in Ireland but those who crossed before us saved us."

"My story as well," Kathleen said.

"Same for my family…," Mr. Goldenberg said, "but we barely have enough to cover the needs of the Jewish Community here in Portland."

"I know," Mr. Goodman said with a sigh. "I propose we talk to each family individually and see what we can gather."

A week later, David and Celeste walked to the Khasina's home and gave the little money they managed to gather to Robert.

"I don't know how much this will help," David said of the paltry sum.

"William, me, and Nathan with some of our friends shoveled out a stable and gave the money to dad to give to you," Celeste said.

"Thank you Celeste. Relatives from the east coast are sending money as well. With what you've added, we should get at least six out of there." He shook their hands with both of his. "I can't thank you enough."

Chapter Seventeen: William's Calling

Late Saturday, on a warm, sunny afternoon, a tall, thin, out of breath, man pounded on their front door of the Kaplan's home and yelled, "I'm looking for William Kaplan. Dr. Beckham needs him. There's a medical emergency. He said he needs William and his little sewing needle."

William, shocked, turned to David, who said, "Don't look at me. Get the needle and go!"

The thirteen-year-old jumped from his chair and bounded across the room, grabbed the box which held the needle and headed out the door.

Nathan entered the parlor and asked, "What's all the yelling?"

"Medical emergency. Dr. Beckham asked for William."

Nathan raced out the door after his brother.

Celeste, who was teaching seven-year-old Shifra how to knit, put down her work, grabbed Shifra's hand and ran after her brothers.

William's feet slapped down the dirt street, then pounded the boards of the wood sidewalk which fronted the shops. Celeste, Shifra, and Nathan, weren't far behind. He ran into Dr. Beckham's office. A mother in tears, tried to soothe a terrified infant. His knee, lower leg and ankle were covered in blood soaked wrappings.

The grim faced doctor told William. "There's tiny shards of broken glass in the wounds plus he needs surgical repair. If we don't accomplish that, I'll have to amputate his leg."

"Please, no," pleaded the mother who cried and buried her tear streaked face in her husband's chest.

William glanced at the gruesome injuries as Dr. Beckham uncovered them.

"He's tiny," Celeste exclaimed. Shifra turned away after a brief glance.

The doctor said, "He was born premature. My arthritic hands can't pick out the broken glass in his wounds. We've joked about your ability with noodles but now it's serious. This child needs your ability, William."

The thirteen-year-old shook his head. "Oh hell no."

The doctor said in a firm voice, "I'll tell you what to do. Clean your hands. I'll clean your needle."

William briefly stared at the little one, then turned and began soaping his hands.

As the doctor began advising him, William took two deep breaths and using tiny, delicate, and precise movements, carefully followed each of the doctor's instructions. William's intense concentration caused beads of sweat to form. Mrs. Beckham wiped his brow.

An hour-and-a-half later the last piece of glass was removed and the final suture in place.

"I'm glad that's over." William said, using his forearm to wipe sweat off his forehead. "Will his leg be okay?"

Dr. Beckham said, "I won't know for a few weeks…maybe a few months. Poor little fellow lost a lot of blood. That leg may still have to be amputated but we did our best today. That's all we can do for now. Thanks for showing up."

"I was told it was an emergency but I didn't think…"

"Please consider, you may have saved an infant's leg today."

William shook his head. "You knew what to do. I didn't."

"I held the knowledge but your hands did the work. When you complete medical school you'll know what to do."

"I'm going to be an engineer. That's what I've planned. I dislike working on people."

The doctor shook his head. "What can I provide to convince you, this is the kind of work you should aim towards?"

"Maybe a magnifying lens?"

Dr. Beckham looked over the top of his glasses. "I meant, what could motivate you to become a doctor?"

William again shook his head. "This isn't for me."

Dr. Beckham seemed saddened. "And next time I need your ability?"

The thirteen-year-old stretched the tension out of his shoulders by rolling them a few times. "Next time…please find someone else."

William put his little needle in the box, the box in his pocket, and walked out of the office.

His grinning brother and sister followed close behind him. William glanced at them over his shoulder. "Quit grinning."

"You're going to be a doctor like Abbey and me," Nathan said.

William's face reddened. With jaw set firmly and clenched fists, he turned to face his brother and declared, "I hated doing that stuff. If I screwed up, he might lose his leg. I'm going to be an engineer and now I'm going for a walk…alone…so I can forget this ever happened."

***

Proud Celeste told her parents, "While he worked on the baby, William wore the expression Dad gets when he's angry." She giggled. "If angry looks can heal, the little boy will be fine."

"How old was the child?" Myra asked, while she helped Ciara hem a dress.

"Six days." Celeste said.

David slapped his forehead. "Six days and needed William."

Shifra held her hands a foot apart. "He was only this big. Almost his whole leg was red with blood."

"Premature birth Dr. Beckham told us." Nathan shook his head. "You should have seen the minute movements my brother used."

William returned from his walk and joined the family.

Myra said. "You hungry?"

William shook his head.

His mother said quietly, "Nathan told us Dr. Beckham couldn't have done it without your hands."

"I was born with a skill. Lucky – that's all."

Ciara considered his answer then said, "No. That baby boy was lucky; lucky you were around to help repair him."

William shook his head.

"What's wrong?" Shifra said. "You fixed his leg."

Ciara asked, "Why aren't you proud of what you did?"

He glared at them. "I'm going to forget this ever happened." He looked at the others. "I'll be furious with anyone who tries to remind me." He stormed out of the room.

"I'll talk to him," David said. "He has an incredible gift."

Celeste said, "Don't push him, Dad. He'll make the right decision."

David opened his mouth as if to reply, hesitated, and turned to Myra who shrugged her shoulders.

***

"Rabbi Rifkin, why don't girls have Bar Mitzvahs?" Celeste asked about the Jewish ceremony for thirteen-year-olds.

Rabbi Moshe Rifkin arrived early that morning for William's Bar Mitzvah. Celeste and William met with him at Dov's home.

"Women have different responsibilities than men."

"What about an Aliyah? A Torah reading?" William asked. "Celeste knows the Torah blessings as well as I do."

"Having an Aliyah is a Mitzvah, a good deed, for men. If she has an Aliyah then she prevents a man from performing a mitzvah."

"Why isn't it a mitzvah for a woman to have an Aliyah?" Celeste asked in a voice tinged with anger.

The rabbi said, "We have traditions that go back thousands of years…"

Celeste continued, "And why don't women count toward a minyan? I don't like that I don't count."

"As I said, women have different…" Rabbi Rifkin removed his glasses and rubbed the area where they contacted his nose. "Celeste, do you have a Hebrew name?"

"No."

"Would you consider taking the name Chana? It was my wife's name."

Celeste smiled. "Chana is lovely."

"You ask questions," Rabbi Rifkin said, "with the same fervor as she did. One of her greatest desires was to read Torah." He sighed and momentarily stared at the floor. "She died before I could think of a way to arrange it." His gaze returned to Celeste. He gave her a warm smile. "The Torah teaches us, Chana was the first person to pray quietly to God. She is most well known for being the mother of Samuel the prophet. But she was also a prophetess in her own right. We learned many fundamental laws about prayer from her."

"Chana is a lovely name," William said.

"I wish my Chana could have met you, Celeste."

"Sounds like we'd have lots to talk about."

"Nathan told me of your love of Judaism and its values. I have something for you and your brother."

He left the room briefly then returned with two cloth sacks, each containing a prayer shawl. With a radiant expression, he handed one to each of them.

Celeste's eyes widened. "A tallit for me? Thank you."

William opened his. "Thank you, Rabbi."

Celeste wrapped hers over her shoulders. "It is lovely but I didn't think women could wear them."

"A girl can wear a tallit as long as it doesn't look like a man's."

"Rabbi Rifkin, Celeste studied as much as me and she knows the blessings and Torah portion probably better than me. Isn't there anyway we could be Bar Mitzvah'd together?"

The Rabbi shook his head.

William's shoulder's drooped. He turned to Celeste. "I tried. It doesn't seem fair."

On the walk home, Celeste stopped walking and said to William who also stopped walking then turned to face her. "You stood up for me." She briefly embraced him.

William wore a questioning expression.

"What?" Celeste asked.

"I guess it's been a long time since we hugged."

"So?"

" I felt your chest things against me. That's new."

Celeste laughed hysterically and they continued walking.

***

"Hi Celeste. Hi Ciara. Can I sit with you?" Shifra asked before William's Bar Mitzvah began.

Celeste glanced at Shifra's mother who nodded.

"Sit over here," she said. Ciara sat on one side and Shifra on the other.

Celeste wrapped her tallit around both girls and Ciara occupied herself playing with the garment's fringes.

At the end of his analysis of the day's Parsha, William added, "I must thank Uncle Dov for teaching me Hebrew and Yiddish plus preparing me for this day. Also, thanks are due to someone who spent as much time as me studying the prayers and analyzing today's Torah portion. When I didn't feel like taking the time to get things right, she reminded me I would have the opportunity to read the text Jews have been reading and studying for thousands of years. Thank you, Celeste Spire."

Chapter Eighteen: The Flu Strikes

Mid-morning on a rainy damp late fall day, William sitting across the kitchen table from his mother, put down the novel he was reading. Myra was occupied knitting a sweater for Ciara. He asked, "Is that Shifra Khasina in Abbey's bed?"

"Yes," Myra said.

"Have you heard anything about her mom?"

Myra stopped knitting, her expression one of sadness. "It hurts me to say but Esther is deathly ill. She's had a weak heart since childhood. Shifra's birth nearly killed her...and this flu epidemic may finish the job. Mr. Khasina is ill as well."

"Is that why Mrs. Khasina is always out of breath when she moves around?"

"Yes. Keep this to yourself but Dr. Beckham thinks she only has a few days left. With Shifra close to Celeste and both parents so ill, they decided it was preferable that their daughter live with us."

"Nathan's lucky he left for Philadelphia last summer to study with Rabbi Rifkin."

"The newspaper wrote that the flu is spreading across the country. They're referring to it as an epidemic."

"I heard school won't open for at least another week."

"That's what I was told. William, I want you to head over to the Holts. The flu's hit them like everyone else. The twins finished with the flu last week and are staying with the Anchotes. I heard Monica's not eating. I made a container of Scotch broth which should be ready in a few minutes. I know she and Kim like it. It's sleeting out so dress warm. I don't want you sick again."

"Mom, I'm not a babysitter." Myra simply eyed her youngest son. He shrugged his shoulders as he knew there would be no changing her mind.

"Mrs. Holt and Monica like to read poetry," Celeste suggested handing her brother a book. She coughed; a deep hacking cough.

"Celeste," Myra said. "Pour yourself a hot cup of tea, add honey and lemon and you get right back in bed."

"Yes Mom."

"How's Shifra?" Myra asked as her daughter stirred honey into her tea.

"Sleeping like a baby and her head isn't burning up like it was the last couple of days."

***

William trudged through howling wind, rain, and ankle-deep-mud to the dress shop. His boots made a sucking sound as each pulled out of the muck.

Entering, he found Kimimela hemming a dress by lantern light. "Mom sent soup over for you and Monica." He removed his boots near the front entrance of the store.

Kimimela said, "I'm busy. Can you get it on the stove and heat it? Don't be surprised if Monica won't eat."

William noticed a rain soaked young man peering through the front window.

"Mrs. Holt, that man is staring at us."

The man pronounced her name and left.

"He looked familiar." She shrugged, seemed momentarily pensive and returned to sewing. "Not many people call me by my Indian name."

William proceeded to their residence at the back of the store.

"Hi William." Monica was reading a book, wrapped in a blanket while seated on a wing back chair in front of the fireplace. The orange glow of the fire reflected on her face.

William said, "Mom sent soup over for you guys."

"Scotch Broth?"

"With chicken."

"Normally I'd love to, but…"

Monica, keeping her blanket wrapped around her, followed him to the stove.

William opened a burner, put kindling inside and ignited it. He moved a kettle over another burner after starting kindling below it. While stirring the soup with one hand, he put the other on his hip. "I slogged over here in this messy weather. You'd better eat."

She smiled. "Are you going to bang your fist on the table to get me to eat?"

He laughed. "Sit down. A few minutes and the soup will be heated through."

"Have you eaten dinner?" she asked.

He shook his head.

"Eat with me?"

"You eat and I'll eat."

She sighed. "I will. Weren't your folks worried you might get the flu over here?"

"Mom and I finished with it last week. Dad got over it before us and he's next door helping Aunt Kathleen's family. I guess once you get it you don't get it again. Celeste, Shifra and Ciara are flat on their backs at our house."

William checked the pot, gave it a stir, and replaced the lid. "Couple more minutes." He heard the water in the tea kettle boiling. "Tea?"

"Love a cup."

He filled two cups and set them on the table.

Celeste added sugar to hers then asked, "Did you see my mom?"

William sipped his tea before replying. "She's working on something."

"Was she sweating?"

"Lots."

"She's sick but won't rest or close the store. Mr. Anchote is home taking care of his family."

"The stores in town are all closed."

They sipped their tea in silence for a while.

William checked the soup. "Ready." He moved it to the side and closed the stove's dampers. The thick, aromatic broth was ladled into two bowls.

"Mom puts in turnips, onions, carrots, dried parsley, and celery besides the barley and chicken," he said.

He filled his spoon and glanced at Monica who hadn't moved.

"You eat and I'll eat. You agreed."

She lifted her spoon and ate a few spoonsful.

Kimimela entered and sat at the table.

"I closed the shop for a while. I can hardly work. My muscles are sore and my joints ache; I must lay down."

"Mom," Celeste said, "You need to eat."

"Not now. I haven't the strength."

"You haven't eaten for two days."

"Later."

"Eat something or I'll quit eating."

William jumped up and filled another bowl which he put in front of Kim then poured a cup of tea for her.

Kim's shivering intensified while she ate. "I can't seem to get warm."

With obvious effort, she emptied the bowl. "I'm going to lie down. William, there are down-filled quilts near the front of the store. Will you please bring two of them?"

"On my way."

Returning with the quilts, he knocked on Kim's bedroom door.

"Come in," a weak voice called out followed by coughing.

"Here's the quilt, Mrs. Holt." He placed it over her.

"Thank you. Keep an eye on Monica please."

"Yes Ma'am."

Monica was sound asleep on the couch in the living area. William placed the second quilt over her. Returning to the kitchen, he washed their dishes and placed the soup pot on their back porch. William read for a few hours while the others slept. He added logs to the fireplace, pulled on his boots and coat, then slogged through the mud to his own home.

***

"How are the Holts?" Myra asked.

"Not so good," William said while pulling his heavy boots off and hanging his coat. "One time, you said a room brightens when Monica enters. Not today. She looks pale, tired, and worn. Mrs. Holt tried to keep her store open but closed it to rest. By the time I left, she was in bed shivering and sweating."

"Oh my Lord. There's no one to cook for them. William get the ingredients for Colcannon. Also lemon, tea, and a jar of honey."

"Does Mrs. Holt know how to make colcannon?"

She looked at him over the tops of her glasses putting both hands on her hips. "No, but you do."

"Mom, no" he pleaded.

She appraised him with a stern visage then grabbed his shoulders. "Listen to me. People are deathly ill all over this town, not to mention country. The Holt's have to eat or they'll get worse. Mrs. Holt is in no condition to cook."

"But Mom…"

"You're fifteen now. Old enough to handle responsibility. Besides, you have your father's determination in you. Time to use it."

"Determination?"

"I've watched you shut out the rest of the world when you set your mind to a task; and seen your face when you get angry. You're truly a copy of your father; so I know you'll get this done."

He shrugged his shoulders. "Ingredients for Colcannon on the way."

They boxed the items on their kitchen table.

"I've included dried apples, sugar, and barley for you to make for their breakfast."

"Breakfast?"

"You've haven't lived through illnesses like this. I have." Myra shuddered. "My family suffered through a tragedy like this during the Irish Potato Famine. You do exactly as I say. Poor Mr. Anchote has already delivered his precious little son Lucas to the cemetery." She gazed at the ceiling. "Lord, please take care of that fine boy." Myra looked at her son. "You stay at the Holt's and do whatever you can. Heat a kettle so it's ready for tea. Be sure to add lemon juice and honey. Serve it to them whenever they're awake. I'll bring more food tomorrow morning. Until they're on the mend, the only reason you come home is for more food. If one of them becomes incoherent, find Dr. Beckham. Remember! They don't eat, they don't heal."

"I'll get an oil cloth to wrap the box."

"Take books so you have something to do in-between taking care of them. Make sure you keep their home as warm as possible."

***

The freezing rain turned to wet snow during his return trip. William's cowboy hat prevented most of the snow from landing on his head but wind-driven-water from the trees caused icy rivulets to course down his neck. He shivered with each. Arriving at the store, the fifteen-year-old pulled off his coat and boots before entering the living area.

Monica, still covered by the quilt and lying on the sofa, briefly opened her eyes and whispered in a weak voice, "Hi."

"How are you?"

"Tired and sleepy. Better than yesterday but my muscles still ache. It feels good to sleep in front of the fire."

"Your mom?"

"Don't know."

William placed more logs in the fire place and briefly looked in on Kim.

"How's my mom?"

"Shivering but sleeping."

"Thanks for checking."

"I'm making tea and I have stuff to make for evening meal."

"Can I help?"

"You're sick. I'll manage."

"Why did you decide to come over?" she asked.

"My Mom. She figured you guys might need help with meals and keeping the house warm."

"She was right."

William walked their chamber pots to the outhouse. He thought, "*I hope the food I make doesn't smell this bad after they eat it.*" He chuckled.

He was about to begin peeling potatoes when Myra's voice echoed in his head. "Everyone wants to eat clean food and clean food starts with clean hands."

"Yes, Mom." He laughed as he soaped his hands.

"Who you talking to?" Monica asked, wrapping the down quilt around her before sitting down at the kitchen table.

"My mom. Ever notice, even when they're not around, your folks talk to you when you're about to do something they wouldn't like?"

She laughed. "Plenty of times."

While the potatoes boiled, William melted beef fat in a heated pot then added flour and stirred until it darkened. He added cubed, boiled beef, a mashed garlic clove, a bay leaf, and water. He finely chopped an onion and sliced cabbage, both of which he blanched in boiling water. After mashing the potatoes, William drained the cabbage and onion, mixed them with the potatoes and added minced dried parsley.

He placed the potato mixture on a plate, made a depression in the middle and ladled the beef in.

"Mom calls this American Colcannon. When she lived in Ireland, they put butter in the middle instead of meat."

He placed the dish and a cup of tea in front of Monica who looked up at him.

"I know," he said. "You're not hungry. Please eat what you can. I'll reheat the Scotch Broth for your mom. When I was sick, it seemed easier to eat soup."

William knocked on Kimimela's door. Not hearing a reply, he opened the door and peered at her sleeping, blanket covered form.

"I have evening meal," he said, loud enough to wake her.

She opened her eyes briefly to see who it was. "I don't have enough strength to eat. Thank you but let me sleep."

William left the room then returned with a chair which he placed next to the bed.

He slid an arm around her back and lifted her to a sitting position while arranging her pillows to support her.

"What are you doing?" Kim asked.

"I'm doing what I imagine my dad or mom would do."

William sat on the chair and fed her Scotch Broth and tea.

"Thank you, William. I must rest."

He checked on Monica who slept soundly. William cleaned the kitchen, added logs to the fireplace, and opened a book.

A few hours later, Monica's coughing woke her. William looked up from his reading. She asked, "Are you going home?"

"Not tonight."

"Where will you sleep?"

"I'll pile blankets on the floor by the fire."

She smiled. "Good."

"Why good?"

"If I wake, I'll see…my cousin and not feel alone."

He chuckled. "Go to sleep, Cousin."

At two in the morning, William thought he heard a distant voice. He listened but didn't hear more sound so refreshed the dwindling fire. The sound occurred again. After lighting an oil lamp, he checked Monica; she slept soundly. The fifteen-year-old peered into Kimimela's room. She was speaking in a language he didn't understand.

"Mrs. Holt," he said, approaching her bed.

She smiled. "Andre, I'm glad you're here."

"Mrs. Holt, I'm William. Would you like tea or something?"

"No Andre. I enjoyed the meal you fed me. Just like the first time we met."

"Mrs. Holt, you're drenched in sweat."

"I'm warm. You're furs always keep me warm but my body hurts everywhere. I don't know how much longer I'll last."

"Don't say that, Mrs. Holt. Monica and the twins need you."

"Yes Andre. They need me." After a gentle sigh, she rolled on her side and closed her eyes.

William put a hand just below her nose and thought, "*Shallow but breathing. With all this sweat, her body must need more liquid.*"

He hurried to the kitchen, heated water then placed tea in a tin mug. William added water when it boiled and stirred in lemon and honey.

Returning to the bedroom he forced Kimimela to a sitting position.

"Please Andre. Let me rest."

"Drink this Mrs. Holt."

"Must I?"

"Yes," William replied with more anger than he intended.

She swallowed a bit of the liquid. "Enough Andre," she pleaded. "I'm so worn."

In a firm voice, William told her, "Not until you finish this." He held the cup up to her lips.

"I will but please don't raise your voice."

It required a number of minutes but she drained the last of the tea. William helped her lie back and pulled her blankets up to her chin. He watched her for a while and checked her breathing.

"Thank you, for that," Monica said. She stood in the doorway to her mother's room.

He retrieved the empty cup and took it to the kitchen.

Still wrapped in the down quilt, Monica followed.

As he washed the cup he glanced at Monica and said, "She thought I was your dad."

"I heard. When you raised your voice, you sounded like him."

"I didn't mean to get loud. You should get back to sleep."

"Mom's awfully sick."

"She is."

Monica said, "Some folks are dying."

"Lots of Indians as well. Mom said Dr. Young went up to Ft. Vancouver to help them."

Her lower lip quivered. "It was bad enough when Dad died. I don't want to end up just me and the twins." A tear rolled down her cheek.

"You won't be alone. You've got family...cousins at least."

Monica smiled and nodded. She crossed the room and stood close; then put her arms around him, resting her head on his chest. "Thank you, Cousin."

William returned her embrace. "The rest of the night, I'll stay by your mom. Get back to sleep. I don't need you as sick as she is."

Chapter Nineteen: The Death Toll Rises

The following day, William rose with the sun. Mrs. Holt slept quietly and no longer shivered he noted. Passing the fireplace on his way to the kitchen, he made a mental note to bring in more wood.

Placing barley in boiling water, he took dried apple slices and chopped them into small pieces. He had just finished filling a kettle for tea when he heard footsteps entering the residence.

"Hi Mom."

"How are your patients?" Myra asked.

"Monica is still sick but she's eating. Mrs. Holt's head was hot and sweat covered last night. She was talking to me as if I was her husband."

"Not a good sign. Is she eating?"

"Yes, but I fed her like a baby."

"Dr. Beckham stopped by yesterday. He said to keep everyone eating, drinking, and praying."

"How are things at home?"

"Celeste is doing well. She'll rest today and tomorrow. If she continues to improve, I'll send her over to help you. Shifra slept through the night so she's on the mend. Ciara is alternating huge sweats and shivering. Her head was on fire last night. She keeps having nightmares but seems to be hanging on."

"Aunt Kathleen's family?"

"Brace yourself."

"Oh no."

"Jack may not make it another day."

"Uncle Jack's only child."

"Aunt Kathleen's started hallucinating. They're having a terrible time trying to get her to eat or drink. Aunt Daire is helping with Angela and Jack but suffering terrible coughs. They're talking to Dr. Beckham about what to do."

"Anyone else I know real sick?"

"Esther Khasina. The flu killed her." Myra stopped speaking to take a deep breath before continuing. "Robert, her husband, is so upset he can barely talk. I heard he hasn't eaten since his wife died."

"Does Shifra know?"

"We told her about Esther this morning. She's wrapped herself around Celeste."

"Anyone other folks?"

"There will be. Mr. Goldenberg and Mr. Goodman stopped by to see your father. They're going to ask everyone in the Jewish community for donations to buy more land for the Jewish cemetery."

"How are you, Mom?"

Myra smiled. "Thank you for asking. Tired but okay. Glad I got over this when you did."

"Something smells good," Monica said, entering the kitchen. "Oh. Hi, Mrs. Kaplan."

"Feeling better, Monica?" Myra asked.

"I'm hungry for the first time in a week."

"Good sign," Myra said with a grin.

William put food and tea on the table for them.

"Will you please check on Mom?" Monica asked.

"Of course, dear. Right away."

William and Monica ate until Myra returned.

"Your mother recognized me but still has a fever. When you've finished get her a meal with tea. Make sure she rests. That includes you, Monica. Getting up too soon can make you sick again. I've brought ingredients for Irish stew."

Monica smiled. "Lots of Irish meals."

"I grew up with them as did my children. It warms me to serve them." Myra smiled. "Monica, when you're finished eating, would help your mom eat?"

"Sure."

"Take a scoop of the cooked barley and stir in a little molasses. It's already got raisins and dried apple in it." Myra sighed. "Heading home. Lots to do over there."

***

"Good morning," Kim said as Monica entered her room carrying the bowl of breakfast barley and a mug of tea. "Crazy dream last night. I was talking to your father. He told me I must get well so I could take care of you and the twins." She stretched. "I feel so weak. Help me sit up. Someone chopping wood?"

"William. He sat with you most of the night."

"Is he taking care of you?"

Monica nodded. "One of Mr. Anchote's children died. Lucas, I was told."

"That happy little boy…how sad. Have any customers come by?"

"The streets are deserted. Until this sickness ends everyone's afraid to leave home."

Kim took a deep breath. "What's the delightful smell?"

"William's baking Irish soda bread. Mrs. Kaplan brought ingredients for bread and stew. William said taking care of us was Mrs. Kaplan's idea."

"The Lord bless her for her kindness."

Kimimela sipped her tea. "William is quite the young man. How's their family?"

"Healing. Mr. Kaplan is living full time at his sister-in-law's home to help them. All bed ridden and their son Jack is deathly ill. William said many Indians are dying. Dr. Young went up to Ft. Vancouver to help. We were worried about you."

"Every joint in my body aches but I have so much work. I should get out of bed."

"No," Monica said, putting a hand on her mother's shoulder. "Mrs. Kaplan said if you do too much right away you'll get sicker. Besides. I'm well enough to help him."

"Help him?"

"And you."

"Monica, he lives in a different world than we do."

***

Myra arrived home. Celeste sat in the kitchen with Shifra.

"You need to eat," her daughter said to the nine-year-old. She ate two spoonsful of barley cereal, dropped the spoon, sobbed and reached for Celeste who pulled her onto her lap.

"Need anything?" Myra asked Celeste.

"Check on Ciara. She's got an awful fever."

"Oh no. God no."

Myra ran into the children's room with Celeste and Shifra following.

She checked Ciara who responded to her touch with a weak smile. "Celeste," Myra said, "Get tea for

Ciara. Warm but not hot." Her daughter scampered out of the room but returned quickly.

"Here Ciara," Celeste said as she lifter her sister's head. "Warm but not hot." She brought the mug up to Ciara's lips. She swallowed twice but coughed on the third sip. "Take your time. Shifra and I are right here with you, little sister."

Ciara took a deep breath and continued sipping the tea.

***

"How are things at Aunt Kathleen's," Celeste asked David when he entered their home. Ciara and Shifra, on either side of Celeste and leaning against her, were bundled in blankets while the trio sat on a couch in the parlor.

David's expression was grim. "Jack seems to be better today. I haven't told your mother yet but after two days of delirium and high temperatures, Aunt Kathleen died. We tried and tried to get her to eat and drink but to no avail. I dread having to tell your mom."

"She's resting in her room."

David shook his head. "It's hard to believe, Kathleen was strong as an ox then is brought down by this sickness."

He gazed at Celeste. "How are you feeling?"

"Weak but much better overall."

"Someone from the family needs to tell William about Kathleen. If he needs anything, he'll have to let us know or come get it himself."

"I'll go." She turned to her young charges. "Ciara you stay here and try to get some sleep." Ciara nodded and put her arms out toward David who picked her up. He held her for a bit then placed her on the couch and tucked a blanket around her.

"I'll be with Mom," David said.

"Shifra, I'm walking to the Holt's. Want to come?"

She nodded. Using both hands, she wiped tears off her cheeks.

Celeste gathered warm outer wear. Someone knocked on their front door. Dr. Beckham stood there wearing a sullen expression. "I heard Shifra was staying here."

"She is."

"Can I talk to your dad?"

They heard Myra scream.

"Dad must have told her about Aunt Kathleen's death."

He looked down and shook his head. "I feel so damn helpless against this shit." His gaze returned to Celeste. "Sorry about the language." Dr. Beckham noted Shifra standing behind her. "Celeste, step outside and close the door."

She turned to Shifra. "I need to talk to Dr. Beckham. Please wait here."

In a quiet voice, he said, "Shifra's father died this morning."

Celeste sucked in her breath. "I heard he was ill."

"Someone needs to tell Shifra."

"We're close so it should be me. Poor girl. She's going to feel so alone."

"Can she stay here until we find a place for her?"

"Of course."

***

With a hood pulled over her head and a scarf wrapped across her face, only Shifra's eyes shown as the thoroughly bundled twosome trudged to the dress shop in an icy wind.

Celeste related their aunt's death to William.

"How's mom taking it?"

"Rough. Really Rough."

"Poor Mom."

"Dad's with her. She was crying and crying when we left." Celeste and William exchanged sad expressions.

"Aunt Kathleen," William said, "survived the Irish Potato famine, the abusive man who paid her passage to the U.S. and worked endless hours running the warehouse until we came out."

"She was so strong. I remember Dad teasing her about being a cowboy."

William shook his head. "All that and this damn flu crap destroyed her. How can a young one like cousin Jack survive but not his strong-as-can-be

Mom? I get the feeling doctors know next to nothing about diseases like this."

"Perhaps our generation will step up and find something. I'm not sure," Celeste said, "how to describe this but…you know how we say Ciara's eyes always sparkle? The sparkle is gone and she's not animated like before. She was burning up for a few nights."

"I wonder how that affected her."

Celeste dragged a rocking chair over to the fireplace.

"Let's sit down over here Shifra. I have something to tell you."

"Is your face sad because so much death?" Shifra asked.

Celeste lifted Shifra onto her lap. "Your father died."

The young one shook her head. "No. He's fine. He told me he wasn't so sick."

"Something happened after your mom passed."

"I don't have a mom or dad anymore?"

Celeste shook her head. "Shifra, I'm so sorry."

"So we girls need my dad."

"He's gone, sweetness."

"What's going to happen to me? Where will I live?"

"I don't know. But for now, we girls will stick together." Celeste held the youngster's head against her chest. Shifra's body quaked as she wept.

An hour later, the wind howled and rattled the building. Gazing out a window, Celeste saw snowflakes the size of cotton balls. She cursed. "This damn weather is making everything worse."

William put a hand on his sister's shoulder. "I think you and Shifra should stay here. I checked their root cellar. We've got enough food for today and tomorrow." He patted Shifra. "I'll walk over to our house when we need more."

"Celeste," Monica said. "You're sweating."

"I think the walk over here tired me."

"You can sleep in my room. I've been sleeping out here on the couch."

"C'mon, Shifra. We'll rest for a bit."

***

A few hours later, the twins appeared in the kitchen where William and Monica were preparing dinner.

Alex said, "Mrs. Anchote brought us home. She's going to her sister's funeral today."

Monica said, "Go take your coats off and come back to the kitchen for a mug of tea."

"How is your family?" Andre asked.

William placed a steaming mug in front of each of the boys.

"Sick but healing."

Andre asked, "What about Ciara?"

His brother stated, "Andre thinks Ciara is his girlfriend."

Andre said, "Knock it off. We're just friends."

Alex opened his mouth to reply but a look from William silenced both. The boys returned to sipping their tea.

After emptying his cup, Alex asked, "Why do they have funerals?"

"They bury the body and people say goodbye to their loved one," Monica answered while chopping carrots.

The young boys leaned toward each other and engaged in a whispered conversation and then giggled.

Monica eyed them. "What's so funny?"

"You guys look like a mom and dad," Andre said.

"Why?" Monica asked with a smile.

Alex explained, "You're taking care of everybody and smile at each other so much."

The teens exchanged embarrassed glances.

"Alex," Monica said. "Tell Celeste and Shifra that dinner is ready."

"What happens at a funeral?" Shifra asked Celeste as they ate.

"Your parent's bodies will each be in a box and they'll be placed in their final resting place."

"When will it happen?"

"Tomorrow."

"I wish I could talk to them."

"You can still talk to them in your head. I've done that for years with my parents and brother."

"Will you stay next to me?"

"Of course."

***

At the Jewish Cemetery, grim Shifra remained wrapped around Celeste as they both choked back tears.

Dov Rifkin cleared his throat. "We've gathered here today to say goodbye to family and friends."

After the ceremony, David addressed Andrew, "Shifra needs a place to live."

"My niece is welcome to stay with me," Andrew said.

Hearing this, Shifra wrapped her arms around Celeste. "You always say, we girls need to help each other. You need to help me stay with you."

Celeste's eyes pleaded with David. He turned to Andrew. "You have every legal right to have her live with you but for whatever reason, she feels closer to Celeste."

Andrew opened his mouth to say something but choked on a few tears first. "You're right, David." He turned to Shifra. "If you live with Celeste, will you still visit Cousin Jack, and Uncle Andrew?"

Shifra eyed Celeste who placed her arm around the young girl's shoulder. "Of course she will. Family is most important for…us girls." Shifra nodded. Celeste continued, "In fact we were hoping you and cousin Jack might join us for the Sabbath once this sickness ends."

On the walk home, Myra said to Celeste, "This will be a huge burden on you."

Celeste put her arm around her mother's shoulders. "I'll be fine. Nearly all my life, I've been watching you Myra raise someone else's children as if they were her own. Besides, I think I was born to raise children."

Chapter Twenty: More Family Changes

In the midst of another snow storm and late at night, an old woman knocked on the door of the dress shop. Monica unlocked the door and greeted her. She was thoroughly bundled in a scarf and leather clothing. The woman brushed snow off her clothing and stamped her feet.

Monica asked, “Can I help you?”

“Kimimela please,” the old woman said with a thick accent. She pulled down her hood and opened her jacket.

“Kimimela is my mother,” Monica said, thinking it odd as few people used her mother’s Indian name.

"Yes," the old woman said while nodding and smiling. "Kimimela mother." She pointed to herself.

Monica's jaw dropped. She took two fast steps toward the residence, then spun around and ran back to her grandmother, embracing her. She pointed to herself. "Kimimela's daughter."

The old woman grinned and put her hand on Monica's cheek. The fourteen-year-old assisted her while she peeled off her jacket and snow boots, then held her hand while entering the residence.

"Mom has been sick," Monica said.

"There are many sick people and many deaths."

Kim sat on the couch in front of the fireplace, knitting a sweater.

"Mom, Grandma's here."

"Who?" She stood up.

They hugged, cried, and spoke in a language Monica, but for an occasional word, didn't understand.

"Sit down Grandma," Monica said while moving a chair near the couch for herself.

The old woman sat at Kim's side.

Monica's mother asked, "How did you find me?"

"A young man from our tribe saw you and told me. I went to Ft. Vancouver. A kind doctor told me how to get here. The streets are empty."

"Lots of sickness."

"Much death among our people. Before, more than one-hundred in our clan. Now eleven."

Kim sucked in her breath, then asked, "My father, sister, and brother?"

"Gone."

"Your sisters and brothers?"

She shook her head as tears rolled down her cheeks. "Many think the whites have poisoned us."

Kim said, "The whites are ill as well."

"They brought this sickness and are evil."

"There are good whites," Kim said. "My business is with white people. Monica studies with a white family every day after school. A white boy is taking care of Monica and me."

The old woman engaged in a deep sigh, pushed her hands into her lap, and asked in a shaky voice, "Kimimela, my heart is heavy to add a burden to your life, but my body is weak with age and I no longer have a place to live."

"Of course. You stay with us."

Grandma bowed her head. "Thank you, Daughter." She glanced at Monica then back to Kimimela. "One day one of your children or grandchildren will do the same for you."

"Grandma," Monica asked, "what's your name?"

Grandma said a word that Monica couldn't say. The old woman and Kimimela laughed at Monica's attempts to pronounce it.

"The whites can't say it either so like them, you may call me Susan."

"Mom, you're breathing hard," Monica said. She turned to her grandmother. "Mother needs to rest."

"Yes. Rest and heal." She patted her daughter's shoulder and smiled at Monica. "My beautiful granddaughter."

William entered the room with a load of kindling. He kneeled in front of the fire place and poked the fire.

Monica said, "William, I want to introduce my grandmother."

He rocked back onto his feet and approached.

"Kimimela son?" she asked.

"No…cousin," Monica responded with a sly grin.

The old woman appeared confused.

"I'll get my brothers."

"How about some warm tea?" William offered.

"Warm. My old bones could use warm," the old woman said.

***

Four weeks after the flu epidemic ended, Andrew watched as Daire put Jack and Angela to bed.

They returned to the parlor. "Daire, I appreciate you living here and taking care of the children and me."

"You're welcome. Thanks for entertaining Angela while I helped Jack with his lessons."

"She's a doll." He became quiet for a moment, then said, "I'd like to discuss a more permanent arrangement."

"I'll help you raise Jack as a Jew but Angela and I will remain Catholic. You and I can marry in a civil ceremony to keep the family together."

"You've thought this through."

"Yes. Sweet Angela's been dependent on me since her mother died and Jack is a constant and joyous reminder of Kathleen."

"Do you want to remain in your own room?"

"It's only four weeks since my sister died so at least until we're married."

He nodded.

Daire smiled an rested her hand on his arm. "Give me some time. I know men have needs. Believe it or not, so do women."

With reluctance in his voice, Andrew said, "Your sister and I didn't do well…" He nodded to the bedroom.

"I know but I'm not my sister." She smiled. "You definitely put a star in my constellation."

"A star in your…?" He laughed. "It's a great relief knowing you'll be here."

"We continue to take care of each other and who knows—we might become more than married housemates."

Chapter Twenty-One: Noah Katzoff

Sixteen-year-old William read while seated on the front porch of his parent's home on a warm late spring day. He sniffed the air.

"Burning wood," he mumbled

He walked into the middle of the street and turned toward the center of town. A column of black smoke rose into the air. The fire bell clanged.

"That's near the orphanage."

His feet dug into the soil covered street while accelerating to a full sprint.

Gazing out the front windows of the dress shop, Monica saw him running past. She headed out the door, hoisted her skirt with one hand and ran after him. Approaching the burning buildings, they heard children crying and screaming. The building adjacent to the orphanage had flames pouring out of its roof. Smoke curled out of the second floor windows of the childrens' home. Men running to the scene organized a bucket brigade as directed by the volunteer firefighters.

One of the firemen, identified by his red shirt, ran out of the orphanage carrying three small children. He was unsteady on his feet while gagging and coughing.

"Let me have them," William yelled over the cracks and pops of the burning wood.

"Get the children away from the buildings," the fireman said in-between rasping coughs and gasps for clean air. "More structures are likely to catch fire. You stay out here and keep the kids together. I'm going back for more."

A nun stumbled out carrying a baby in one arm and pulling a young boy. Two coughing, gagging children walked behind her, holding tight to her skirt. Her hair was singed, her face streaked with black, and her habit smoldered in places. The sound of a window exploding caused the children to shriek. The high pitched noise added an exclamation point to the crackling sound of the fire as it consumed the wooden structures.

"Give me the baby," Monica called out. She took the tiny one and placed his head against her shoulder. He repeatedly coughed; each accompanied by a puff of smoke. His entire body convulsed with each attempt to clear his lungs.

"This is Noah Katzoff; six-months-old and a good boy," the nun said patting his back. She turned to her young charges. "Follow this girl away from the fire," Before re-entering the building, she pushed aside the fireman who beseeched her to remain outside.

David and his workers from the warehouse rushed past and joined the bucket brigade.

"Here comes the fire pump!" a voice in the crowd yelled. Pulled by a team of six horses, the heavy pump slowed them to an exhausted rapid walk despite their driver's entreaties to move faster. The equines arrived covered in sweat and breathing heavily.

"Poor things pulled that monster from over two-miles away," someone said while passing a bucket to the man next to him.

Men stretched out the pump's hoses which led to the river while a team of men moved the long handles of the mechanical pump. Two firemen guided the stream which barely made it into the second story windows. As the men at the pump tired, others from the bucket brigade took their place. One fireman threw buckets of water on the horses to cool them.

William ferried numerous little ones to an area up the street. Drs. Beckham and Young examined the children and a few adults.

Monica clung tight to Noah who emitted pitiful cries in between coughing fits. She noticed his saliva was filled with black specks.

Dr. Beckham examined him. "Run your finger around the inside of his mouth to get as much of that stuff out as possible. Don't let him swallow it if you can." He examined child after child and bandaged their burns. "William, as soon as you get the children away from the fire I'm going to need help."

A screaming boy ran out with pants and shirt on fire. Three of the volunteers drenched him with water. William pealed the child's pants off and discovered some of the material embedded in ugly looking burns. The acrid scent of his burned flesh added to the smell of the burning buildings.

"He's stopped breathing," William said. Dr. Young checked the boy and shook his head. William carried him to where other bodies were being collected and covered with blankets.

A second nun came out of the building with two toddlers. Handing them to William, she turned to re-enter the burning structure. Two fireman restrained her.

"There are more children inside," she pleaded while trying to push through their restraint.

"It's too dangerous now," a fireman beseeched her. "The injured children who've survived will need you."

The Sister reluctantly allowed herself to be guided away; her body wracked with sobs.

William approached Monica with a toddler in each arm.

"The front wall's coming down," a terrified voice yelled.

William turned away from the buildings and pulled the two children close. He arched his body over them as debris flew past him. Firemen ran to the horses to steady them after the loud noise.

He checked the youngsters. They weren't hurt but cried and trembled. One of them pointed. Monica was flat on her back, twisting and moaning, while Noah cried at her side. A nasty three-inch-gash just below the baby's hairline bled profusely.

William kneeled at Noah's side. Monica sat up, holding her head with both hands. "Ouch that hurt. Something hit me."

He brought the edges of Noah's laceration together then screamed for Dr. Beckham.

The doctor examined the wound, opened his medical bag and handed William a needle and thread.

The fifteen-year-old's eyes widened. "I'll keep it closed until you…"

"Damn it! Close that laceration or he bleeds to death. Your choice."

William steeled himself. "How far apart?"

"Same as the newborn."

Monica moaned and asked, "What happened? What's going on? How's the baby?"

"I have to close this. Keep him still."

She put him on her lap then steadied Noah's head with one hand and kept his hands from interfering with the other. The little one screamed anew with each needle insertion.

"Done," William said with a sigh.

Dr. Beckham approached and examined his work. "Get a bandage from the Sister and cover his wound, then see Dr. Young. He has more for you to do."

Monica cradled Noah against her and patted his back. The little one cried loud sobs. She said, "It's over, it's over. You're going to get better now."

***

Kim and Victor Anchote arrived at the scene. He joined the bucket brigade.

Kim watched kneeling Monica who still held Noah while William sutured a gash in a toddler's leg. "What happened? Poor little one. Is he alright?"

"He'll be fine," Dr. Beckham shouted over the sound of the children who screamed due to their burns.

"Momma, hold the baby. I feel dizzy. William, help me sit over there."

William assisted her to her feet. He kept an arm around her while they moved to the wood planked sidewalk. Dr. Young yelled for William.

"I'm needed."

William walked away but looked back over his shoulder at Monica. She gave him a proud smile.

Kim said, "I should get you and this little one home."

"Not yet. Who's watching the twins?"

"Grandmother."

Tiny Noah began a violent series of coughs. His entire body convulsed with each.

Monica cleared his mouth and wiped his chin. "Go ahead without me. I want to sit here and watch my future husband repair children."

"He comes from a wealthy family. Surely they will chose a wife from a wealthy family."

"Look at him. Just like the doctors. Repairing child after child. He truly has a doctor's hands."

"You said he didn't wish to study medicine."

"Like you've told me many times, we don't know His plans for us."

A nun handed Monica a bottle for Noah.

Two hours later, the fire was out; three buildings reduced to smoldering ash plus piles of brick and stone where the fireplaces and chimneys once stood. A few fireman walked around pouring water on any remaining hotspots. Dr. Beckham shook William's hand and Dr. Young slapped him on the shoulder. Their reluctant assistant grinned sheepishly then approached Monica and her mom.

"How's your head?" he asked.

"It hurts."

"Dr. Beckham asked if you could watch the baby for a few days."

"I will," Monica said. "William, we're going home. Please walk next to me. You can steady me if I become dizzy."

Kim raised an eyebrow at her daughter then turned to William. "Many badly injured?"

"A number of dead including one of the nuns."

"The children?"

"Some weren't breathing and had no heartbeat when I checked them. Half the children I worked on will be okay but the others will need lots of time to heal. Many sustained awful burns and lacerations. I lost count of how many sutures I put in."

Kim said, "You put your ear to a thing, then pressed the other end to the children's chest."

"Dr. Young taught me to check for heart and breathing sounds."

In front of the dress shop, Monica tripped and stumbled into William who quickly wrapped his arms around her torso to support her.

"Are you dizzy again?"

"Yes. I may have tripped over something."

"Let's get you inside," he said.

He helped her to the residence and onto their couch. "I better get back; they'll need help with cleanup."

Monica gave him a radiant smile. "Thank you, William."

"Sure. Dr. Beckham said he'll want to see the baby in a week."

"I'll remember."

Kim watched the door close behind him. She turned to her daughter and wagged a finger. "That was a cheap trick."

In an innocent tone, Monica replied, "What was?"

"I may not have much book learning but one thing I know for certain. My daughter is as sure footed as a mountain goat."

"I felt his arms around me today. Who knows when that might happen again."

"He's white. You're not."

"I'm half white."

"He's …"

"Jewish," Monica said.

"I fear you'll be sorely disappointed."

Monica leaned back, cuddled Noah against her, and closed her eyes. "William and I rescued children today."

"Get a blanket to wrap the child."

She folded a blanket and placed Noah on it. He cried. Monica picked him up and the crying subsided. Placing him back on the blanket he cried again.

Kim said, "He's scared, poor thing. Keep holding him. Noah doesn't know us yet but if we hold him and talk to him he'll feel secure."

Chapter Twenty-Two: William's Choice

Five hours later, William stopped by the dress shop. "Dr. Beckham wants to know how the baby was doing; he said the coughing should be subsiding."

"It's slowed considerably," Kim said. "He's scared but no other injuries," She held out the baby. "Would you mind holding Noah while we get some chores done?"

"Hi little guy." He put him against his chest and patted his back while walking around the room. "You can hold your head up pretty well for such a tiny person." He received a brief smile with a cheery vocalization. The little one rubbed his nose against

William's shoulder then, after a deep cough, turned to rest his forehead against his neck.

Kim and Monica kept glancing at William while he continued patting and talking to his little charge. Occasionally Noah would lift his head, babble, and laugh as if replying to William's conversation.

"Look at them," Kim whispered to her daughter. "The baby felt secure the moment William held him."

Monica grinned and whispered, "As did I."

Kim asked, "William, how did you manage when you dealt with…"

"Children who died?"

"Yes."

"I kind of put them out of my mind and concentrated on the next patient…can I call them patients? I'm not a doctor." He slowly shook his head. "A few died while I worked on them. They're faces will haunt me. One little boy, covered in burns, grabbed my arm. His eye's pleaded for relief but there was little I could do." He patted Noah for a while. "I felt pain in the pit of my stomach when I saw how many bodies were lined up. So sad we couldn't save more."

"You saved many of them," Kim said.

"I assisted Drs. Young and Beckham and followed their orders. That's all."

***

"I can run real faster than everybody and jump real higher than everybody," a three-year-old said demonstrating a mighty three-year-old leap.

With the little one, Dr. Beckham, David, Monica and William sat on the Kaplan's front porch.

"Billy," Dr. Beckham said, "would you mind showing us your scars."

The three-year-old pulled up his pant leg.

"These are scars where a doctor fixed me here and here." He pointed at his knee and ankle.

Dr. Beckham turned to William with raised eyebrows. "Your handiwork."

"Lucky hands. That's all."

The doctor said, "Besides incredible hands you have an excellent mind. Father McMahon said you're one of the best Latin and German students he's ever taught. That's indicative of a superb intellect and we haven't even discussed your mathematical prowess."

"My dad's taught me math since I was young."

"Another man with a fine mind."

David said, "William, the Lord's given you an incredible set of gifts. You have a responsibility to use them."

He gave angry looks to David and Dr. Beckham and stormed off the porch.

"Oh my Lord," said Monica. "Did you see his expression? He's decided on medical school."

"What?" David said. "All I saw was anger."

Monica grinned and chased after him. Over her shoulder she called to them. “Excuse me. I need to accompany William.”

***

Monica walked at William’s side.

“Don’t say anything.”

“I’m just walking with you.”

They walked in silence until William stopped walking and blurted out, “Enough. Say what you’re thinking.”

They faced each other.

Monica said, “I’d give up every bit of my drawing ability, if I could fix one child’s leg.”

“I’m going to be an engineer.”

“Yes. You’ll engineer fixes to children’s’ bodies.”

“I’ve made up my mind.”

“I know. I’ll miss you when you’re at medical school in Salem.”

“How do you know what I’ve decided?”

“The William Kaplan I know is the type of person who runs toward a burning building; not away from it.”

“You ran toward it as well.”

“Only because you led.”

They walked in silence for a while.

William shook his head. “I’d be crushed if a little one died because I made a mistake.”

They walked back to his house. William asked to be alone and went to his room. After a few minutes, Monica entered.

"You're not supposed to come in here."

She turned and locked the door. He sat on his bed with his back against the wall.

"Monica, if I do something and a child dies…"

Monica lifted her skirt, climbed on his lap, facing him, with her knees on either side of his legs.

"Then you'll have to be comforted by the knowledge you did your best."

"And if I make a mistake?"

"It will prove you're human."

She put her hands on William's face. "You won't be able to fix all of them but others," Monica grinned, "will run real faster than everybody and jump real higher than everybody."

***

Dr. Fine, chairman of the department of medicine in Salem was visiting Dr. Beckham's office and talking to William. "Dr. Beckham said you're an excellent student. I think you'll enjoy the classes we offer."

"I'm looking forward to it, sir."

"I'd like you to consider something else. Dr. Beckham and I are recruiting a team to teach and do research on improving medicine for children."

"I'm just a beginner."

"But I'm told you can set emotion aside when needed."

"I can during an emergency."

"Should be useful when treating children. We're in Salem now, but over the next few years we'll have space at the University in Seattle."

"I'll be moving there sometime this year," Dr. Beckham said.

Dr. Fine continued, "We could use someone about the time your classes end. With talented hands like yours, I'd suggest research to improve surgical techniques."

"I enjoy teaching," William said, "and research sounds interesting."

"One day, when we know enough, there will be doctors who work with children exclusively. For now, it's a science still in the womb…our level of knowledge about the differences between adults and children is rudimentary at best. Dr. Beckham and I will teach you all we know."

Dr. Beckham said, "I'm hoping you'll join our team, provide help with sick children, teach, and perform research to broaden our knowledge of medical science as it pertains to children."

William addressed Mr. Fine. "You know I'd plan to become an engineer most of my life."

"So I've been told. Once you've completed your medical studies, there's not a reason in the world which would prevent you from taking engineering courses. Your mathematical background will be as good as gold for those classes. Maybe you'll find engineering principles to aid in our medical research." Dr. Fine looked over the tops of his glasses. "If you joined our team at the University, the engineering courses would be free."

William slowly nodded. "I like the sound of that."

***

William, holding Noah, glanced skyward. "Sun's breaking through the clouds."

"At last," Monica said.

The threesome swayed on a glider on the back porch of her home.

"Dad's selling his business and bought another one in Seattle," William said. "My family is moving in a month or so."

"Your mother is moving the dress shop to Seattle as well. Mom, Grandma and I will move with her."

Staring at the sky, William said, "I understand I can bring my wife with me to college."

"Wife? If you're taking about me, you haven't even asked my mother for permission to court me."

"The college hopes I'll remain there after medical school to teach, treat patients, and do research. That means I won't have as much salary as a doctor with his own practice…won't make near as much as my father's business. I adore teaching and the thought of doing research is most appealing."

"Is this your way of asking me to marry you?"

"I apologize that I don't have an ounce of romance in my body but I have this feeling."

"What are you talking about?"

William momentarily stared at the neat rows in Kim's garden then off to the side. "This is difficult for me but…remember the nights I slept in front of the fireplace during the flu epidemic?"

"Sure."

"I smiled each morning because the first person I saw was you."

"You never told me."

He shrugged and stared at the tops of his shoes. "I didn't know how. And I was afraid you'd laugh."

"I wouldn't have." She smiled. "Remember when we danced at the summer fair?"

"One of my favorite memories."

"Mine too."

He took a deep breath. "I want to wake up with you next to me for the rest of my life."

"Are you certain?"

"If I had to give up medical school to accomplish that, I would."

Monica rapidly shook her head. "You can't and you won't. Too many children who will be born in the next fifty years will be depending on you."

"I'll continue to see patients while I teach, so I may be called away at a moment's notice."

"I'll explain to Noah and whoever, someone who is injured needs you."

"Noah?"

"Mother's given me total responsibility for him."

"I didn't know. He'll come with us?"

"Is that a problem?"

They sat in silence for some minutes.

"William?"

"I was just thinking of the smile Noah gives me when I pick him up and how his little fists grip my shirt."

"He cries when you leave."

"Since when?"

"You'll take both of us?"

"Of course."

Without looking at him, she said, "William, I'm not Jewish."

"Neither was my mother when I was born. Not until five-years-later. I'm not supposed to know but I saw the date on her conversion certificate and Katuba."

"Their what?"

"Jewish wedding contract."

"Your brother Nathan; can he make me Jewish?"

"Yes, but so can Dov Rifkin."

"How long will it take?"

"Some months of study."

"So I won't be waking up next to you before some months from now."

"Well…"

"I will not live with you until we have a proper wedding."

"By then I'll have a good start on my schooling."

"How will we pay for our wedding? My mother doesn't have much."

"I'll talk to my parents."

"You need to talk to my mother first."

***

A few months later, William, Monica, and Noah were taking a buck board ride on a Sunday evening. "Are you glad your conversion is over?" he asked.

"We can begin planning a wedding now."

The skies darkened and a large rain drops struck them. "This feels like a serious rain," Monica said.

William urged the buckboard's horse into a trot as it pulled their conveyance down a muddy trail.

Monica said, "Noah might get sick from becoming wet and chilled." She wrapped him as best she could inside her coat.

"We'll be home soon. I didn't think it would rain when I suggested a ride."

After shivering when the rain penetrated her dress, Monica said. "You're going too fast."

"He's a young horse. He'll manage plus I'm a great buckboard driver." William used the whip to urge the horse to greater velocity.

The right front wheel of their conveyance struck a basketball sized rock. The axle, worn from years of use, couldn't endure the sudden increase in load. It split with a resounding crack. The frightened horse tried to get away from the sound by suddenly veering left. Monica screamed. The buckboard pitched on its side, delivering it's human cargo into the trees which lined the road.

Noah was launched from Monica's arms. She collided face first into a large oak, her body spun, her left leg breaking on a fence post. Monica, fell to the ground in a groaning heap. Landing on her left shoulder, she broke her collar bone. Noah cried. Barely conscious from the excruciating pain, she reached out with her uninjured arm and clawed at the wet soil to pull herself across the muddy terrain toward his voice.

William, in substantial pain from blows to his head and chest used an oil lamp to examine Monica and Noah. *"Noah just seems scared, but Monica's barely coherent,*" he thought. He turned to a teen who'd arrived with his mother. "We need transportation to get us to town."

"I'll get blankets from my home," the woman said.

The rain gradually diminished as William attended Monica whose eyes and occasional moan pleaded for relief from her pain. "We'll head to my parents' home shortly," he told her.

William felt relief as he saw his Aunt Daire, a rugged cowgirl like her sister, driving a wagon's team with David riding shotgun and eleven-year-old Jack standing behind them. She hauled back on the rein's while simultaneously applying force to the wagon's break lever. The combination brought the large wagon to a halt.

David dropped the freight wagon's tailgate while William gently lifted Monica into the wagon.

William said, "Dad, I'll stay in back and keep an eye on her."

David said, "I'll take Noah. Dr. Beckham is meeting us at our house."

The freight wagon rumbled into town, the bumps often eliciting groans from Monica.

Monica woke up in the girls' room at the Kaplan's home.

"What happened?" she asked.

Dr. Beckham responded, "You were in an accident."

She sat up. "My left eye…"

"Swollen shut."

"Noah and William?"

"Noah's fine," David said.

"William's chest and head are covered in bruises," Dr. Beckham said. "He needs to rest."

***

Dr. Beckham shook him. "Wake up, William. Monica asked for Celeste but she wants to talk to you next. She's in the girls' room and may not have much time left."

William looked around his bedroom and saw Dr. Beckham, David and Myra staring at him; all with grim expressions. He put a hand on his head which throbbed with pain like it was being crushed in a vice.

William tried to stand on wobbly legs. David held his arm and guided him toward the other bedroom.

Celeste was leaving the room, her face ashen.

Her head covered in bandages, Monica gave him a weak smile. "Promise you'll take care of Noah." He sat on the edge of her bed and grasped her hand.

"We'll both take care of him."

"Please promise."

"I promise."

Monica tightened her grip on his hand and closed her eyes. She took a few labored breaths and stopped breathing.

"Monica. Please. Stay with me. Noah and I need you."

Dr. Beckham entered the room, examined her and shook his head. "I'm sorry."

William staggered out of the room.

"William?" Myra said, looking at his tear streaked face.

"Gone…She's gone," he said.

She embraced her son as he dissolved into loud sobs.

Myra said to her husband. "Someone has to tell Kim."

David said, "Celeste went to find her."

Kim and Grandma Susan hurried into the house. Monica's mom took one look at William and embraced him. They sobbed in each other's arms.

***

"Where is he?" David said, an hour later after walking Kim and her mother home.

"Sitting on the back porch holding Noah," Myra replied. "I don't know if I should leave him alone or talk to him."

"Neither," David said shaking his head. "I'll get Celeste."

Five-minutes-later, Celeste returned to the house. Myra pointed to the back porch.

"Hi," William said, standing up.

She gave him a brief embrace.

William said, "This is really shit."

She nodded. "I know."

"I'm glad you're here." His eyes filled with tears. "She… hold Noah." He handed the little one to Celeste and covered his face with his hands. His entire body shook as he wept.

"The undertaker is here," David shouted from the kitchen.

"Let him take her. I can't watch."

Celeste moved Noah from her shoulder to her lap. He looked up at her and smiled. "Pretty smile, Noah." She bumped a finger into his nose and he laughed. "Accidents happen."

"I know." He stared at the floor.

"It's not your fault."

"I know."

"William, it's not your fault."

"I understand."

"You did nothing wrong."

He yelled. "She's dead because I wanted to prove I could handle the buckboard at high speed."

"Dad said the axle hit an obstruction. It split because it was worn."

"Monica told me I was going too fast but I was only concerned with demonstrating my ability instead of being safe."

Celeste put a hand on his shoulder. "It could have happened to anyone."

"But it happened when it was my responsibility and resulted in her death."

***

After each of the mourners put a three shovels of dirt on Monica's casket, Kim tried to talk to William but anguish stifled her words. Grandma Susan put an arm around her daughter and spoke to him. "Monica's purpose was to be a joy to her mother and ensure William would become Noah's father."

William tried to speak through his grief but just nodded.

***

Celeste found William on the porch again.

"When will you leave for college?"

"I'm not."

"What?"

"I have to take care of Noah."

"You could apprentice with Dr. Beckham. He's moving to Seattle with us."

"Who's going to take care of Noah while I work? I can't stay with Mom and Dad. They look and talk to me with such pity. I can't stand it."

"I'll take care of Noah."

"You have Shifra. I feel I've disappointed so many people. They look at me and see Monica's executioner."

"You're the only person who feels that way."

William sat up straight and folded his arms across his chest.

Celeste continued. "We can get a place near Dr. Beckham's office. You and Noah could live with Shifra and me."

He rubbed his face with his hands then turned toward her. "I won't earn much money as an apprentice."

"Dad was going to spend a large sum on your college. Maybe he'll let us have part of it for living expenses. I'll bring home work from the dress shop so I'll have some income."

"Let's see what Dr. Beckham says," William said. He watched Celeste playing with Noah. The tiny one giggled and laughed. He sighed and said, "My future looks grim."

Chapter Twenty-Three: The Goulds

Families gathered in the courtyard of the synagogue after Saturday morning services in Philadelphia, Pa. It was late May, 1864. Light rain fell from the steel grey sky. A man with a sad expression slowly walked into the courtyard. He turned up his collar and yelled, "I'm looking for Joyce Gould."

"I'm Joyce Gould," a thin woman of less than average height said.

"Wife of Ruben Gould?"

"Yes."

He walked to where she stood under the eve of the synagogue and removed his hat. "My son is serving in the war with your husband. We just received this." He reached into his coat and handed her a letter. "I'm sorry."

The woman slowly unfolded it. As her eyes moved across the lines, she began trembling then wiped away tears.

"Is it about Dad?" a little girl, standing at her side, asked.

Joyce nodded and tried to speak.

The girl asked, "When is he coming home?"

"He's not," the woman said. The color drained from her cheeks and her eyes rolled upwards.

Nathan Kaplan threw an arm around her upper body as she collapsed. He put his other arm under her knees and carried her into the synagogue.

The little girl, hysterical by now, stood at his side as he placed her mother on a bench. He checked Mrs. Gould's breathing. "Give her a minute. She'll come around." Nathan dropped to his knees and put an arm around the little girl. She turned to him and buried her face in his shoulder.

Mrs. Gould opened her eyes. "Someone please help me sit up."

Nathan assisted her.

After a few minutes, Rabbi Rifkin said, "When you feel ready, Mrs. Frey will walk you home."

They helped the woman to her feet. She briefly turned to Nathan. "Thank you." He nodded. Steadying herself on Mrs. Fry's arm, she and her daughter left the synagogue.

"Did you read the letter?" Nathan asked Rabbi.

"Mr. Gould's body was torn apart by a cannon ball. Poor man couldn't be identified except for the remnants of the shirt he was wearing."

Nathan's thoughts went to his sister Abbey, who was doctoring soldiers in some part of the war.

***

"Didn't you carry my mom?" a radiant little girl with a head full of soft brown curls said. She stood in front of Nathan after Saturday services.

"I'm Nathan and yes, I did."

"I'm Naomi and I'm six. Mom told me she got dizzy and couldn't stand."

"It's been four weeks since then. How is she?"

"When everybody asks how is she, she tells them empty."

"Empty?"

"That's what she says. She used to laugh and tell me funny stories, but not anymore."

"I'll bet she needs lots of hugs."

"Has she been telling you family secrets?" Joyce said with a weak smile as she approached the twosome.

"He said you need lots of hugs cause you feel empty."

"At least hugs," Joyce muttered, then turned to Nathan. "I feel like a rung-out dishrag."

"I'm sure your family is supporting you."

"My folks live in Texas and my in-laws never liked me so I'm on my own."

"I understand you paint portraiture."

"It's a mostly ethical way to make a living."

"Mostly?" Nathan asked.

"Besides portraits, I paint the occasional immodestly dressed strumpet for display in bars."

He laughed.

Joyce regarded him for a bit. "Nice talking to you…"

"Nathan Kaplan."

"Thanks for the assistance when I collapsed."

"My pleasure."

She grabbed Naomi's hand and turned to leave but hesitated then regarded him once more. "You're the one who saved Mrs. Ornstein."

"Not sure if saved is the right word."

"They say she'd have bled to death if you hadn't stopped her hemorrhaging."

Nathan shrugged and smiled, "I did what I was taught."

Bright eyed Naomi asked, "Will you teach me so I can save someone?"

"If your mother agrees, I can teach you."

"She's too young," Joyce said.

"I was about her age when I learned."

"Please, Mom."

Joyce, with a pensive expression, asked Nathan. "What do you do Sunday afternoons?"

"Read or take a walk if the weather is pleasant."

"Can I walk with you? Please," Naomi asked. "Mom has a sitting tomorrow afternoon so I have to stay in my room and not make any noise."

Joyce glanced at Nathan who said, "Fine with me."

"Good. Naomi will have a happy person around her for at least a few hours."

"We'll have fun," Naomi said.

Rabbi Rifkin approached. "Are you feeling better, Mrs. Gould?"

"Managing. How are Mr. Kaplan's rabbinical studies progressing?"

He smiled at Nathan. "His Uncle Dov prepared him well. After a day quizzing his knowledge of Torah and Talmud, I'm certain he'll become a rabbi in a year or so of additional study with me."

***

"We walked and talked and talked and walked, Mom," grinning Naomi said, late the following afternoon. "And we counted robins, sparrows and flycatchers."

"How many?"

"I don't remember how many we counted but it was a big number. We even saw a bald eagle."

"I hope she wasn't too much," Joyce said.

"She brightened my day."

"Will you please stay and have something to eat with us?"

"You've just lost your husband. It wouldn't be…"

"I'm a widow. I don't have a disease."

"I know…"

Joyce put her hands on her hips. "Then why does everyone avoid me? Why won't they talk to me? I'm being treated like an outcast. The only looks I get from people are expressions of pity. If people say anything it's only to convey condolences and quickly get away from me."

"They probably don't know what to say."

"You're Rabbi Rifkin's grandson. You should know what to say when people are in emotional pain."

"Not because I'm his grandson but I do understand your pain."

"How?"

"I lost my parents and brother when I was two. A family took me in and raised me. Although I was little more than a baby, I remember the depth of my grief and how often I cried."

"What did they do?"

"They held me and talked to me."

With a tear running down her cheek she folded her arms across her chest. In a scolding voice, Joyce said, "I have no one to hold me. I don't expect you to do that but at least stay and have a meal with us."

Nathan considered her thoughts. "Where can I wash my hands?"

During dinner, Nathan asked, "If it's not too painful, tell me about Ruben."

"He was six-years older than me. I was fifteen when we met. His good looks swept me off my feet. We'd been married a year when Naomi was born. She was not quite four-years-old when he left."

"I hardly remember him," Naomi said.

Joyce continued, "We lived with his parents. He felt strongly about keeping the Union together so he joined the Army as soon he heard about Ft. Sumter. His mother and I mostly fought so I moved to my own place and began painting."

Chapter Twenty-Four: A Relationship Grows

"Before we begin studying Talmud, I have a question," Rabbi Rifkin said to Nathan the following week. "Did you spend an evening with Joyce Gould?"

They sat in the rabbi's study. The rabbi at his desk, his secretary Shlomo at a desk off to the side, and Nathan in a chair facing the rabbi.

"I did. She's lonely as can be."

"You won't see her again. She's a widow who's recently lost her husband. It's not proper that a single man spend time with her. It's too soon."

"We enjoyed each other's company."

The Rabbi peered over his reading glasses. "It won't happen again."

Nathan became pensive. After a minute's silence, he said, "Does her widowhood preclude her having visitors?"

"Of course not."

"She said no one talks to her."

"Other than civil greetings, conversing with her is not your responsibility."

"I enjoyed spending time with Naomi as well. We'll be getting together for a picnic next Sunday and if Joyce permits me, I'm going to visit them at least weekly."

The Rabbi leaned toward him and shouted. "Mrs. Gould should be sitting Shiva. Not entertaining guests."

Nathan replied in a quiet tone. "She struggles to earn a living. I doubt she has time for Shiva."

The rabbi raised his voice a second time. "You live in my house. You follow my rules."

"As you wish." Nathan stood up. "I'll gather my things and leave."

Rabbi Rifkin laughed. "Where will you go? What will you do?"

Nathan grinned. "My Aunt Sarah taught me bookkeeping. I've seen plenty of signs on businesses looking for bookkeepers. When I earn enough, I'll head home." Nathan turned to leave.

The rabbi appeared incredulous. "Wait. Stop. Please. Consider what you're doing. Your father, myself, my father and grandfather were rabbis. Surely you wouldn't throw away your heritage?"

Nathan's brow furrowed. He leaned forward with hands on hips and said through gritted teeth. "Stay or leave, if I believe visiting a widow and her daughter is the right thing to do, I will."

"Alright." Rabbi Rifkin threw up his hands palms forward and breathed a sigh of relief. "Visit her." He gestured at the empty chair. "Sit down…Please."

"If you ever threaten me again, I will be out the door quicker than a lightning strike."

The Rabbi muttered, "Your father warned me you were strong willed."

"Excuse me?"

"Nothing. Shlomo, some tea please."

***

Nathan encountered Joyce and Naomi purchasing cloth and notions at the general store a few days after Rosh Hashanah, the Jewish celebration of the New Year.

"I heard you and Rabbi had an argument about me."

"That was some weeks ago," Nathan said. "Besides, the disagreement wasn't about you. It was about who was running my life."

"What was decided?"

"We decided I was."

Joyce nodded to Naomi who cleared her throat and said, "Mr. Kaplan, will you please join Mom and me for the break-the-fast meal after Yom Kippur, last day of the New Year's celebration, next week?"

"It would be an honor."

Joyce appeared pleased until he added, "May I invite my Grandfather?"

"Are you sure?"

"Nearly everyone in the shul has invited him but if I ask him, I'm sure he'd join us. May I help carry your goods home?"

Joyce's smile returned as she handed him the items. He held them in one arm and offered her the other.

At her home, Naomi said, "You still have to teach me to bandage people."

He turned to Joyce. "I'll need a yard of two inch wide cloth and a pair of scissors."

"You'll have it shortly."

While Naomi concentrated mightily on Nathan's instructions, her mother stood at her easel, studied them and applied paint to a canvas.

***

At Joyce's home and just before the break-the-fast meal, Rabbi Rifkin, with sparkling eyes and a lilting voice, mesmerized Naomi with a bible story about Ruth. He then discussed how God is always with us.

"Even the minute I wake up?"

"Yes."

"I feel sleepy in the morning. Sometimes I don't want to get up."

"That's why the first instruction in the Code of Jewish Law is: Be strong as a lion when you wake up in the morning to serve your Creator."

"Strong as a lion?"

"Precisely."

"I'll try."

"Your soul goes to heaven each night to be re-invigorated. We thank God for choosing to return it each morning."

"How should I thank Him?"

"We have a prayer that we say as soon as we wake up."

"Will you teach me?"

"I'd love to. It's called Mode Ani."

***

"Thank you for a lovely evening, Mrs. Gould."

"My pleasure, Rabbi," she replied.

"I'll be along later, Zadie. I'm going to help with cleanup."

Nathan ignored his disapproving glance.

"Bedtime young lady."

Naomi hugged her mom then ran to Nathan and hugged him as well.

Joyce started scrubbing dishes. Nathan dried and stored them.

"Naomi thinks the world of you."

"I know," he said while drying a soup tureen then stored it where Joyce indicated.

She put on hand on her hip and said, "I'll bet you don't have a clue." Joyce began washing cups.

He took a plate from her hands and began wiping it. "I just received a firm hug from her and know she looks forward to our Sunday afternoon walks."

"Naomi was playing with friends in our back yard yesterday. She told them she was going to be a doctor. One of the friends replied that girls can't be doctors." Joyce stopped rinsing the dish she held and turned to face him. "My daughter yelled that her father's sister was a doctor healing soldiers in the Civil War."

Nathan was motionless for a moment then asked, "She said that?"

"She did." Joyce picked up serving plate and scrubbed it. She handed it to Nathan who began drying it. Joyce continued, "I showed Rabbi the painting of you and Naomi when you were teaching her how to bandage a wound."

"Did he comment on it?"

"He smiled at first but the smile slowly disappeared. I asked what he thought. Lovely he said, but something saddened him."

"I wonder what?" Nathan said.

The last of the dishes were stored. Joyce said, "Remember playing pretend as a child?"

"Certainly."

"I'm going to turn down the lamps. You and I are going to pretend that I'm not four-years-older; that

I'm not a widow with a child. We'll pretend we've known each other for longer than a few months and have a future together. With all that in mind, sit on the couch and let me cuddle against you."

***

On three consecutive December days, a snowstorm of massive proportion closed down Philadelphia. The windows of Joyce and Naomi's home rattled as the wind-driven-blizzard dumped many inches of frozen precipitation.

"I don't like being inside all the time," Naomi complained.

Joyce shook her head and said, "Only the devil would venture out in this weather."

They exchanged wide-eyed-glances as someone knocked on their front door.

Naomi ran to answer.

"I brought dinner," Nathan said, using his hat to slap snow from his clothing while holding up an oil cloth covered basket.

Naomi put on a mischievous grin. She turned to her mother and shouted, "Mom, the devil is here and he brought dinner."

The adults laughed.

"This has been an interesting week," Nathan said, as he plated corned beef and cabbage.

"How so?" Joyce asked.

"Zadie introduced me to a young woman he thinks I should marry."

"What happened?" Joyce asked.

"I was cordial. It was obvious she was only interested in marrying the son of a famous Rabbi. She made no attempt to get to know me."

"If she had?"

"It wouldn't have mattered."

"Why?"

"She's not four-years-older than me and doesn't have a daughter named Naomi."

"Rabbi doesn't approve of me."

"His concern. Not mine."

Joyce shook her head. "What would your parents think?"

"Before I left home, my father said it was my decision who I marry. He's dying to meet you and Naomi."

"He knows about us?"

"Since our first dinner."

***

"You're quite the cook," Joyce said as the meal ended.

Nathan said, "My mom is so clever. Everyone helped prepare meals. I was learning cooking from a young age and didn't even realize it because it was part of our daily routine."

After Naomi was put to bed, Nathan said, "I'd like to talk about us."

"I'm a widow with a child and I'm four-years-older than you."

"Joyce, listen to me. The age difference is nothing and I adore Naomi. You and I have enjoyed each other's company almost weekly for six-months."

"You have your rabbinic studies to complete. Let's talk when you're ordained."

***

The sun had almost set. Rabbi and Nathan hurried home after a trip to the butcher. Two men blocked their path.

"Hey, Marv," one of the men said. "It's that rabbi and he's got one on his students with him this time."

"Out for a lesson Jew boys?" Marv said.

Rabbi Rifkin noticed Nathan's clenched fists. In a quiet voice he said to his grandson, "Ignore them."

One of the bullies laughed. "Ignore us? I think you need a lesson. From us. I'll bet you Jew boys got plenty of coin on you." He grabbed one of the Rabbi's side curls.

"Leave me alone," the Rabbi said as his head was cruelly yanked sideways.

"Fucking Jews don't fight back." He stepped in front of Nathan and threw a roundhouse at his head. Nathan ducked.

"No fighting, Nathan," the Rabbi yelled.

In a high pitched voice, the assailant mocked, "No fighting, Nathan."

"Hey look, Marv. Nathan's angry." If Rabbi Rifkin had ever seen David Kaplan's face when he became angry he would have known what was coming next.

The would-be mugger threw a punch at Nathan's face. It was easily knocked aside. Using the blocking motion which rotated his body, he threw a fist into his assailant's face which snapped his head back. Blood spurted from his nose and cut upper lip. Both wounds were accompanied by a scream. The other man threw his arms around Nathan, pinning them to his sides.

Spitting blood the other walked back to Nathan. "Now you're going to get it, Jew boy." He drew back a fist.

Nathan brought his foot into the man's crotch with enough force to lift him off the ground. The assailant grabbed between his legs and collapsed to his knees. Nathan used the same foot to bring all his weight down on the top of the other's foot.

"Ma foot!" the second assailant yelled, finding it painful to put weight on. "We didn't mean nothing. We was kidding around."

"Laugh at this," Nathan said. He grabbed the man's hair with both of his hands then yanked his face into his rapidly rising knee which flipped the man onto his back. The other assailant struggled to his feet and ran at Rabbi Rifkin. Nathan shoved the Rabbi aside and delivered a set of withering combinations to the man's face and mid-section. He hit the ground a second time.

"I suggest you stay down," Nathan said standing over the prostrate figure.

Breathing heavily and spitting blood, the man raised his hand and nodded.

Rabbi Rifkin pushed Nathan. "We have to get out of here."

"We'll go to the police station and report them."

"No. Absolutely not. We don't make waves."

"Zadie, this is not Europe."

"I know about these things, believe me."

***

"We heard there was an altercation near Main," one of two policeman said, standing in the entry to the rabbi's home.

Nathan stood next to trembling Rabbi.

"There was," Nathan said. "Two toughs attacked Rabbi and me."

"One of our patrolman found them shortly after the altercation. I was told they looked like someone knocked the hell out of them."

"I was defending myself and the Rabbi."

"We don't put up with crap like this, sir. We believe those two are responsible for mugging an elderly preacher and his wife last week. I'd appreciate if you'd come down to the police station, identify them and press charges. The preacher's on his way down to ID them as we speak."

"I'd be happy to," replied Nathan. "Be there shortly."

The policeman left.

Rabbi Rifkin breathed a sigh of relief and said, "Thank heavens that's over."

Nathan chuckled. "Those two are lucky William wasn't with us."

"William? Your younger brother?"

"He's not tall but built like an ox." Nathan laughed. "If he'd been with us, those two bums would have needed serious medical attention."

Chapter Twenty-Five: Gould Family Upheaval

"I'll get to call your rabbi in two weeks," Joyce said on a late spring day. They sat on the couch in her parlor. "When are you going home?"

"Two years from now."

Her expression one of surprise, she asked, "What will you do for the next two years?"

"I'm going to medical school here in Philadelphia."

"You'll be a rabbi and now you want to become a doctor?"

"Since I was a little boy, my primary goal in life was to become a doctor. I'll teach Jewish studies on the side."

"Does Rabbi Rifkin know?"

"Not yet."

"If he wants you out of his house, where will you go?"

"You and I have been together for nearly one year. We've put off talking about it long enough. I want to marry you."

Her expression brightened. "Naomi will be thrilled if we…"

A gentle knock at the front door interrupted them.

Joyce pulled it open, froze briefly, then gasped. The color drained from her face.

In front of her stood a one legged man on crutches. His sallow skin was tight against his bones; his sagging Union uniform threadbare, soiled and disheveled. One pant leg was rolled up to mid-thigh where his leg ended. He gave her a near toothless grin.

"Ruben," she said.

"Hello, Joyce. It's been years but you still look lovely."

"Please come in."

He hopped to a chair, grimacing with each step.

"We were told you were killed."

"I was captured. Sent to a prison in Andersonville, Georgia. Got an infection. Started as a small cut just above my ankle. When it got bad, they kept chopping more and more of my leg off until this is all that's left. When the war ended they sent me home."

"This is my friend Nathan Kaplan. He's about to become a Rabbi."

"A Rabbi. Nice to meet you Rabbi."

Nathan approached and shook his boney hand. "You two must have much to catch up on. I should leave."

"Nathan, please stay," Joyce said.

"Sit," Ruben said. "I'm glad my wife had a rabbi to talk to during my absence."

"I'll get Naomi," Joyce said.

***

"Nice fellow, that rabbi," Ruben said after Nathan left. "Joyce, I apologize for the way I look."

"Don't be. I've read about the conditions at Andersonville. Newspaper articles and such."

"Before I do much else, I'd like to bathe and then I could use some rest."

"I'll fill the tub and get some of your old clothes."

Tears welled up in Joyce's eyes when her husband took his shirt off.

Ruben noticed. "I know. Nothing but skin and bones."

She helped him into the tub. The clear water turned murky. Joyce scrubbed his back and washed his hair.

Naomi walked in.

"Out," her mother yelled.

The youngster spun around then shouted over her shoulder, "Sorry. Not used to having a man in the house."

"Ruben, does your mother know you're home?"

"No. Will you get word to her?"

"I'll invite her to dinner tomorrow night. That will give you a chance to rest."

"Why did you move out of her house? It would have been cheaper to live there."

"Your mother and I don't get along. You know that."

"It's different now. I won't be much help making a living."

"I make enough to get by with my painting. You used to make wood sculptures. You do that and we could sell them."

"It'll be easier living with her. Another person to help with my care."

In an angry tone, Joyce said, "I was little more than your mother's servant and scullery maid when we lived in her house. I was young and didn't know any different but when she started acting like Naomi's mom, it was over. We found this place and moved in."

"My mother has good intentions."

"No! She's mean and manipulative."

"Joyce…"

"I'll get your crutches. You should get some rest."

***

"Good evening, Mrs. Gould," Joyce said, opening the door of her home.

Her mother-in-law entered. "Joyce, how nice of you to invite me. Except for an occasional glance at synagogue, I haven't seen my granddaughter in…what…a number of years?"

"Mrs. Gould…"

"Still won't call me mother, eh?" Brenda Gould turned to her son. "Ruben how wonderful that you've made it home."

"I'm glad too," he said. Ruben struggled to stand with the help of his crutches. They briefly embraced.

"Ruben! You're so thin. Isn't she feeding you?"

"He just arrived home yesterday," Joyce said.

"And yet you waited until today to tell me."

"He wanted a day to rest."

Ruben said, "Let's eat shall we?"

They gathered around the kitchen table.

"If you lived with me," Brenda said to Joyce, "I could help you take care of Ruben."

"We'll be fine."

Brenda tried the chicken soup. "Joyce, you made chicken soup with celery root. And you put in turnips instead of potatoes."

"Naomi likes it that way."

Mrs. Gould turned to her granddaughter and smiled. "Don't worry Naomi, now that your father's home, you'll come to live with me and I'll teach you the correct way to cook."

Joyce slammed the table with her hand. "That's it."

In an innocent voice, Mrs. Gould said, "Did I say something wrong?"

"Get out!" Joyce screamed.

"Joyce," Ruben said.

She raged at her husband. "She doesn't come to my house and insult me. I won't stand for it."

Mrs. Gould again feigned innocence. "What are you taking about, Dear?"

"Joyce," Ruben repeated. "Mother's just trying to be helpful. You should appreciate that. And I think she's right. If you don't want to live at her home, she could move in here."

"What?" Joyce yelled. Her expression one of shock.

Mrs. Gould suggested, "I could share Naomi's room."

Naomi appeared terror stricken.

Joyce stood up. "Like hell you will. Get out now. If you don't leave, I'll take one of Ruben's crutches and beat you bloody."

"Ruben, did you hear what she said to me?"

"Mother, I'm sorry…"

"Sorry?" Joyce grabbed one of his crutches and slammed it on the table.

Brenda Gould stood, balled up her napkin, and threw it onto the table. She spoke in a sanctimonious voice. "In order to keep peace in this family, I'll make a great sacrifice and terminate my visit with my son and granddaughter."

Ruben pleaded, "Mother, don't…"

"Beloved son," she put her hand on his cheek then turned and sneered at Joyce. "When your wife regains her mental balance, we can discuss your future." She stormed out of the house.

***

One week later, Rabbi Rifkin, with Brenda Gould at his side, knocked on the door of Joyce's home.

She welcomed them and they, plus Naomi, gathered in her parlor. Joyce noted Ruben wasn't surprised at their arrival.

Rabbi cleared his throat and said "Brenda has informed me, there is some conflict among family members. I'd like to help resolve it."

Joyce sat in a chair and crossed her arms. Mrs. Gould arranged three adjacent chairs which faced her. Off to the side, Naomi sat on their couch.

"Three against one?" Joyce asked.

"You see?," Mrs. Gould said. "She immediately impugns our motive for coming here."

Rabbi asked, "Joyce, would you like to resolve the conflict?"

She hesitated then said, "Yes."

"Your mother-in-law believes she can be helpful in Ruben's care."

"We're doing fine."

"Even Ruben told me more care would help."

"All she does is criticize…"

Mrs. Gould interrupted. "I do no such thing. She is too sensitive."

The room rattled as someone pounded on the front door. It exploded open. Nathan stormed in like the three Furies of Greek mythology.

"You shouldn't be here," Rabbi said.

Nathan put his hands on his hips. He glared at his grandfather. An angry voice emanated from deep in his throat. "Shlomo said there was a chance to see you resolve a family conflict. I didn't want to miss that."

"Sit next to me," Naomi said in a cheery voice. She patted the cushion next to her.

Joyce uncrossed her arms, straightened, and had difficulty suppressing a smile.

"He's not needed. This is a private matter," Brenda said.

Rabbi observed Nathan's expression was little different than the one he wore when the two young toughs attacked. He seemed to be radiating anger as he sat next to Naomi.

"Rabbi, tell him to leave," Brenda said.

The rabbi said in a quiet tone, "I have as much chance of moving him as I would a ship's anchor." He turned to Joyce. "You were saying…"

"I said Mrs. Gould criticizes…"

"There she goes again. I give her advice…"

The windows rattled as Nathan thundered, "Don't interrupt Joyce when she's speaking."

***

"I don't think anything was resolved," Rabbi said as he and Nathan walked home.

"Brenda Gould is a witch."

"I realize that now."

"Would you have realized it if I hadn't shown up?"

"You talk to a person once a week but you really don't know them. I believed her complaints were legitimate."

"There will be no more ganging up on Joyce."

Rabbi laughed, "After your performance tonight, no one would dare."

***

A month later and after Saturday morning services, Naomi approached Nathan.

"Mom explained to me why you're not visiting us anymore but could we still go for walks?"

"Does your mom know?"

"She said I could ask you."

"Does your father know?"

She nodded.

Nathan offered his arm. "Off we go."

After five minutes of talking about school, Naomi said, "Mom spends all her time painting or taking care of Dad."

"It must be hard on her. Do you help?"

"Sometimes."

"How's your father's health?"

"Good some days but awful other days. He got all sweaty and hot last week. The doctor removed more of his leg."

"Do you talk to him?"

"I try. Really, it's like we're strangers."

"Be patient. Things will improve as you get to know each other."

***

"What was prison life like?" Joyce asked her husband.

Ruben shuddered as memories flooded his mind. "Mostly bad, but we all tried to help each other. We were crowded in a small area with a stream that ran through the center of the compound. The stream was our drinking water and toilet."

"No wonder dysentery was rampant."

He rubbed his chin and stared at the floor for a while then said, "There was this lady doctor who arrived at the prison after the war ended and not long before they let us go. With little to work with, she spent sun up to sun down and sometimes all night trying to save lives. She begged, pleaded with, and yelled at the officers to provide her with more medical supplies" He giggled. "I think they complied just to avoid confronting her."

Naomi asked, "What was her name?"

Ruben leaned back and stared at the ceiling. "Pity but I don't remember. Tall woman. We just called her Doc. A real angel she was...come to think of it the officers called her Dr. Kaplan."

Chapter Twenty-Six: Career Change for Nathan

"As I've completed rabbinical studies, I'd like to talk about my future," Nathan said. He and the rabbi were in the rabbi's study.

"I've been waiting for this discussion." Rabbi folded his hands across his belly as he sat in a big leather chair.

"You know?"

"Please...sit." He motioned Nathan to a chair. "You lived here a few days when Mrs. Ornstein was run over by that buckboard."

"I remember. She sustained painful injuries."

"You spoke to her while you examined her injuries, bandaged and put splints on her. Her shoulder was crushed and she was in terrible pain."

"I did what I was taught."

Rabbi's expression brightened and he leaned toward Nathan. "It's the way you talked to her and touched her. She was suffering terribly and thinking she might die. But as she watched you and listened to your confident demeanor she calmed."

Nathan shrugged, "It was nothing special, a couple of splints and a few bandages to control her bleeding before we took her to the hospital."

"You engaged Moshe and Lana who quickly came to your assistance. They followed your instructions to the letter. I'm proud you've completed your rabbinic studies but prouder yet of the healing you'll do as a doctor."

"You knew?"

"Each of us has a purpose. You discovered yours before you met me."

"You're not upset?"

He shook his head. "For quite some time, I ignored thinking you belonged in medical school; until I saw the painting of you teaching Naomi to bandage a wound. With paint and canvas, Joyce faithfully reproduced your skill and reminded me of the depth of your compassion when you helped Mrs. Ornstein. It hurt but I swallowed my pride. Maybe one of your children will be the next Rifkin to lead a Jewish community."

"I'll be happy to talk to them about doing that."

"I have no doubt, if one day you find yourself in a Jewish community lacking spiritual leadership, you'll provide it…if only temporarily."

"Thank you, Zadie."

"I hope you'll continue to live with me while you attend medical training."

"Thank you. I will."

"I'm retiring when you complete your studies. Dov has offered me a place in his home. I propose we head to Seattle together."

"The family will love having you live nearby."

"Nathan, please know, your father and mother are proud of you."

***

"Hello Rabbi. I need to see Nathan," Joyce said on entering his office.

"I know he's been on occasional walks with Naomi but it's been nearly two years since he last visited your home."

Joyce nodded.

"Go home and take care of your husband."

"Please Rabbi. I need to talk to him."

"Nathan will finish medical school in a few weeks and return to Seattle."

"I saw him enter the house a minute ago so I know he's here. Please let him know I wish to speak with him."

Rabbi shook his head.

Joyce smiled. "I'll begin screaming and not stop until Nathan finds me. After which, I'll let you explain why you objected to my visiting him."

The rabbi mumbled in a subdued voice, "You two deserve each other."

"I'm sorry. I didn't hear you."

The rabbi pointed down the hallway. "His room is next to the kitchen."

She walked down the hall and called out, "Nathan, it's me, Joyce."

"Come in."

"Hello Nathan."

He looked up from the material he was studying. "Joyce, please have a seat."

She sat on a chair in front of his desk and spoke without looking at him. "I wanted to talk to you before you returned home."

"How's Ruben?"

"Up and down. He needs to have his leg looked at again. There's almost nothing left."

Still not looking at him, she said. "Naomi will miss you."

"Joyce…"

"I'm not the same person Ruben married."

Nathan sighed. "I know. You and I grew during his absence. We're both stronger for our relationship."

With fury in her eyes, she looked into his and said, "You're a rabbi. Tell me. Why did the Lord put us together and allow us to grow and find joy in each other only to cruelly tear us apart?"

Nathan became pensive, ran a hand through his hair, and leaned back in his chair. "Perhaps to give us the strength to do the right thing when a crippled soldier returned home."

"I love you, Nathan."

He took in a deep breath and let it out slowly. "You married Ruben before I met you and he needs you."

She twisted on her chair and folded her arms across her chest. "When you return to the Northwest, may we correspond?"

He thought for a moment while rubbing his chin. "No love letters. Only what's going on in our lives."

"Agreed."

"And no secrets. Ruben needs to know."

"He's sensed how much you mean to Naomi and me. He's told me he won't mind if I write."

"We'll be a continent apart."

Joyce rapidly shook her head. "No. You'll always be right here." She put her hand on her heart.

Nathan covered his tearing eyes. "Good bye, Joyce."

Chapter Twenty-Seven: William and Celeste

William studied at a desk in their parlor. Celeste and Shifra were busy knitting.

Noah walked over to his father's side. "Daddy, play blocks with me?"

"Not tonight, Noah."

"I'll play," Shifra said.

The toddler stamped his foot. "No. Daddy play."

"Dad," Shifra said, "He wants to play with you."

William growled. "Not now."

"You've ignored us the last few days," Celeste said to him.

William wore a troubled expression. "I've been questioning my career choice lately."

"It's been over a year. Why now?"

"Two-months ago, four-year-old Mary Chris Riley trapped her leg in farm machinery."

"You and Dr. Beckham worked on her for a number of hours. Neither of you thought she'd live."

"She lived but will use a crutch for the rest of her life. The leg we tried to save is so weak it's nearly useless."

"You've experienced setbacks. Why is this different?"

"I was explaining," William said in an anger tinged voice, "to her family she'd be on a crutch the rest of her days. My eyes were full of tears. I apologized for not being able to do more. Mary slid off her mother's lap and put her little crutch under her arm." William crossed his arms and sighed. "With halting steps she came across the office; the crutch making a thumping noise each time it hit the floor. She held her arms out and I pulled her onto my lap. Mary momentarily rested her head on my chest, then put her little arms around me, and said, 'Don't be sad. You did your best.'"

"You can't expect to repair every injury," Celeste said.

He shouted a reply. "A four-year-old shouldn't be looking forward to using a fucking crutch the rest of her life."

Celeste glared at him, stood up and yelled through gritted teeth. "Then use your anger to bury yourself in engineering and medical books and engineer a fucking solution instead of taking your frustration out on your family."

William's expression became one of shock. Celeste never raised her voice and never used profanity.

"Come children," she said. "We'll retire to the girl's bedroom and leave Dr. Kaplan with his problem. Perhaps he'd like to go for a walk until his anger subsides." She glanced at William over her shoulder.

He nodded.

Two hours later and the children asleep, William returned with a stack of books. Celeste busied herself assembling a knit sweater.

After an hour's silence, she glanced at him. William pointed to the books. "My dad's mechanical engineering course work." He wrote a few notes, dropped his pen and gazed at her. "Celeste …"

She interrupted. "I'm going to put the kettle on for tea. Favor a cup?"

He nodded.

Celeste took a few steps toward the kitchen. William jumped up and blocked her path.

"What?" she asked.

He threw his arms around her. She slowly closed her eyes as she wrapped her arms around his neck. He put his lips on hers.

She leaned away from him. "William … "

"Celeste, will you marry me?"

An expression of satisfaction bloomed. "But…everyone who knows us thinks we're brother and sister. They may not approve."

"Anyone who doesn't approve can go to hell."

"William! The children have heard enough profanity for one night."

He kissed her forehead. "Let the whole world hear. I meet dysfunctional families every day. I know fathers who dread going home and wives who dread their husband's arrival. Dr. Beckham's first marriage was like that. Depression nearly buried me after Monica died. I doubt I could have maintained my sanity without living in your home."

"It's our home."

He shook his head. "No matter what the results of my medical efforts, you're proud of me. Coming home to you, Noah, and Shifra, gives me strength to endure failures. You know when to cheer me up and when to get upset with me." He kissed her again. "If love was visible, the world would see the children and me wrapped in and protected by the cocoon of your love."

She leaned her forehead against his chest. "When we were children, I was desperate to gain your attention. If that meant doing something mean, I didn't care. All I cared about was you focusing on me." Celeste smiled and briefly tightened her embrace. "As we grew, no one dared put a hand on me because they'd face your wrath."

"All brothers do that."

"Not all. I was so proud of the way you stood up for me during your Bar Mitzvah, I began making plans on how we would live as husband and wife."

"But Monica came long."

"Yes. Summer dance. The way you and she looked at each other…I cried for days."

"I didn't know. Lately, I've caught myself fantasizing about making you my wife."

"Nothing would make me happier."

They engaged in another long kiss. Celeste caressed the back of his neck. "The children are both asleep in the girl's room."

They proceeded to the boy's room, undressed and slid under the blankets.

***

Celeste cuddled tight against his naked body. "That was beautiful. I had no idea doing it would feel so wonderful." She kissed his lips. "You seemed to know just what to do. Is that because of your medical training?"

"Dad told me."

"I'll have to thank him."

"Funny thing. When I said I appreciated his telling me, he laughed. Said I owed thanks to a mud puddle."

***

The sound of rain pelting their home's windows provided a rhythmic background to the evening's quiet.

"You guys are sitting different," Shifra said, looking up from her school work.

"In what way?" Celeste asked.

"While you're reading, you're sitting leaning against each other."

"Shifra, you're the first to know."

"What?"

"We're getting married."

She wrinkled her brow; her gaze returning to her school work. "It's about time."

The adults laughed.

Thunder echoed through the neighborhood followed by the ripping sound of a tree being cleaved in half after it was struck by lightning. The shutters on their modest home rattled as the wind picked up and the rain intensified. A hand pounded on the front door and a voice yelled, "Dr. Kaplan, Dr. Beckham needs you."

"On my way," William yelled as he pulled on a coat and reached for his medical bag.

Chapter Twenty-Eight: Bad Air?

"Within a few days, half the town was squatting in the shallows of the river. Every one of them with the runs."

Dr. Beckham and William were interviewing a young family which had just arrived from a small town east of the Cascades.

"Accompanied by severe stomach cramps?" Dr. Beckham inquired.

"That's right, doc," the wife said. "If people ate anything, it just went right through them."

The husband continued, "They's a lot of folks dying over there. We lived in Andersonville a few years with eight other families who pioneered the town just east of the Cascades from here. Lost my wife and little son to the sickness. We thought young Brian here wouldn't make it as well but he's doing better last couple of days and he don't have the runs if he eats something."

"What did you do for a living?" William asked.

"Livery and blacksmith during the day. Had a bar I ran at night. Made my own beer."

"Were you sick?"

"Not a lick." He thought for a while and said, "Something odd. One couple was untouched by the sickness. Nice folks. Just came here from England. Funny thing about them, they drank tea with all their meals."

William turned to the little boy. "How do you feel, Brian?"

"Just tired. Don't have the awful stomach pains like before."

Dr. Beckham turned to William. "Sounds like Cholera."

***

David, Myra, and Ciara arrived for Sabbath dinner at William and Celeste's home. After lighting candles and listening to Shifra and Ciara chant the blessing over them, William announced, "Let's sing the Shehechianu blessing tonight. Celeste's agreed to marry me."

They sang and then engaged in a round of hugs.

"I have another announcement," William said. "I've secured a part-time position at the University.

I'm teaching and conducting research on childhood diseases."

Midway through dinner Myra quietly talked to Celeste. "The year you went camping with the Holts, David told me you and William were more like boyfriend-girlfriend than brother and sister."

Celeste thought for a bit and said, "I was young but felt that."

"It must have hurt when he chose Monica."

She nodded. "It did."

"Monica wouldn't have wanted him to be alone."

"I know. On her death bed, Monica made me promise to take care of him."

"I had no idea," Myra said. "Blessed Monica."

They ate in silence for a few minutes.

Myra cleared her throat. "I'd be honored to help plan a wedding."

"We wanted to wait until the weather improved."

"Seems reasonable."

"Not anymore."

Myra's face brightened, "You're…"

Celeste's cheeks turned red. "Since we agreed to marry, we can't keep our hands off each other."

Myra laughed. "Thought of names?"

"Jonah, after my father or Leah, after my mom."

"Thoughtful choices." Myra grinned at David.

"What?"

"Your…son's spear found it's mark."

"Spear?…Oh." He turned to William who nodded. David slapped him on the shoulder.

"Ciara has news," Myra said.

Myra's youngest sat up straight. "Andre Holt sent me a letter asking that I move to Alaska and help him with his business…it's a restaurant and bar."

"That's a long way and quite a risk," William said. "I'd heard he was gold mining."

"He was but used the gold he mined to start the business."

Celeste said, "Are you sure…"

"Andre's the only boy who ever showed any interest in me. I've already answered his letter. I'm leaving in two-days."

They ate in silence for a while.

"On a different note," William said, "One of my university colleagues, Dr. Nelson, is retiring and moving to Yakima, Washington where his brother owns a tree and fruit farm. He said it's lovely in the fall and invited us to visit."

William appeared lost in thought. When he mentally joined the others again, he said, "Dad, travelers arrived from a tiny town east of the Cascades. We think one of them had cholera. He lived but just barely. Most in the town were sick and many were leaving."

"Cholera has killed millions over the years," Myra said.

"I've read what I can about the disease. The texts indicate it's related to bad air."

"How can you tell when the air is bad?" Celeste asked.

"I don't know. One source said it happens when many people are living in close proximity," William said.

"Like shanty towns with people living cheek to jowl?" Myra asked.

William nodded.

"That doesn't make sense," Celeste said. "Why wouldn't the bad air move away from the shanty town and cause illness in other areas?"

"Most doctors agree it's related to bad air," William said. "I'm going to take the train out there with another doctor from the University. If the disease crosses the Cascades, I want to learn all I can before it gets here. We'll leave the train and travel on horseback to the town. Maybe we can learn something new about the disease." He turned to his father. "Want to come along?"

"Don't know what I can contribute but sure...I'll go."

"We'll make pasties for you," Myra said.

"And me!" Noah shouted. After an angry glance from his mother, he lowered his voice and quickly added, "Please."

William said, "I've been using a microscope at the University. You wouldn't believe the zoo of tiny creatures which live in a drop of water."

"Can you bring it home so we can see?" Shifra asked.

"I'll do that."

***

As their wedding ceremony concluded, William crushed a glass under his foot and everyone shouted "Mazel Tov." He put his arms around his bride. The engaged in a long kiss. She placed her cheek on his and whispered. "And, bless the Lord, a little girl lived to see this day because the man I just married, noticed the girl's injury, and took appropriate action that prevented her from bleeding to death."

Chapter Twenty-Nine: Cholera

A number of miles east of the Cascades, the train slowed until the cattle car with their horses fronted an earthen ramp.

Dr. Bradley Simpson, William and David took to their mounts, waved to the trainmen and proceeded south on a trail which roughly paralleled a river.

At noon, they entered a small town which was abuzz with the sound of hand saws and hammers. Five homes and one building were in a state of construction. The only other structures were the tents where the families and workers lived until the structures were completed.

"Let's talk to these folks and eat," Bradley said.

They introduced themselves and explained their mission.

"Hell, I left that town even though we lived there four-years. Near every family was touched by that damn sickness. Two families wiped out completely. One of my boys was fine at dinner but dead four-hours later. You get this watery diarrhea, a person's skin turns kind of greyish, and you suffer terrible muscle cramps. When it hit me, I was in so much pain, I was ready to meet my maker. With such bad air around, leaving was an easy choice."

"How did you know the air was bad?" William asked.

"Easy. We all got sick."

"Did the air have a distinctive odor?" Bradley asked.

Another man laughed and said, "With everybody suffering the runs the whole town distinctively smelled like shit."

They all laughed.

"Men upstream and women downstream" one man said as the meal ended. He turned to the new arrivals. "Haven't found time to dig pits for outhouses yet."

"If you visit that town," one man said, "don't stay long. The air is bad, I tell you. We believed it was a great place to live as there seemed to be a constant spring and summer breeze from the west or southwest during the winter."

"Keep following this trail next to the river and you'll be there right quick," another said.

***

"I counted seventeen graves," David said. "Mostly youngsters and elderly."

"The wind is coming directly from the Cascades today," Bradley said.

"So bad air came across the Cascades without affecting Portland and hit this little town but no other towns in its path?" William said shaking his head.

"I'm going to make some notes on how the town is laid out," Bradley said. "Maybe that'll help us make sense of this."

***

"Here's the report I wrote on our trip," William said to his father as Sabbath dinner ended. "If I've forgotten anything, let me know."

"The paper you gave me last week, authored by John Snow concerning the Cholera outbreak in London was fascinating," David said.

"Not everyone accepts its findings," William said.

"Maybe we should plot cholera victims around here. Perhaps we can trace it to a bad water supply like Snow did."

"We should do that but how would that account for Cholera in the abandoned town?"

"Is there a way to determine bad water?"

William shrugged. "Not that I know of and Snow doesn't mention it."

David read William's paper. "You wrote about the barman who brewed his own beer but not the English couple who didn't become sick."

"Oh yes. The tea drinkers. Don't know how that could relate to what we've found so far."

"Just one more fact."

William nodded. "True. I'll add a note about it."

Someone knocked on the front door. Shifra answered and returned with a note for William.

He scanned it and said, "More Cholera. Dr. Simpson wants to meet with all the doctors in town. I need to leave."

"Can I show Zadie the drawings I made with the microscope?" Shifra asked.

"Sure."

"You let her use that delicate and expensive instrument?" David asked.

William patted his daughter's head. "Not only does she use it with great care, but I have some of Shifra's drawings at school to demonstrate to my students what careful observation can yield."

She ran to her room and returned with a stack of drawings.

"You saw all this through the microscope?" wide-eyed David said to his granddaughter as he paged through her drawings. "Shifra, this is amazing,"

"They're mostly drops of water from around town," she said. "I annotated the source and date of each material I put under the microscope."

"What's this?"

"A leaf slice from one of our peach trees. Dad said most life seems to be made of connected cells like a honey comb."

"And this one?" David pointed to a drawing with lots of round structures.

"I got in lots of trouble for that one. I made a little cut in my finger and put a drop of blood on a slide. Dad was upset because I cut my finger but then spent hours reviewing the three drawings I made. I think one of those drawings is on the wall in his office."

"My granddaughter the scientist," David said as the gave her a brief embrace.

***

Following dinner a week later, Shifra approached William.

"Dad, we learned about science experiments in school this week. We each have to do one but I'm not sure what to do."

William became pensive. "Try putting water on a slide then observe it. Add a drop or so of beer, let some time pass and observe again for changes. Also take another water sample from the same source, observe it, then heat the sample hot enough for tea and see if there are any changes. I'll provide the water samples."

***

Max Unger leaned over the bar to address the young girl who walked into his tavern.

"You looking for someone?" he said.

"I need some beer, please" Shifra said.

"I don't sell to children without a note from their parents."

"My Dad sent me for a few drops."

He smiled. "Drops?"

"Yes, sir."

"And your father is?"

"Dr. Kaplan."

"He knows you're here?"

"Yes sir. You can put them in this, please." Shifra removed the lid from a tiny jar.

He put a small amount of beer in her jar and held it up to the light. "That's about ten drops. Enough?"

"Yes, sir. How much does it cost?"

Max thought for a moment and said. "You are one polite young lady so there's no charge. What are you going to do with the beer?"

"It's for a science experiment."

The proprietor's broad smile couldn't be missed. "You have a nice day young lady."

***

A week passed. William asked, "How was your science experiment?"

She retrieved a paper from her room and handed it to him.

"You received a top grade. Excellent work." William quickly scanned the paper then handed it back to her. "Wait. Let me see that again." He re-read her paper. "Where are the drawings you made for the experiment. Shifra found them and handed them to her father. He reviewed the supporting microscope observations. "Oh hell." He stood and put on his coat. "Celeste! I'm going out. We need to have a school board meeting."

"You had one two days ago. What's going on?" Celeste asked.

"No time. I'll tell you later." He ran out the front door; Shifra's science papers still in his hand.

Celeste turned to Shifra. "What was that about?"

Her daughter shrugged.

***

Celeste was busy knitting while seated on a rocker in front of the parlor's fire place when William returned late that night. He plopped into an overstuffed chair which faced the fireplace.

"Tell me what's going on?" she asked.

"Your daughter's science experiment."

"Caused a school board meeting?"

"Everything I've studied about cholera says it's caused by bad air. Even though it makes less and less sense, I've been telling folks that for years."

"And?"

"What if it's bad water? John Snow's analysis of the London cholera outbreak implies something in water is the cause." He hoisted and waved Shifra's paper. "I told our daughter to add beer to a water sample and boil another sample. Her science experiment lends credence to the idea that bad water is at the root of this disease."

"How did she demonstrate that?"

"She put a drop of water under the microscope and observed the usual creatures moving about. Shifra added a drop of beer. They quit moving."

Celeste laughed. "Even people quit moving if they drink enough beer."

"She checked them a day later and there was still no movement."

"The beer killed the waterborne creatures?"

William nodded. "Same with boiled water. If you remember, the beer brewer and the tea drinkers survived the cholera outbreak."

"How did this necessitate the school board convening?"

"Last meeting, we appropriated money to move the school's outhouse closer to the school. Miss Pringle asked for that so the children don't get soaked when it's raining."

Celeste consider his words. "Closer would mean closer to the well the children drink from."

"Exactly. What if, somehow, bad water from the outhouse reached the well? Fortunately, tonight everyone agreed to move it to the other side of the building. We'll have to add a door to that side of the school but it should be safer. I'll spread the word to the other doctors. We'll attack this disease like water is the problem and see what happens."

Chapter Thirty: More Babies

"Good news," David said, holding up a newspaper as he entered their home. "Lee surrendered April Ninth. The Civil War is over."

"Thank heavens," Myra said. "Abbey and the soldiers will be coming home."

"Many are crippled."

"How will they be employed?"

"I'll talk to my supervisors. We'll need lots of ideas for that."

Six weeks later, Myra's face was radiant as she shouted to David. "We received a letter from Abbey," Myra said. She sat next to her husband, tore the letter open, and scanned it. "She's staying on the east coast.

A fellow doctor from the war offered her a place in his practice."

"Won't have much chance to see her if she's out there."

With an expression of concern, Myra said, "She said she'll be out here some months from now. Our oldest wants to have her baby in our home."

"Baby? What baby?"

***

The rare early January sunshine warmed them as they swayed on rocking chairs on the front porch of Myra and David's home.

"I'm so happy you came home to have your child," Myra said.

Abby said, "I almost didn't when I learned of the cholera outbreak."

"It was decided to close some wells in the crowded parts of town. The disease seemed to end after that."

Abbey twisted on her chair. "I can't seem to get comfortable."

"How was your trip?"

"Miserable. What a blessing when the railroads completely cross the continent instead of riding between trains on those wretched stagecoaches. I'm glad to be home but I'll be returning to my practice on the east coast."

"How was doctoring in the war?"

"A nightmare."

"Tell me about it?"

"I've developed huge muscles in my back, shoulders and arms."

"How?"

"Sawing off limbs and restraining men who were about to have limbs amputated."

"What a horror. I can't imagine how you handled that." Myra folded her hands in her lap and said in a quiet tone, "Is that all that's troubling you?"

Abbey looked away.

"You've been depressed since you arrived home? Why so sullen?"

"Nothing I'm willing to talk about."

"You and I were always close. Even when you were six. My eyes filled with tears the first time you called me Mom."

Abbey took a deep breath and folded her arms across her chest. "I was a child who needed a mother."

They both stared at the street while slowly rocking. Thirty minutes transpired without conversation. Finally, Myra turned to her oldest daughter. "Pregnant, no husband, extreme anger and bitterness…and you won't talk to me."

"Talking won't help. Getting this damn child out of me will." She tried to cross her legs but her belly got in the way. "Ouch!"

"What?"

"It keeps kicking me."

"Most women find joy in that."

Abbey twisted uncomfortably on the rocker. "Most women…" She stopped talking, her angry eyes followed a carriage bouncing its way down the rutted street.

"Abbey, I want to help no matter what…"

"It's too painful to discuss."

"Talk to Dad. Talk to William. Please, it can't be good to keep whatever this problem is bottled up inside you."

Abbey said with a smirk, "Believe me. I know about the danger of bottled up emotions."

"Then talk…"

Abbey gripped the arms of her rocking chair so tightly her knuckles turned white. "Let it go, Mother, or I'll stay at a hotel."

Deep sorrow etched Myra's face.

Abbey added, "You're making me think it was a mistake to come home."

Myra leaned forward, her shoulders drooped as she stared at the street. "I won't bring it up again." She turned to Abbey. "Celeste and William will be bringing their newborn Jonah to synagogue tonight. I hope you'll come with."

"The last thing I want is to be around a newborn."

Myra put a hand on Abbey's. Her daughter jerked her hand away, stood and walked into the house. Myra shook her head as she listened to Abbey's footsteps while she climbed to the second floor.

***

Her just delivered son was placed on her belly.

"GET IT OFF ME," Abbey screamed.

Celeste gently lifted the tiny one, waited until the umbilical was severed then wrapped him in a blanket and cuddled him to her chest. Leaving the room she whispered, "Don't you worry. There's plenty of love for you in our home."

Myra screamed, "No! Celeste, come back here. She has to hold her child."

"I WON'T HOLD THE DAMN THING."

"Stop it, Abbey. This is your son."

"BE QUIET MOTHER."

"Dad," Celeste yelled. "Get Mom out of there. She's upsetting Abbey."

David entered and moved between Myra and Abbey. "You're making things worse."

"But she didn't even hold him."

He put an arm around her and guided her to their bedroom.

"Something awful must have happened."

"When she's ready, she'll tell us." David shrugged. "Or not."

***

Abbey called William to her side that evening. "Please close the door so we can talk privately."

He did and sat on a chair next to her bed.

"I need your help. I want my bags packed and I want you to help me get to the train station before sunup tomorrow."

He leaned back in the chair. "I'll help you leave with two conditions."

She eyed him suspiciously. "What?"

"When you're back on the east coast, you'll talk to someone about what happened to you."

"It's not anyone else's business."

"You're killing my sister."

She folded her arms. "I am not killing myself."

"If you don't get help…"

"This is my problem; not yours."

"We're family. It's our problem."

Abbey shook her head.

"Either promise me or I'm walking away." He stood up.

"Fine. I give you my word I'll talk to someone as soon as I'm back east."

"A professional."

She nodded.

"And you'll ask him to write me a letter stating he talked to you."

Abbey didn't reply.

"I don't want to know what happened; just that you're getting help."

Staring at William with an angry expression. She sighed noisily. "I will."

"What about your child?"

"I don't care what you do with it."

"I'll be right back." He returned with a sheet of paper. "Read, then sign and date this."

She read the document aloud. "I hereby give up all legal and parental rights to the child born this date and transfer them to William and Celeste Kaplan."

***

"You helped her leave?" Myra asked William at breakfast.

"Yes. With some conditions."

"Which were?" David asked.

"First, she's promised to talk to a professional about what happened. From what I've learned, my blessed sister won't begin to heal until she can discuss what happened."

"I'll pray it will help," David said.

"Abbey also signed a paper transferring legal and parental rights for her son to Celeste and me."

David and Myra exchanged surprised glances.

Celeste said, "William and I had a long discussion about this when it became apparent Abbey had no interest in her child. Andrew Khasina created a legal document for us. William and I decided this would be best for her child."

After giving her parents a chance to digest the news, Celeste switched to a cheery voice. "I propose naming him Ethan after my brother." She shifted slightly and put Ethan on her breast.

Myra said, "You've gone from two children to four in a matter of weeks."

William said, "I've found a larger home."

"I'll arrange for men from the warehouse to help move your things," David said. "On a different subject, I've been talking to Fred Levin. He has a proposal for a new business. We'd be getting into boat building. It could be a good time as the war has ended and Alaskan commerce seems to be picking up."

Myra turned to Celeste and put a hand on her shoulder. "I can stay with you as long as you need help."

Celeste smiled. "That will be a blessing." She studied Ethan, ran a finger down his cheek, and kissed him. "When Dr. Beckham came over to check on Ethan, I expressed my concern that I won't have enough milk for two babies. He said, 'Your body will adjust just like a mom with twins.'" Celeste blushed. "Now I know why the Lord gave me such a large chest."

Laughter filled the room.

Chapter Thirty-One: Arranged Marriages

"Mordechai," Ismael Gershom the baker said to his son, "Bring me two cups of flour."

"Yes, Papa." The nine-year-old carefully filled the two-cup-measure.

Approaching his father, he tripped. The flour measure went flying, depositing its contents in a wide swath across the floor.

Mordechai jumped up trembling. "I'll clean it up."

"Clean it up? Who's going to pay for the flour." He slapped and kicked his son.

Eighteen-year-old Sophie pushed between them. "Papa stop hitting him. He said he'd clean up."

He stepped back; fury still etched in his face. Mr. Gershom slapped the side of her head and punched his daughter in the belly. She doubled over in pain.

"Both of you! Clean up this mess." He left the room as his wife Bessie, walked in.

"Mama, can't you stop him?" Sophie pleaded, putting a cold rag on her head to calm her raging headache.

"If I interfere he beats me. If he kills me, who will care for you and your brother?"

"One of these days he's going to kill Mordechai."

"You on the other hand, are old enough to leave."

"No. Better he hits me than Mordechai. Is there no one you can tell?"

"Your father is widely respected. Who would believe me?"

***

"How dare you set this up without telling me?" Sophie Gershom raged at her parents. She raised her arms in exasperation and stamped her foot. They were standing in the living room of their home, located over her parent's bakery.

"This is a wonderful match," her father said. "You've known him all three-years we've lived here. Matis, the butcher's son, is a good boy and one day he'll inherit his father's business. You'll bring the bakery and he'll bring the butcher shop. Both of you are Orthodox. What could be better?"

Sophie stamped her foot again and crossed her arms. "I want an educated and intelligent man…someone who knows Torah and Hebrew better than I do; at least someone who is as smart as I am. Not some dolt!"

Ismael turned to his wife. "Listen to this. Who filled her head with these crazy ideas? I didn't!"

Eva said, "You should be proud you have an educated daughter."

"I'm proud…but how much does she need to know to be a good wife? She already knows ten times as much Torah as me and I've been studying Torah all my life." He shook his head. "I can't tell you how many times I've been sitting with the Rabbi discussing a Torah portion and I relate an idea He looks at me with that knowing smile and says, 'A brilliant thought, Ismael.' But I can see it in his eyes. He thinks it came from Sophie."

"If we'd been discussing a son, you'd be walking around bragging about him."

"Please Eva, help me. You know I've already talked to Yaakov the butcher. He thinks it's a good match as well."

Eva turned to her daughter and pleaded. "Please Sophie, listen to us. We only want the best for you and Matis is a nice boy!"

"Fortunately for the people in this town," Sophie said in a voice dripping with sarcasm, "Matis is smart enough to know which end of a steer to butcher but he wouldn't know the difference between Rabbi

Akiva and the Pharaoh of Egypt if they stood in front of him. I want better than that for myself."

Ismael put one hand on his hip and wagged a finger in her face. "Parents have been arranging good marriages for their children for centuries and we are doing the same for you."

"Rabbi Akiva's father-in-law," Sophie said with a smirk, "wouldn't allow him to marry his daughter until Rabbi Akiva became an educated man. Go tell Matis the same thing!"

"How dare you talk to me like that!" A slap echoed across the room.

Sophie put a hand to her cheek and the other in front of her face thinking she'd have to ward off a second blow.

Her father turned to his wife and threw up his hands. "Now she wants Rabbi Akiva? Your daughter is crazy." He slowly turned toward Sophie with fury in his eyes and threatened her, shaking a fist in her face. "You do as I say or else."

"Sophie," Eva said, "we'll talk about this later. I need you to deliver a cake and two dozen bagels to the Warshawsky family. They're having a Simcha (blessed event) tonight. Put their order together and go."

***

Sophie walked along Puget Sound on the way to the delivery. It was a pleasant day with puffy clouds scattered in the deep blue sky. She stopped for a moment to admire the view of the Olympic Mountains. *Is it because I'm plain looking?* She peered at the sky and, with a heavy heart, pleaded with God. She thought, "*All my life, I've prayed for an intelligent man to spend my life with.*"

The eighteen-year-old took in a deep breath of the cool late fall air and shook her head. Tears formed while she contemplated spending the rest of her life with someone she didn't love and who could barely discuss the ideas that mattered to her.

A thin man, about her age and height, with sand-colored hair, penetrating blue eyes, and a warm smile was walking past her when he stopped, eyed her slim figure, and said, "Careful miss, you need to stop crying or you'll get tears on the items you're carrying."

"I'm not crying. I have something in my eye."

"It must be a big something to affect both eye's at the same time. I have a clean handkerchief. Let me take a look and maybe I can help you."

"I don't need help and besides I don't talk to strange men."

He nodded. "Certainly! I understand; always a good idea. You shouldn't talk to me. Instead, just listen and I'll talk about a broad, fast moving, and powerful river. The Columbia River starts in the Canadian Rocky Mountains and in Eastern Washington it is joined by a mighty river called the Snake. I hear the Snake River starts from three tiny headstreams in Wyoming, and courses its way through southern Idaho."

Sophie eyed him suspiciously.

"The river's name changes to the Columbia and finally passes Portland on its way to the sea. Both rivers start as melted snow from tall steep sided mountains. Can you imagine how many billions upon billions of snowflakes would be needed to fill a huge river like this?"

"And how do you happen to know all this?"

"I learned stories from a French trapper who told me about the mountains where the river starts. He canoed down the Snake River and into a valley east of a broad range of mountains which are known as the Grand Tetons. He said you could hear a popping sound in the shallow water. Small birds could be seen which nested in the banks of the river plus white pelicans flew overhead."

Sophie warmed to his descriptions and the enthusiasm in his voice. She was further entranced by the sparkle in his eyes.

"North of there, the trapper saw a place where hot-bubbling-mud came out of the ground, as well as blue ponds of hot water. They remained hot all year long, and were rimmed by gold-colored-rock where the hot water spilled over the edge of the ponds."

"That sounds far-fetched."

"He also told me of a place near there where a column of steaming water would shoot high in the sky every hour."

"If a place like that existed, I'd love to see it."

"Maybe I'll take you one day."

"I doubt that," she said, laughing. Sophie found it difficult to look away from his ebullient expression.

That and the way he smiled at her when he talked made her heart beat faster.

He added, "I find the natural world endlessly fascinating."

A sharp cry, almost a scream, grabbed their attention. It came from a bird circling high above them.

"A bald eagle," Sophie said. "I love their distinctive white heads and unique call. They glide so gracefully in large circles then dive down to the water to grasp a fish."

"So you love the natural world as well," he said.

"The Torah teaches us to appreciate the Lord's creation."

"The Torah?" the man said with a questioning expression.

"You wouldn't know about that," Sophie said.

"Look!" he exclaimed.

They watched an Osprey fly low over the water, reach into the dark surface of the Sound, and trap a salmon in its talons. As it flew up to tree height, the bald eagle dived on it, causing the Osprey to panic and lose its grip on its prize. Before the salmon fell to the water the eagle swooped down and retrieved the Osprey's catch.

"A fish thief on our Sound! How scandalous!" he yelled, putting one hand on his hip while shaking a fist at the eagle and displaying mock anger.

When Sophie finished laughing, she said, "I need to complete my delivery."

"Thank you for spending time with me," he said with a huge smile. "I'm going to be here next Sunday morning about seven o'clock to go for a buckboard ride along the north edge of the Sound if you'd like to join me. We'd see many more birds and I saw quite a few deer up there a few weeks ago."

"That's impossible. A woman doesn't go for rides with strange men."

"Certainly! I understand. Always a good idea…But if you were willing to break your rule about talking to strangers, I was thinking maybe you'd break the rule about not going for rides with strangers."

"And why would I do that?"

"So we can continue to share our enjoyment of nature. Personally, I think sharing this kind of beauty is good for the soul. Thank you for that."

She replied slowly, "You're welcome. I've enjoyed...our…sharing." Sophie sighed. "No, I can't come with you." She shook her head. "It's impossible. My parents would never allow it. Good day, Sir."

***

"What took you so long?" Ishmael asked.

"I…I walked along the Sound."

"Alone?"

"I met a friend."

"Who?"

"I'm eighteen. I don't need my parents keeping track of my friends."

He slapped her, snapping her head sideways. "You'll do exactly as I say or I'll throw you out." She put a hand up to her cheek and turned away. He punched her in the lower back. "The floor of the bakery needs scrubbing. Get busy."

Chapter Thirty-Two: Nathan Aaron

All week long, Sophie couldn't get the stranger out of her mind. She smiled each time she reviewed their brief encounter.

"I would look forward to doing that again," she whispered as she sliced and boxed an apple strudel.

"You're talking to someone?" her mother inquired.

"Just myself."

Her memory kept replaying his bright expression, their shared enjoyment of the natural world, and particularly, their shared laughter. At one point she tried to imagine what it would be like to have his arms around her but quickly pushed the idea from her mind. Sophie thought, "*Impossible relationship. He's not even Jewish… but he warms me when I think of him.*"

***

Sophie awoke at daybreak the following Sunday. The slim man was waiting for her standing next to a freshly washed buckboard which was hitched to a fine looking chestnut horse.

"Good morning," he said with the same warm smile below the sparkling eyes she remembered so vividly. "We've been blessed with a clear sky and comfortable temperatures."

"If we're going to ride together perhaps you should tell me your name."

He hesitated then said, "Nathan Aaron."

"I'm Sophie Gershom."

He held out his hand to assist her as she climbed on the buckboard.

"Have you eaten breakfast yet?" Sophie asked as the chestnut began a gentle trot.

"Only ate a piece of bread as I was busy getting the buckboard ready."

"I have a few things," she said. "Why don't we travel for an hour or so and then find a shady place to stop."

They passed a grove of white barked trees. Sophie sighed at the beauty surrounding them. She glanced skyward and viewed seagulls wheeling overhead and calling to each other.

"Sophie asked, "What do you do for a living?"

"I'm a helper at a warehouse."

She laughed. "You'll never earn enough money to support a family doing that."

He smiled. "You're probably right."

They stopped at a grass covered area surrounded by wildflowers at the edge of a cliff above the Sound. Nathan secured the horse and watered him while Sophie gathered firewood. Across the water, gentle foothills could be seen that lead into the snow-covered peaks of the Olympic Mountain Range.

Nathan opened a blanket. Sophie unpacked her basket, and put out poppy-seed bialys with sweet onion-garlic spread, tea, and a cherry tart.

"Everything was delicious," Nathan said as he helped her repack her picnic basket. "I have an activity for us," he said with an impish grin. "I have play-books for Macbeth. Let's act out the scene from Macbeth where she goes mad."

Sophie began reading without any emotion.

"No, No, No," he said. "Lady Macbeth is going mad. Twist your face into a mad person's expression like this." He looked at her with one eyebrow raised and the other lowered while twisting his lips and flaring his nostrils. He began reading the lines, alternating between normalcy and madness.

Sophie laughed hysterically. "Nathan stop. I have the idea. Let me try."

She leaned forward from her waist and rubbed her hands. "Out, damned spot! Out, I say!—One, two. Why, then, 'tis time to do 't. Hell is murky!—Fie, my lord, fie! A soldier, and afeard? What need we fear who knows it, when none can call our power to account?"— Sophie changed her expression to one of fear and she cowered. "Yet who would have thought the old man to have had so much blood in him."

Nathan, a blank expression on his face, stood without moving.

"How was that?" she asked.

He grinned then shouted, "That was marvelous. You nailed Lady Macbeth! Fantastic!"

Sophie beamed.

In their excitement they embraced.

Sophie moaned.

"Are you alright?" Nathan said.

"My ribs are sore."

He dropped his arms. "What happened?"

"I…fell against a table yesterday."

Nathan suggested, "Let's continue, but seated on the blanket."

"Yes, but please lean against me while we continue our reading."

Back to back, they continued their dramatic readings of Macbeth.

Sophie took a deep breath. "A few friends and I are gathering for a meal where the water from Union Bay enters the Sound, just before sunset this Thursday. Would you like to join us?"

"I'll have to talk to my boss to see if I can get the time off but I'll see what I can do."

They gathered their belongings and headed back to town.

"I enjoyed spending time with you," she said, as their horse trotted on the trail next to the Columbia River.

"I as well," he said giving Sophie a warm smile.

She stared at the sound for a while as they began their ride back to town.

"I love the view of the Olympic Mountains," she said. "Each peak is beautiful but the combination of peaks is so majestic compared to any peak on its own."

Sophie smiled and took in the mountain's majesty like a thirsty man drinking water.

Nathan said, "That's how families can be when two people get together; if it's the right two people, of course. They become more than the sum of two people. The combination of their thoughts, emotions, and ideas come together to build a strong home where children can be nurtured and educated in a safe and loving environment. My parents demonstrated that as we grew."

Sophie's smile broadened and she leaned against his shoulder. "Nathan Aaron you think like I do. You see much of life like I do." She straightened, her expression saddened. Sophie folded her arms across her chest. "It's not fair."

"What's not fair?"

"I'm promised to someone. It's like a contract which my parents made for me. I can't get out of it so I really shouldn't see you again. I'm being a terrible person by spending time with you."

He was quiet for a moment. "Sophie, do you want to see me again?"

She twisted on the seat of the buckboard and stared at her lap. "Yes."

"Do you still want me to meet with you and your friends on Thursday? If not, we can meet on Sunday morning again."

"I'll see you Thursday. I…I shouldn't say this but I'm drawn to you like rivers are drawn to the ocean."

"Thank you. A beautiful metaphor."

Without looking at him she continued, "Since the day we met I rarely have a thought that doesn't include you."

Nathan stopped the horse and put his arms around her.

She pushed him away. "NO! We can't do this. It's wrong."

He held up his hands and leaned away from her. "I'm sorry."

Sophie stared at the water for a few seconds then turned back to him and threw her arms around him as tight as she could. He slowly put his arms around her. He slid one of his hands up to the back of her neck and began caressing it.

"This is nice…I wish you were…"

"Wish I was what?" he asked.

"Nothing. It's something selfish."

"So next Thursday?"

"Yes," she said.

"I still have to get permission to take time off from my job."

"I understand," she said. They ended their embrace and continued the ride back to town.

***

When she arrived home, Sophie's parents were waiting in the parlor for her.

Ismael inquired, "Where did you go and who were you with?"

"A friend."

"Who?"

"A friend. That's all."

The sound of a slap echoed across the room. Sophie saw stars and put a hand out to steady herself.

"This will not happen again. You will inform your mother or me before you leave the house. Is that clear?"

"I'm meeting friends from synagogue near the river this Thursday."

Her father inquired, "Will Matis be there?"

"Yes."

"Fine. You can go. Sneak out again and I'll throw you in the street...after I knock the hell out of you."

***

Late Thursday afternoon, Sophie and her girlfriends arrived at the edge of the wide shallow river which connected Union Bay with Puget Sound. They and a few of the boys were the first to arrive. She'd known most of the group since her family arrived in Seattle three years earlier and became part of the Jewish community. She considered them extended family. While they laid out blankets, Sophie kept glancing towards town.

A young man arrived carrying a fish net. The others didn't know him, but Sophie's expression brightened as soon as she saw him. She walked around with Nathan introducing him to the group.

"Look at Sophie." Rose Goodman leaned towards her longtime neighbor Lazar Katz. "She invited a stranger. That was a lot of nerve, her being promised to Matis."

"He looks familiar but what in the world is she thinking inviting a stranger?" he said.

By stranger, they meant someone who was non-Jewish.

***

Nathan showed Sophie the net he intended to use for fishing.

"The wife of a trapper showed me how to use this. C'mon, let's try it."

He walked to the stream's edge, removed his shoes, rolled his pants above his knees, and waded into the stream.

To her friends' horror, Sophie removed her shoes, pulled off her stockings, tucked her skirt up above her knees, and followed the stranger into the water. She stumbled and screamed. He steadied her with one arm around her waist. The both laughed.

She tried to net a fish tail first.

"Not like that," Nathan said. "Scoop from the head end. You touch their tail and they dart away."

When she finally caught one, they embraced in celebration. The others looked on in horror.

Laser whispered to Rose, "A public display of affection is entirely unacceptable behavior."

They sat on the bank putting on their shoes. Nathan asked, "Have you heard about the new theatre that's just been constructed?"

"Yes. Why?"

"An orchestra from San Francisco is going to perform there next Sunday afternoon. They're going to play selections by Mozart. I have an extra ticket you could use if you'd like to attend."

Her eyebrows went up. "I'd heard those tickets were expensive. How could you afford…" She shook her head. "No, I couldn't attend. Not possible...my parents wouldn't let me…they wouldn't let me stay here if they saw us fishing together."

"I see."

While Sophie tied a shoe lace, she said, "I've never heard an orchestral performance."

Nathan's expression brightened. "I have and I assure you it's not to be missed. It's a similar kind of beauty which you and I adore in nature. I'm certain you would enjoy the concert."

"That's presumptuous of you. How can you be so sure?"

"My heart tells me you would, but," his demeanor changed to a taunting expression and voice, "you'll have to meet me in front of the theatre at one o'clock next Sunday to see if I'm correct."

Sophie shook her head. "Thank you for inviting me but it's unlikely I can get away."

Nathan cleaned their catch, cut it into strips, and placed it next to the fire, supported by small sticks.

"Where did you learn to cook a fish like that?" Lazar asked.

"The wife of a trapper. I'm really smoking it instead of cooking it. It takes longer but has a richer taste in my opinion."

Sophie added another log to the fire.

"Lazar, do you like to read poetry?" Nathan asked.

Lazar's face brightened. "Who doesn't?"

"I brought a book of poems. We could do readings before we eat."

"Let me see what you have." Lazar paged through the book.

"Keats' A Draught of Sunshine is one of my favorites."

"Attention everyone," Nathan announced. "We are most fortunate today. We are to be honored with a dramatic reading by Lazar…what's your last name?"

"Katz, but I don't…"

"Mr. Lazar Katz will provide us with a dramatic reading of a Keats poem."

Nathan applauded. Sophie did the same then the other's followed.

Lazar walked to the front of the group and cleared his throat. His voice was shaky at first but soon steady and confident as the emotion of the poet's words took hold of him. He finished the reading with a lilting tone in his voice.

Everyone applauded.

"Anyone else?"

"I memorized a poem for school by Rebecca Hammond Lard," Rose said.

She walked to the front of the group. Sophie noticed she glanced to ensure Matis was watching before beginning.

"Lovely, thank you, Rose," Nathan said as the applause died down. "If I may, I've just discovered what is called a nonsense poem. With your permission, I'll read it."

His reading of, "The Owl and the Pussycat," was regularly interrupted by substantial laughter. Sophie beamed while she clapped for him.

"Now ladies and gentleman, I wish to announce the presence of a fine Shakespearian actress."

Sophie gasped. "Nathan no."

"If we encourage her, she will provide a dramatic reading of Lady Macbeth's monologue."

With much applauding, she stood and walked to the front.

Sophie turned her back to her audience. When she turned to face them again, she wore a mad woman's twisted face and rubbed her hands. She performed the lines with her expression and demeanor alternating between madness and fear.

There was silence when she finished followed by thunderous applause.

Nathan approached her. "You were great."

"Time to eat," Rose announced.

"You've invited a stranger to dinner, Sophie?" Rose said in a quiet but remonstrating voice when away from Nathan.

"He's a friend so I invited him to join us."

Rose moved to stand directly in front of Sophie and shook a finger in her face. "Don't look at him like you've been doing when Matis is around."

"What are you talking about?"

"Your face glows when you look at the stranger."

"That's silly. We just had a little fun fishing and we're just friends. Nothing more. Obviously, we have no future as he's not Jewish."

"The two of you embraced and you both laughed and screamed when you caught the fish. That certainly was inappropriate. When you were wading in the river, I'm sure your carrying on could be heard to the other side of the city."

Sophie wouldn't look directly at Rose. "You don't know what you're saying."

"You are not being fair to Matis who expects to marry you," she said in a voice suddenly tinged with anger. "It's like you're teasing him. That's mean of you, Sophie."

She turned to face her friend. "Rose Goodman…you're in love with Matis."

Now Rose avoided Sophie's gaze. "Yes, as it happens. We've been good friends since childhood. He may not be the brightest man in town but I know we would be perfect for each other. However, the match is between you and him. My family has nothing. My parents wouldn't even think about approaching a wealthy parent like Yaakov the butcher for a match."

Sophie stared at Nathan who was laughing with the other men while they sampled the salmon. With hands on hips and determination in her voice, she said, "Rose, I will not be marrying Matis."

"But the match…"

After dinner, Sophie overheard Matis having a private talk with Nathan.

"Stay away from Sophie. She's obviously attracted to you. A match has been made and I'm to be her husband."

"I see. How does Sophie feel about that?"

"It doesn't matter how she feels or how I feel. As I said, a match has been made. We're Jews and we have traditions we live by. She thinks she needs a Tzadik, but what she's going to get is a butcher. I'm sorry but you wouldn't know what a Tzadik is."

"Tzadik…an interesting word...meaning a learned man," Nathan said. He began speaking Hebrew.

Sophie gasped and put a hand over her mouth.

Still speaking Hebrew, Nathan explained the origin of the word Tzadik, its numerical value, its significance in the holy Gemara and how it was related to the Hebrew word for charity, Tzedakah. 'Shalom, Matis." Nathan shook his hand and walked away. Matis just stood there, wide eyed, jaw dropped, and thoroughly astounded at what he had just heard.

***

Sophie was trembling, her mind spinning as she gathered the last of her things and began walking home.

Out of breath, Rose ran up to her and excitedly exclaimed, "Sophie, stop walking, and listen to me. Lazer just told me, Nathan gave Matis a thorough lesson on the word Tzadik. Not only that, but the entire lesson was given in…Hebrew. From what he said, Nathan must be Jewish."

"I know. I heard him." Sophie shook her head. "But it can't be. Surely he would have told me by now."

Sophie's body stiffened as her expression changed from confusion to one of determination.

"I don't know how but I'm going to marry him."

Chapter Thirty-Three: Ishmael Gershom

"So you were out by the river with some stranger I'm told," Sophie's father raged.

"I was. I'm capable of making my own friends."

Her father slapped her and grabbed a fist full of hair at the back of her head. "As long as you live in my house you live by my rules."

"Yes, Papa."

Tears welled up in Sophie's eyes.

With a slap to the other side of her face, her father continued, "I'll tell you when you can go out and who you can go out with."

***

Late Sunday morning, Sophie changed into her finest dress.

"What are you doing?" her mother asked.

"I'm going to the new theatre to hear the San Francisco orchestra. I'm meeting a friend there."

"After your father finishes working in the bakery this morning, we have guests coming."

"I'm going to miss them."

"Sophie you have to stop acting like this. Your father and I have made a match for you."

"So…" she said, stamping her foot. With hands on hips Sophie glared at her mother. "You've invited them and didn't tell me. Were you going to surprise me when they arrived at our front door?"

Bessie said in a pleading voice, "Sophie, please be reasonable."

"Reasonable? You and father go sneaking around behind my back trying to force me to marry an ignorant man? Is your opinion of me so low you think I have no mind of my own?"

Bessie put her hands together as if praying and continued to plead, "Sophie, you're my daughter and I love you dearly but you're not a pretty girl. You're eighteen. Another year and no one will want you. How do you expect to attract a man without a match?"

She stood tall while remembering Nathan's smiling countenance while he carefully considered her thoughts and ideas. With utmost confidence she stated, "With my mind, mother; with my mind. How sad you refuse to see that."

Sophie's mother drew back a hand to slap her.

"If you strike me, I will be happy to explain to everyone at the theatre, being slapped is preferable to spending one's married life living in intellectual poverty."

Her mother eye's widened in anger but she didn't move. Sophie pulled on her bonnet and neatly tied its strings into a bow. She checked her appearance in a mirror one final time, pulled on her gloves, and put her purse over her arm. "Have a pleasant afternoon mother. Please give my best to Matis and his family."

***

Sophie approached the man standing in front of the theatre who wore a finely tailored suit and top hat. The minute she saw him, she tried to remain calm but her heart beat increased and she couldn't suppress the smile that spread across her face. He greeted her then noticed the bruises on her face.

"Who hit you?"

"Please, we have a pleasant afternoon in front of us."

"You expect me to ignore someone striking you? Not on my watch." He seethed.

Sophie saw his fists were clenched. "Please Nathan. Let's go in and we'll talk afterward."

He hesitated then slowly offered his arm. She grasped it firmly and sighed deeply.

While waiting for the music to begin, she turned to Nathan. Speaking in Hebrew, she inquired about a complicated question provoked by that week's Parsha. He answered in the same language and then Sophie explained why, in her opinion, Rabbi Hillel's interpretation was superior to Rashi's.

Nathan wore an ear to ear grin. "A superb analysis, Sophie. I am humbled by your learned mind. We must have more discussions like this."

Sophie beamed. "Most men get upset and don't want to listen when I argue an interpretation of Torah."

"How utterly foolish of them. I on the other hand, get the benefit of your superb intellect."

As the music began, she positioned herself so she was leaning against his shoulder.

After applauding the first piece, she hooked her arm around his and held it against her. "My favorite melodies during services are the before and after Haftorah blessings."

"I agree with you. It lifts my heart to chant them."

As they stood to applaud the orchestra at the end of the concert, she said, "You were correct. I could listen to music like this every Sunday for the rest of my life."

When they were walking out of the theatre, Nathan asked, "When can I see you again and when can I meet your family?"

"It's complicated with my family."

"What shall we do about that?"

She tightened her grip on his arm. "I can't begin to tell you how much I enjoy spending time with you.

You make me proud to be who I am. I have to work something out with my family but I'm not sure how."

"Perhaps I'll think of something."

His countenance darkened and he stopped walking. "Sophie, did someone in your family strike you?"

"You don't understand what's going on."

"You're a grown woman. No one has the right to strike you. You should leave. You can stay with someone in my family."

"I can't."

"Why not?"

She tugged at his arm and they continued walking. "If I leave, there'll be no one to protect my little brother."

"How do you protect him? And from who?"

"If he, my father, is beating my brother I interrupt him in a way so he focuses his anger on me."

"Sophie …"

She glanced up the street, stopped walking and covered her mouth. Sophie gasped.

"Who is that?"

"My father…and my brother."

"He's going into the medical office."

They ran up the street. When they entered, they heard Ismael say in a firm voice, "He fell."

"What about these other bruises?" William asked.

"None of your Goddamned business little doctor."

Nathan and Sophie entered the office.

"What wrong?" Sophie said to her trembling brother.

"He fell," her father repeated while glaring at her. "Go home. You're not needed here."

"Did you break his arm?" Sophie asked.

He back handed her across the face. She toppled sideways, her head striking the edge of a desk. Nathan grabbed her.

William's features twisted into his father's angry countenance.

"Get busy, Doctor or I'll give you a good one," the baker said.

Mr. Gershom stood directly to the doctor's left and he was at least a foot taller. As fast as a rattler's strike, William's left fist rose from his waist to his shoulder then directly into Mr. Gershom's nose.

The man screamed and put a hand to his face. Blood spurted out between his fingers. William handed him a bandage. "Hold this on your nose." He placed an armless chair behind the injured man. "Sophie and Mordechai need to live with Celeste and me for the time being. Sit down. You'll give your permission now."

The baker shouted, "The hell I will."

Just before his butt hit the seat William pulled the chair away. The cruel father screamed again as he hit the floor. The doctor put the chair, which had foot rails, over him and sat on it; thereby preventing Mr. Gershom from rising.

"You bastard. You can't do this to me. I have friends."

William spoke slowly in a measured tone. "I'm a doctor who's carefully inventoried your son's injuries.

Who do you think the police will believe? A baker who beats his family or a doctor?"

"I have a great reputation in this town."

"You won't when I get done spreading the word you've just broken your son's arm and he's covered in contusions."

"I'll find a way to get even with you."

"You tell Sophie and Mordechai they can leave with us. Either that or Nathan and I will beat you bloody then walk you over to the Police."

"The unappreciative cow can leave."

"And her brother?"

"No."

William kicked the restrained man's left elbow as his left hand held the bandage against his injured nose. The baker screamed in pain.

"Your son?" William shouted.

"Alright. Yes," he said in a subdued tone.

William let him up. Mr. Gershom staggered toward the front door. "You bastards. I'll get even with you." He slammed the office door. William smiled at Mordechai and finished bandaging the young fellow's splinted arm.

"Are you okay?" Nathan asked Sophie.

"My head got slammed but I'm okay."

"What about your Mother?" Nathan asked.

"I've repeatedly asked her to leave but she won't."

Mordechai asked, "Where are we going?"

"Where no one will hit you." William said.

"And Mama?"

Sophie said, "I'll get word to her."

***

Papa died?" Sophie asked her mother the following day in the parlor of the Gershom home. Nathan stood at her side.

"Your father arrived home after a night of drinking. He said, 'One day I'll find them without those damn Kaplans around. I'll beat a lesson into them they'll never forget.' He staggered to his bed, took another swig of whiskey and collapsed in an unconscious stupor."

Bessie twisted uncomfortably. She looked at Nathan. "Sir, would mind waiting outside. I have a private matter to discuss with my daughter.

Nathan nodded and moved to the porch.

Bessie turned to Sophie. "No more hitting…I told him that again and again as I walked to the kitchen and retrieved my ten inch cast iron fry pan. I returned to our bedroom…"

"Mama no," Sophie said.

"I held the handle with both hands then slowly raised it over my head. Using enough force to lift my heels off the floor, I brought it down on his head; again and again thinking of all the times he hit you and your brother while I did nothing."

"Mama you didn't…"

"I only stopped when my arms lacked the strength to lift it one more time. When I finally released my grip on it; I remember a loud clang as it hit the floor. I looked at him for the last time and told him, No more hitting."

"Mama, that's enough."

Bessie continued, "I removed my blood-flecked-dress and scrubbed the blood from my face, arms and hair. After adding two logs and kindling to the fireplace, I folded the soiled dress and put it in the fire. Two more logs went on top. As the fire grew and consumed the dress, I'm sure the orange flames reflected in my eyes." She laughed. "I remember, I even told the fire, No more hitting."

"Mama, I don't think you should be telling me…"

Unperturbed, Bessie continued, "I pulled a clean dress over my head, walked to the general store and returned with a skein of yarn which I left on the couch in the parlor then found a policeman and brought him back to my bedroom. I explained to him, your father came home drunk this morning after a night of boozing, gambling and, I suppose, whoring. I suggested someone felt cheated and came here to get even. I remember, the policeman stared at the body with the barely recognizable face...then at me."

Bessie sighed and grabbed her daughter's hands in both of hers.

"I asked him to have the undertaker stop by for the body. He asked, 'Mrs.–were you angry with him?' I replied, 'Why would you ask that?'"

"He said, 'There've been rumors he was beating you and the kids.'"

"My husband of twenty-one years? Respected by all who knew him? Why would anyone say that? He stared at me for a while then shrugged and agreed to tell the undertaker. When passing through the parlor, the policeman paused and glanced at the fire.

"Warm day for a fire," he said.

I told him, "Thank you for asking. I felt a chill earlier but I assure you I'm fine now. I remember I smiled at the fire and whispered, There'll be no more hitting."

"He asked what I said. I gave him a sweet smile. Knitting, I told him. There'll be no more knitting…until after the funeral."

"Mama, please. You can't tell anyone what you've just told me."

"I won't. I simply thought you should know your mother finally stood up for her children."

They stared at each other, then joined in a tearful embrace.

Chapter Thirty-Four: Children Making Matches

After Sabbath services many of the families conversed in the courtyard of the small building which was used for their synagogue. Sophie saw Nathan sharing laughter with William and Celeste Kaplan. She stood next to her mother and brother when her eyes widened, she stood a bit taller, and then smiled as Nathan walked up to her.

"Shabbat Shalom, Sophie."

"Shabbat Shalom, Nathan," she said with a radiant expression. "I enjoyed hearing you chant the Haftorah blessings. As you said, they lifted my heart."

"It's a lovely day, Sophie. I was wondering if you would like to go for a walk with me and afterwards have dinner at my parent's home."

Nathan held out his arm. Sophie put her hand on it and said, "I would love that. Allow me to introduce you and your family to my mother."

"Pleased to meet you, Mrs. Gershom," Myra replied.

"My pleasure, I assure you. This is my son."

"Hello Mordechai," William said. "How's the arm?"

"Doesn't hurt so much today, Doctor."

Matis' father was watching them. His eyes became so huge, Sophie thought they might explode. With his throat choked with righteous anger he approached the them and demanded, "Take your hand off my future daughter-in-law."

Nathan said, "I'm sorry to correct you but Sophie has her hand on me."

His anger turned to rage. "Remove your hand. Who the hell do you think you are?"

Others in the crowd turned to see what the commotion was.

Nathan pulled Sophie's arm against him. "The man who's going to marry her."

"No. Absolutely not. A match has been made and it doesn't include you."

"I again respectfully apologize but Sophie and I have other plans."

"Who gives a damn what the two of you planned?"

Nathan's smile evaporated. He leaned toward Matis' father and radiated anger, the likes of which, Yaakov the butcher had rarely experienced. In a low and measured voice, he said, "Your son's happiness is worth more than a financial arrangement."

Red faced Yaakov opened his mouth but nothing came out.

Sophie stood on her toes, looked for Rose and waved her to her side.

Matis approached and held out his arm. Rose politely thanked Matis as she placed her hand on his arm. Matis turned to his father, "He's right. You should care what we think."

Now rattled, Yaakov asked his son in a quivering voice, "And why is that?"

"Because your grandchildren will be living in Rose and my home."

Rose tightened her grip on Matis' arm. He smiled at her.

Matis father starred daggers at his son then Nathan. He yelled, "Who the hell are you?"

Nathan's smile returned, "Do you know Rabbi Moshe Rifkin?"

"Of course. Everyone knows that blessed man. He comes from a long line of learned Rabbis. What's that got to do with you?"

"I'm his grandson."

Sophie experienced momentary shock, sucked in her breath, and felt her knees trembling. She leaned against Nathan to steady herself.

Nathan held out his hand to Yaakov the butcher. "I'm Rabbi Nathan Aaron Rifkin."

He, along with many others in the crowed, turned to look at grinning Dov Rifkin who said, "Rabbi Nathan is my nephew."

Barely able to talk, Yaakov mumbled his wife's name while introducing her as he shook Nathan's hand.

Matis turned to Nathan, held out his hand, and said, "Thank you for the lesson about the word Tzadik, Rabbi Nathan. Perhaps one day, you can teach me your fishing technique and we'll have another lesson."

Nathan shook his hand. "I'll look forward to that.

"Matis," Sophie said, "will you and Rose please accompany Nathan and me. We're going for a walk, then to his parent's home for dinner."

Matis looked at Rose who nodded.

"We'd be happy to," Matis replied.

***

As they proceeded on their walk, Nathan teased, "You didn't ask my permission to invite Rose."

With pretend anger in her voice, Sophie said, "Listen to me, Reb Rifkin. You may be the famous Rabbi to other people but in our home you won't be more than Nathan Aaron."

Nathan laughed so hard he stopped walking. He repeated her remark to Matis and Rose who joined his laughter.

As the continued their walk, Sophie leaned toward Nathan and quietly whispered, "Rose is laughing at

Matis' silly butcher jokes. I dreaded hearing them but she's enjoying them. They'll make a great couple."

"So you're acting like a rabbi's wife already by putting those two together."

"She appreciates him for who he is. The way he's looking at her now, I know they'll be great together."

"You're right and I'm happy for them."

"When did you know I was Jewish?" she asked.

"I saw your mezuzah the first day we met."

She smiled and fingered the tiny mezuzah she always wore. "Why didn't you tell me your full name? And that you're a Rabbi?"

"I was assigned a bride a few years ago by my grandfather. When I met her, it was apparent that she was in love with the idea of marrying the grandson of a famous rabbi but didn't have any interest in getting to know me. Did I hurt your feelings by not giving you my real name?"

"No…but you could have told me. Should I be embarrassed that I argued Torah with a learned Rabbi?"

"You may not be embarrassed…because I loved arguing with you. Besides, we weren't arguing. We were discussing." He smiled at her. "When did you think we might have a future?"

She squeezed his arm against her side. "My Tzadik stole my heart the same day an eagle stole a fish from an osprey."

They walked in silence for a few minutes. Nathan noticed Sophie grimace.

"What's wrong?"

"After I fell in your brother's office, my arm tingles and I've experienced a headache which worsens each day."

***

As Sophie and Nathan continued up the street, he said, "That's my parent's business." He pointed to the Kaplan-Kaufman signboard.

"Myra and David Kaplan are your parents? You're a helper at your parent's business?"

"Yes, they are and yes, I am until another opportunity begins. I lost my birth-parents when I was two. They took me in and raised me as their own. Out of respect for my birth-parents, and with the Kaplan's permission, I took my father's name for my middle name and changed my last name back to Rifkin after I finished rabbinical school."

After introductions were made at David and Myra's home, Myra asked Sophie and Rose to help set the dinner table.

"So you're the one making him crazy," Myra said to Sophie as she handed them dishes. "Since he went out one morning for a walk along the river, he can't leave the house without asking me at least three times if he looks okay."

Sophie grinned then turned to Rose, "Matis is positively in heaven when he looks at you. He never looked at me like that."

The family and guests sat down to dinner. Sophie kept twisting on her chair.

"There's nothing to be nervous about Sophie, we're just ordinary people," David said while spooning peas into his shirt pocket. Noting Sophie's amazed expression, he said to her, "Saving these for later."

As everyone became hysterical laughing, Nathan covered his eyes with his hand and shook his head. Myra playfully punched David in the arm.

"What?" he said raising his shoulders and hands in a gesture of innocence.

"You're embarrassing Nathan."

"I know but now Sophie's not nervous."

Celeste said, "I apologize, Sophie, Matis, and Rose but that's what it's like to be around our family."

Jonah said, "Uncle Nathan has lots of amazing abilities. Wait until you see his technique with his spear."

Sophie blushed. "I wasn't aware that was a proper subject for dinner conversation…but I'm looking forward to the day when he demonstrates the use of his spear."

There was immediate silence after which the family became hysterical laughing, Nathan quickly whispered to Sophie.

She closed her eyes and lowered her head as her cheeks reddened further. William told Matis and Rose, "He really does own and throw a spear."

As the meal ended, Myra said, "Nathan, take a moment and give Sophie a tour of the upstairs. Also Nathan, tell Sophie about you know what if you haven't already."

David whispered to Myra, "You sent them upstairs?"

She replied in a whisper, "Sophie is still nervous. A little time alone will help. Besides, I think this is a good time for him to tell her about the other thing."

***

They wrapped their arms around each other the moment they were alone and engaged in a long kiss.

Sophie asked, "What did your mother want you to tell me?"

"I've been educated as a rabbi but after I finished rabbinical school I spent the next two years studying medicine and that will be my primary career. I learned that in ancient times you were required to be a doctor before you could become a rabbi. That's what I did but I got the order reversed."

"What?" Sophie said, as she noisily collapsed to a sitting position on a hallway couch. "I'm overwhelmed."

"Don't be. I need you in my life to remember I'm just Nathan Aaron."

"You don't think I should be impressed that you're a learned rabbi and a doctor?"

"I've been invited to Spokane, Washington to set up a medical practice and become a part-time rabbi for a small Jewish community until they grow sufficiently to hire a full time Rabbi."

"Are you going?"

"Will you come with?"

"We'd be away from family."

"Spokane is a train ride away."

"What will it cost to move?"

"They'll pay for the move and pay one year's rent for a medical office. They're also willing to help me equip the office."

"Then I'm going."

"You love me that much?"

"I loved you when I believed you were a clerk. I ..." Her voice trailed off. She kept trying to speak but seemed to have trouble forming the words. Her eyes widened in fright.

"Sophie. What's wrong?"

She swayed slightly and collapsed.

Nathan began screaming for William.

***

Nathan leaned over her lifeless body, one hand on her cheek. William checked for heart and breathing sounds. He shook his head.

"Sophie," Nathan said, "started slurring her speech and collapsed. She'd been complaining of terrible headaches."

"I'm so sorry. With all the head trauma from her father's beatings, it could have happened at any time."

***

Following Sophie's funeral, Nathan spoke to David and William.

"I'm moving to Spokane. It's far enough from Seattle, I won't see daily reminders of my time with Sophie."

"We'll miss you but I think it's a good idea," David said.

Nathan walked to the desk in the parlor. He took out a sheet of paper and began writing.

"Dear Ruben, Joyce and Naomi, The last few days may have been the worst in my life…"

Chapter Thirty-Five: Moving On

"Congratulations Doctor Rifkin."

"For what?" Nathan said to his office assistant while cleaning and bandaging a laceration on a boy's elbow.

"I just glanced at the calendar. Our Spokane office has been open for six-months today."

Nathan laughed.

"You have a woman and young girl waiting to see you. Not an emergency they said."

"Thank you, Mrs. Cornish. I'm nearly done here. Let them know, I'll meet with them in my office in a couple of minutes."

Nathan washed his hands and crossed the hall to his office.

"Right this way and have a seat," Mrs. Cornish said as she seated the twosome across from Nathan's desk.

Without looking up, he said, "I have to make a couple notes about my last patient. I'll be right with you."

"When I received your letter that Sophie died, I thought you might need a hug."

Nathan looked up; his eyes widened. His pen dropped as did his jaw. "You're here."

Joyce smiled. "I wanted Naomi to continue her walks with you."

"Ruben?"

"Died nine-months ago. They never cured his leg infection."

"You didn't tell me."

"You were involved with Sophie." Joyce twisted on the chair. "Are you…ready...?"

"To move on? Yes. Definitely."

Relief flooded Joyce's expression.

After a long silence Naomi asked, "We brought all our stuff out here. What are we going to do now?"

"Climb ladders," Nathan replied.

"Why?" Naomi asked.

"To gather apples and peaches."

"Apples and peaches?" Joyce asked.

"It's harvest time for families who have an orchard."

"Are we a family?" Joyce asked.

"Am I still in there?" Nathan nodded at her heart.

"Yes. And you?"

"Still have a special place for each of you."

Sounding exasperated, Naomi said, "But does that mean we're a family?"

"Come here," Nathan said as he stood. Naomi raced around the desk and embraced him.

"Let's go home," he said.

"Dr. Kaplan," a young man called out while helping an old woman into the medical office. Grandma fell off a ladder."

"Right this way," Mrs. Cornish said.

"Have a seat," Nathan said to Naomi and Joyce. "I'll be right back." He helped the old woman to an examining table. "Just looks like some bad scrapes but that bump on your knee will take some time to heal."

"Can I watch?" Naomi asked.

Nathan turned to the old woman. "Mrs. Olson, do you mind if Naomi watches?"

"Of course not."

Nathan began cleaning and bandaging. "Perhaps at ninety-three you should give up climbing ladders."

"There were three nectarines that looked so perfect, I had to." She noticed Naomi's rapt attention. "She's keeping an eye on you doc."

"I taught her how to bandage."

She turned to Naomi. "What are you waiting for Darlin'? Give him a hand."

"Naomi, move to my right side and hold this for me," Nathan said as he covered a long thin scrape on Mrs. Olson's upper arm.

"Remember what I taught you?"

Naomi nodded.

"Go ahead."

With each wrap, Joyce's smile broadened.

"Excellent," Nathan said.

"Will four jars of canned applesauce and three jars of peaches suffice?" Mrs. Olson asked.

Nathan glanced at Mrs. Cornish, nodded, and said, "Yes they will."

"Do you often receive goods for services?" Joyce asked as they left the office.

"Yes. Mrs. Cornish has a good idea of what things are worth."

"Do you always leave work at mid-afternoon?"

"Only before the Sabbath."

"Is your rabbi nice?" Naomi asked.

"I like to think so."

"You're talking to him," Joyce said.

"Oops. I forgot." Naomi grabbed Nathan's hand and skipped as they walked.

***

"This is my home," Nathan said, opening the front door for them.

"Where are the fruit trees?" Naomi asked.

"Behind the house and beyond the garden."

Naomi ran off to explore the orchard.

"Thank you for letting Naomi help."

"She remembered everything I taught her."

"Nathan, I hate to do this but I couldn't sleep coming out here. Not knowing what to expect. You know, just showing up and all. I'm totally exhausted."

"My bedroom is upstairs in front. It has the only bed in the house. Where are your things?"

"At the railroad station."

"I'll have them brought here."

They embraced and engaged in a long kiss.

Joyce's eyes filled with tears.

"What's wrong?" Nathan asked.

She kept her arms firmly around his neck and whispered in his ear. "Do you know how long I've waited for that kiss? Believe me. These are tears of joy...pure joy."

He kissed her again.

"Think it's our turn to have some peace in our lives?" Joyce asked.

"I'll pray that's the case."

She held him tightly.

"Joyce, will you marry me?"

"Yes...but soon."

"If I send a telegram to my folks today, we can plan on a wedding in a few weeks."

"Send it."

***

One day later a reply to his telegram arrived.

"My mom wants to take the train out here in a few days to help set things up for the wedding."

"Another mother-in-law. Don't know if I can take that."

"If she becomes a problem, I'll put her on the train back to Seattle. Your choice and I'll back you."

"If it becomes a headache..."

"It won't happen. Besides, you and I need some time alone."

"Who'll watch Naomi?"

"My mom."

"Are you certain? Naomi doesn't need hysteria with new relatives."

***

"Naomi and Joyce, I'm so happy to meet you," Myra said.

"Please have a seat, Mrs. Kaplan," Joyce said.

"Actually, I was hoping to do some shopping. Does Naomi know where a butcher and green grocer are?"

"I do," Naomi said.

"Would you mind accompanying me if it's alright with your mother?"

"Sure."

Joyce nodded.

They headed out the door with Myra asking Naomi about school.

***

"They've been gone over three-hours," Joyce said, twisting on a chair in the parlor.

"I promise. Naomi will be fine."

An hour later they heard Myra and Naomi's laughter. They walked through the front door laden with numerous purchases.

"Your daughter was an immense help," Myra said.

"Mom, I showed Mrs. Kaplan how we pick potatoes, garlic and cabbages. Then I helped her pick out two lengths of cloth so we can make a dress for me."

"Let's put the food away," Myra said.

"Don't forget," Naomi said as they disappeared into the kitchen. "You're going to teach me to cook cold cannon."

"I don't believe my ears," Joyce said. "Naomi volunteering to cook?"

"By the way," Myra said as she returned from the kitchen. "Celeste and Shifra plus Daire and Angela will be out in two days. They'll help me with your wedding dress." She opened her design book. "If you like, we can look through these and gather ideas for your own design."

Naomi's eyes widened as she and her mother paged through the book. "Mom, these are…"

"Gorgeous," Joyce said.

Myra asked, "Will you be having bridesmaids?"

"At least Naomi."

Myra opened a second book and handed it to Naomi. "These are bridesmaid dresses."

"For me?"

"Once your mother settles on a design, we'll make a dress for you that coordinates with hers."

***

Rabbi Moshe Rifkin, with Dov and other friends and relatives, arrived in Spokane Friday morning before the Sunday wedding.

Shifra introduced Naomi to her brothers and other cousins.

During the ceremony, Rabbi Rifkin said, "These two exhibit strength of character which we should all emulate. Once they decide on the proper course of action, they proceed with utmost determination…even with the knowledge the decision may cause them pain." He put a hand on each of their shoulders. "I know how much they mean to each other. Therefore it gives me immense pleasure to pronounce them husband and wife."

Once all were seated for dinner, Nathan stood and waited until the crowd quieted. "I wish each of us would raise a glass to a man who rescued a two-year-old boy from a burning steamboat then returned to rescue others. He died in that attempt. Sadly, we never learned his name. L'Chaim."

"Grandma," Naomi asked Myra. "Some of the kids at school say a girl can't be a doctor so how did Aunt Abbey do it?"

"Hard work and determination."

David added, "You ignore people who say things can't be done."

"Why?" Shifra asked.

"They're usually run over by people doing them."

Naomi and Shifra, sitting next to each other, exchanged glances and laughed.

"I heard you bandaged someone's arm," Myra said to Naomi.

"Mrs. Olson. She fell off a ladder."

"See this scar?"

"That's a big one."

"When your father and Aunt Abbey watched a doctor sew and bandage my arm they decided to become doctors."

David turned to Nathan and spoke in a quiet voice. "Is she bright enough?"

Also in a quiet voice, Nathan said, "Without doubt. She talks of becoming a doctor but her love of science may take her in other directions." Nathan continued in full voice. "Naomi is intelligent like William and has Abbey's mental strength and drive."

"I love astronomy and math," Naomi said.

"I love looking through a microscope," Shifra said then giggled. "You like big and I like small."

Naomi nodded.

In full voice, Nathan said to David, "When Naomi wanted to know how big the moon is, I did the same trigonometry exercises you did with William and me. We started with a talk about right triangles, measured furniture, then the house, and finally a mountain."

"Tangent is my favorite because you can measure so many things," Naomi said. "We drew graphs with the sine function using radians and it looked like a wave." She turned to Shifra. "I found it weird because it never got bigger than one and minus one."

Shifra stared at her lap for a while. "I can't quite picture that. You need to show me."

"Love to," Naomi said.

Naomi turned to Myra. "Grandma, can you help me write to Aunt Abbey? I have some questions for her."

Chapter Thirty-Six: Jonah

During a springtime Sunday dinner at William and Celeste's home, his mother asked twelve-year-old Jonah, "I was putting away your shirts when I found a box with money in your dresser drawer. Where did it come from?"

"Our business."

"What business?" Celeste asked.

"Our candy business. I've been running it since school started."

William said, "Tell us about it."

"Zadie gave me three-cents for sweeping out his office the day before school started. I took it to the general store and bought three pieces of candy. I sold them at school for two-cents each. Next day, I bought twice as much candy and sold it. I just kept doing that. My business grew so I asked Ethan and Noah to help. When we started to sell the same amount of candy every day, we stopped by the Czech bakery and bought some of Mrs. Kurkova's fruit Kolaches. We paid three-cents for each one and sell them for five-cents."

"How much money do you have?"

Noah chimed in. "Not counting the cost of inventory, we have sixteen-dollars and eighty-seven-cents."

"Cost of inventory?" William said with raised eyebrows.

Ethan said, "Zadie showed us how to do …"

"Bookkeeping," Jonah said. "It's how we can keep track of our income and expenses."

"Your business better not be getting in the way of your school work."

"No," Jonah said. "Zadie said we need to have good English skills to write business letters and proposals plus good arithmetic skills to do bookkeeping and finance."

Celeste smiled at her industrious sons.

William eyed the boys in a questioning manner. "I was at a schoolboard meeting earlier this week. We reviewed bids for the new roof for the school house. The lowest bid was submitted by Jenz Kaplan. No one knew who that was."

The boy's eyes widened as they glanced at each other. Jonah leaned toward his father. "The lowest?"

Ethan asked, "Did we win?"

William peered over his glasses. "Who is Jenz Kaplan?"

Noah said, "My business partners and me. Jonah, Ethan, Noah, and Zadie."

William slapped his forehead and turned to Celeste. "Why am I not surprised my father is behind this."

Jonah added, "Zadie agreed to sell us lumber at two-percent-over-cost. I had to calculate that for every board foot we needed. Noah negotiated, with Zadie's help, prices for all the other materials and labor. Ethan checked the dimensions of the drawings to see that we have the right amount and type of lumber."

"And what else are you doing?"

Jonah enthused, "We have to keep our bookkeeping balanced to make sure it's correct and prove its correct to Zadie."

"Who's going to supervise the carpenters?" their father asked.

Noah replied, "We all are."

"But really Zadie," Ethan said. The other boys nodded agreement

"My children," Celeste said, "the businessmen."

Jonah added, "Zadie said, we're trip and manure's."

"Entrepreneurs," William corrected. "And this is the end of these shenanigans."

"Why?" Jonah asked.

"Your job is school. Not working for your Grandfather or running your own business."

"But our grades are okay."

"I suspect they could be much better. Jonah, you especially could be getting more schoolwork done without this distraction."

"I love business stuff," Jonah pleaded.

"None the less, you'll have to find a new love because your first priority is your schoolwork."

***

"I have another letter from Aunt Abbey," Naomi said. She opened it, read a few lines then leaped in the air and shouted. "She's visiting Seattle but will stop here first!"

Her younger brother Joshua asked, "Mom, can I call her Aunt Abbey?"

Joyce replied, "We'll all meet her and yes, you call her Aunt."

Naomi continued reading the letter.

"She's bringing Uncle Benjamin, Shayna and Daniel."

"Wow! More cousins!" Joshua exclaimed.

Joyce asked, "When are they arriving?"

"In two weeks."

***

"Joyce," Nathan said, "now that Naomi and Josh are in bed. I want to talk about a patient. Tod Swenson came home from the war missing his right arm and left hand. He grew up on a farm and thinks he's useless. His wife threatened to leave him and take their children before he agreed to see me. I've talked to him once and insisted he bring his wife to the next meeting. I want you to be there when I meet with them."

"I've already dealt with a crippled casualty of the war."

"Perhaps then, you'll have insight into getting him involved in life again and helping his wife."

"What can I possibly say to his wife?"

"What emotions did you go through when Ruben came home?"

"Well…" Joyce was deep in thought for a while before responding. "I felt like a victim of the war. I know it's selfish but I resented the imposition his injury had on my life."

"If his wife has the same reaction, it might help her feel better knowing you experienced the same thoughts."

Joyce became pensive again. "Not thoughts." She shook her head. "Feelings. Mr. Swenson's wife has to understand her…and his…feelings. It's the only thing that worked for me. Abbey endured horror through the entire war. Perhaps she'll share some insight with me."

***

"Mom," Naomi said as she and her mother walked to the library, "Did you learn stuff from Aunt Abbey?"

"She's given me a list of books to read plus I have to engage in self-reflection. That's not always fun."

"Like what?"

Joyce thought for a moment. "Last year, one of your friends teased you. You erupted and called her a string of vile words."

"She started it."

"How do you think she felt?"

"I don't know."

"You said she cried and ran home." Joyce stopped walking and turned her daughter to face her. "Naomi, how did she feel?"

Naomi's smile disappeared and she stared at the ground. "Sad."

"Only sad?"

"And humiliated."

"You used your powerful vocabulary to sadden and humiliate a longtime friend."

Naomi twisted her foot in the dirt. "I was cruel."

"Now you're going to write her a letter expressing your feelings and apologize."

She nodded. They walked in silence for a while then Naomi asked, "Is that how Aunt Abbey is helping you? With your feelings?"

"Yes. I still have a lot of resentment toward Ruben."

"Like what?"

"Things that are difficult to talk to a daughter about but Aunt Abbey is helping me."

"What will writing a letter do besides make me sad as I relive what happened?"

"It will help you come to grips with your cruel actions. Help you learn self-control and, by understanding the pain you caused your friend, so you will avoid doing that again."

***

William sat down with Jonah just prior to his high school graduation. "Did you use the kit of medical supplies I gave you during your hunting trip?," William asked Jonah.

He nodded. "One of my friends, sliced his palm open when sharpening his knife."

"What did you do?"

"Cleaned the wound site, put in twelve-stitches and a proper bandage."

"So you put my lessons to good use."

"I also put your angry tone to good use; balling-him-out for not controlling the knife while sharpening."

"Good thing you were there."

"I'm keeping that kit near me on any hunt or cross-country trip. His hand bled like a river until I closed it."

"How was the hunt itself?"

"We shot two deer. We divided the meat among the four of us. I cleaned the deer the way Grandmother Kim taught us when she took us hunting when I was twelve."

William took a deep breath. "Your brothers are going to college after summer break but you avoid talking about your future."

"I know what I want to do but you won't like it."

"Does it involve college?"

Jonah avoided looking at his father. "No."

"How will you earn a living?"

"Last summer I helped Zadie put together a deal to ship construction lumber to three ports down the coast. My commission on that deal, most of which I gave to Mom because I still live at home, will pay for one of my brothers first year of college. I live for buying, selling and deal making. That's what I'm going to do."

"Does Zadie know?"

"He's waiting for me to talk to you and Mom before he offers me a permanent position."

"Of all my children, you're the only one with the where-with-all to take my place in my medical practice."

"I know but I have no desire to do that. When you need to expand the hospital or the University, I'm working hard to ensure I'll be one of the individuals who will finance that expansion."

"Without sufficient doctors with the requisite skills, it will be a useless structure." William paused to let his words sink in. "Jonah, when you put your mind to it, you're one of the hardest workers I know...and you're capable of learning anything."

"Zadie makes sure I work hard. Every summer he assigns me new and more difficult projects."

William put a hand on his son's shoulder. "I don't like this." He leaned towards Jonah, lifted his son's hands, and pleaded, "You even the have the dexterity which can perform delicate surgery like me. You have a responsibility to use the gifts God gave you."

Jonah pulled his hands away. "I only want to buy and sell."

"And I only wanted to become an engineer but finally realized how much good I could do as a doctor."

"It's different now."

William sighed. "I'm certain children of every generation say that to their parents. Go talk to your mother. If she asks, tell her how I feel." Wearing a pained expression William leaned back in his chair then rubbed his chin. "If you take the job with my father, you have one week to pack your things and move into your own place."

"But Dad…"

"Perhaps living on you own and paying your own way will convince you of the need for college."

PART THREE

Chapter Thirty-Seven: Riding in Boxcars

A freight train pulled out of the Missoula Montana railyard just before sunlight began to warm an icy cold winter night. A tall, barrel chested man ran alongside, his every exhalation condensing into a cloud. He threw his bag through the half-open door of a freight car and hoisted himself inside. The frontend of the car was filled with crates stacked to the ceiling and the other was occupied by a girl, dressed in waist overalls and a heavy parka. She looked to be in her mid-teens. The teen pulled her hood forward but gave furtive glances in the direction of the new arrival. He put his bag into the corner of the back wall and laid down. Within minutes the swaying of the car plus the rhythm of the steam locomotive's sounds put him to sleep.

***

Jonah awakened to the sound of a knife being sharpened against a stone. He nodded to his traveling companion.

She returned a nod and said, "That's a nice pistol you've got. Colt, isn't it?"

"It is." Jonah removed the pistol from its holster.

"What a huge barrel," the woman said. With an impish grin she added, "You're better off shooting somebody so they have a chance to survive. Hit them over the head with that barrel and you'll kill them for sure."

Jonah laughed. "This is the Cavalry model. Seven-and-a-half-inch barrel, if I remember."

"Is the hammer on an empty chamber?"

He opened the cylinder. "No. Good thing you asked." After removing one round, Jonah carefully closed it and verified the hammer was over the empty chamber.

"Where you headed?" he asked. "Name's Jonah, by the way."

"I'm Beth. Headed to Seattle. Heard the winters are warmer."

"They are."

She pushed her hood back. "You live there?"

He nodded.

Beth's gaze examined him from top to bottom. "You're wearing nice clothes. What're you doing riding like a bum?"

"Did a little card playing last night. I used my train ticket as my last bet and lost…held three kings…lost to four jacks."

She laughed. "How do you normally make a living?"

"Work for my grandfather. He sent me out here to secure lumber contracts for one of his businesses."

"Why didn't he send a new ticket?"

"He's careful with money. I received enough to get out here, stay three days and return. If I ask for more, he'd tell me it was my problem."

"Wise man."

"You have, I believe, a Scottish accent."

She smiled. "Born in Glasgow. Came to Philadelphia when I was nine. My mom died from the flu a year later. Moved in with a mean-as-hell aunt. I worked from twelve to fourteen-hours seven-days-a-week in her bread shop. At twelve I ran away and been living on my own. Met some kids who taught me how to live on the streets."

"How'd you end up in Missoula?"

Beth stared at him for a while as if she was deciding how much to tell him. She took a deep breath and continued. "The cops in Philly got to know my pickpocket habits. Spent a week in a filthy jail with a bunch of street walkers. Rode a train to Chicago. Got picked up for picking a couple coins from a rich woman's purse and this cop beat and kicked the hell out of me." She shook her head at the memory. "Limped for days afterward. I tried to hop a train back to Philly but it was dark and ended up in

Minneapolis. I learned what real cold is." The recollection caused an involuntary shiver. "Heard Seattle was warmer so hopped a train heading there. Hunger overwhelmed me on the ride to Seattle, so I stopped in Missoula to find something to eat."

"Sounds like you need a new profession."

"Don't know what I'm gonna do. Don't have much book learning, but I managed a library card in Minneapolis."

"What do you like to read?"

"I like learning about animals."

He shivered. "The air's getting colder. You mind if I slide the door closed."

She shook her head.

The door closed with a loud thunk. The girl pulled her hood forward. Jonah removed a quilt out of his bag and threw it to her.

"Thanks. You won't need it?"

"Without the wind blowing through here, I'll be fine. Was up nearly all night so I'm going to get some shut eye." He closed his eyes and slept with his head on his bag.

Beth wondered if his help would lead to his requesting she do something unpleasant. She cast a wary eye on Jonah. "Nobody does something for nothing," the thin woman whispered.

***

Mid-morning the following day, a light snow fell as the train approached a three-hundred-foot trestle located seventy-five-feet over a canyon. A rail, which had been improperly secured to a rotten tie some months previous, moved up and down as each train passed causing it's spikes to loosen. Its motion eventually loosened the spikes in the adjacent ties. With a light covering of snow, the engineer and fireman didn't have an opportunity to notice the rail was out of place before the train came off the tracks just prior to the trestle. It plowed down the sloped canyon wall, slowly rotating on its side. The boiler's steam lines ruptured and the locomotive exploded with the sound and force of a nearby lightning strike. A cloud of white steam and black smoke rose high into the air. The forces sent burning embers aloft. Many landed on the wooden freight cars which followed the engine into the drop-off.

Chapter Thirty-Eight: Finding Shelter

Their car plunged into the canyon; they felt a momentary weightless sensation and were lifted into the air. Beth cried out and Jonah swore. When they slammed into the floor they slid forward and into the large crates. Separated from the car in front of it, the steel chassis came to an abrupt halt as it slammed into the rocks and boulders which lined the bottom of the canyon. The large crates continued forward, easily rupturing the thin, wood sheathed, front wall. Wood planks from the sides and rear of the car, plus lumber from the ruptured car behind theirs, piled on top of the two human occupants.

***

Jonah heard the engine's remaining steam hissing into the atmosphere.

He wedged his body against the pile of sheathing covering him. Nothing moved. Rotating his head, he could see the sky between a few boards. Jonah pushed his arm into the small opening. He pushed on one of the top boards with his fingertips, moving it a few inches to the side, which let more sky in. With great effort, Jonah slowly moved one board at a time. Beth moaned.

"Beth, can you hear me?"

There was no response. He tried to take a deep breath but could only manage a shallow one as an iron bar pressed on his chest. He smelled burning wood. His pulse increased until it hammered in his head.

Jonah relived nightmarish sights and sounds; screams of agony accompanied by the acrid smell of burned flesh. A firefighter writhed in pain in his father's medical office. The doctor slowly shook his head in the direction of the waiting firemen and the fireman's wife. During the following two hours, the fireman's screams diminished. Ultimately, his burned lungs responded to their trauma in deadly fashion. They filled with fluid and no longer conveyed oxygen. "Burns are the most painful injury," Dr. Kaplan said on their walk home. "His fate was sealed before he arrived at my office."

Jonah pushed hard and shoved his hand further into the opening, grasping about, trying to find more loose boards to push aside as the sound of the fire increased.

A small hand grabbed his, let go and Beth shoved and lifted debris off him. Smoke wafted across his face. He began coughing.

"Hang on," Beth called out. She strained to push more of the wood and tangled metal aside. The crackling of the burning wood increased. The thin girl picked up a board and used it as a lever to create a larger opening.

"Can you move?"

"My legs are trapped," he said, in between coughing.

He heard Beth climbing off the debris pile and running away. Jonah, in terror, tried to yell, "Please don't leave me," but with the bar pressing against his chest a weak voice was all he could manage.

Jonah felt the heat from the burning sheathing intensifying. He tried wedging against his tomb with all his might; to no avail.

The sound of an ax on wood startled him. Beth grunted with each swing of a full size axe. She coughed as a cloud of smoke briefly enveloped her but continued chopping away at Jonah's prison. The thin girl pushed debris aside. His legs were free.

"My chest is pinned," he said.

She attempted to use the ax handle as a lever to lift the bar which pinned his chest. The end of the axe handle was at mid-belly level. Her arms ached as she strained to lift the bar. It didn't move. Repositioning herself, she bent her knees and put the end of the ax handle on top of her shoulder. Screaming and using the power of her legs to lift the handle it slowly moved the bar.

Jonah squirmed free of the restraint. He gathered his legs under him and forced his way up and out of the debris pile. The twosome ran from the burning car.

Sitting on rocks in clear air, they both puffed hard. He coughed and spit out saliva filled with black specks.

"That was some shit," he said.

Breathing hard, Beth just nodded.

"I owe you," Jonah said.

She waved a hand and shook her head.

A gust of chilled air blew across them.

Jonah glanced at the sky. "Black clouds are headed this way. Likely more snow," he said. "We need to find some shelter."

"Shouldn't we wait here for a rescue train?"

"No. Those clouds are in the western sky. There's a storm coming. If it's heavy, it could be days before another train arrives."

"Nothing left of this train." Beth scanned their surroundings. "Up there. Fifty-yards below the crest of that ridge. There's a cabin."

"At least a six-hour hike."

"We'd be out of the weather."

"The crew members?"

She pointed. "That pile of rubble is all that's left of the caboose. All dead in there. The locomotive exploded. No trace of the occupants."

Jonah shook his head looking in the locomotive's direction. "Let's dig around. See if we can find anything useful to help get us out of here."

Beth gazed at their surroundings. "I'll see if I can find our bags."

An hour's digging in the rubble and Beth yelled, "Got 'em."

Jonah said. "We need to cross the trestle to get to that cabin."

"Why don't we cross the river down there? It's ice covered."

"We don't know how thick the ice is. We fall through and the still flowing water will push us beneath the ice and we'll drown."

Beth shivered. "Don't like the sound of that."

Jonah walked one-third of the way onto the trestle.

"See? It's solid." He jumped up and down to demonstrate. The tie he jumped on split.

Her eyes went wide and she gasped as he dropped.

He twisted his body as it descended. Jonah used both hands to reach for a rail. His right hand solidly gripped it but his left slipped off. His body swayed like a pendulum over the chasm. With his heart in his throat, Jonah tried to remain calm and waited for his motion to bring his free hand close to the rail to attempt grabbing it. With a yell he pulled up with his right arm and securely gripped the rail with his left hand. He steadied his body then did a pull up; with a slight sway left then right, he rotated his right arm over the rail, followed by his left. Straightening his arms, he threw his leg over the iron beam. He took a moment to catch his breath and let his heart rate subside then slid forward on the rail. He carefully stood, keeping his feet on the tie but close to the rail. Jonah walked to Beth's side.

"Thought I lost you," she said.

"Two close-calls in one day."

"You need to be more careful before you run out of luck."

Despite the cold air, he wiped sweat from his brow. He glanced up the mountain. "We need to get to that cabin."

As if in reply, snow fell and the wind picked up.

"We can use some of the siding and place them on the ties next to the rail," Beth said. "It'll spread our weight out and be closer to the trestle's support. We'll move them as we proceed."

Jonah smiled briefly. "Let's do it."

Carrying a board each, they returned to the beginning of the trestle.

"How will we carry our bags?"

Jonah pulled out the belt and suspenders he'd secured from the deceased trainman. "I'll cut this into strips and build us backboards. There's probably an axe at the cabin but I'll carry the one you found just in case."

After securing their bags to the backboards, he slid the first board out on the trestle and cautiously walked to the end.

Beth walked out with slow precise steps; a board under one arm, the other arm straight out from her shoulder to help maintain balance. She carefully transferred the board to Jonah. He placed it and walked to its end.

This was repeated numerous times. They're journey across the bridge was made more dangerous as wind gusts assaulted them. At two-thirds distance, a strong gust forced Beth off balance.

"Bend your knees and get low," Jonah bellowed, as she flailed her arms to regain her balance.

She lowered her body and steadied herself by grabbing the rail. After the wind died down, her breathing and pulse slowed. Beth took a deep breath, straightened her legs and continued.

Once both were across the trestle, they smiled at each other. Beth breathed a sigh of relief. Jonah placed his hand next to his face to block the blowing snow and stared toward the ridge. "It's a steep climb and the snow is blowing nearly sideways. I can barely see the cabin. We need to get moving."

After three-hours of trekking up steep snow-covered-terrain, plus stopping occasionally to make sure they were still moving in the cabin's direction, Jonah looked back at Beth. The drifted snow was half way up her thighs. Her face grimaced with each step. She appeared exhausted. He strained to see, then moved to her side.

"I can't locate the cabin." He needed to scream to make himself heard over the whistling sound of the wind driven storm. "Hell, I can barely see ten-feet. Don't know if we're going the right direction."

Fright etched her red cheeks as she used the edge of her hood to try and keep the snow out of her face. "We can't stay here," she yelled.

Jonah surveyed their immediate surroundings. "Follow me," he shouted as the bitter cold wind and blowing snow whipped around them. He hiked a short distance to where a huge drift lay against the side of the mountain. Using his gloved hands, he dug a tunnel into the snow. Beth moved close and kneeled next to him, trying to use Jonah's body to shield herself from the wind whipped snow crystals which felt like razor burn on her cheeks. After many minutes of furious digging, only Jonah's feet were showing. He slithered out of the opening.

"I'm going to open it up to make a cave but we need pine boughs to cover the floor."

"I'll cut them."

"Don't go far or you won't find your way back."

***

With constant pain in her thighs plus sore abdominal and hip muscles, Beth sawed off branches. Each time she accumulated a good sized bundle, she leaned into the fierce wind and trudged back up to the cave. Kneeling in the snow she pushed her load through it's opening.

Her heart pounded, her head felt like it was being crushed by a vice, plus her feet and hands hurt with each movement. She'd walked ten paces from the tree when Beth realized she wasn't sure if she'd come this way. She retraced her rapidly disappearing footsteps to the base of the last tree. Beth strained to see through the blowing snow. Her entire body trembled as she realized she'd lost any sense of where the cave was. Forcing her mind to quell the increasing sense of panic, Beth decided to walk twelve paces from the tree's base. If she didn't see the cave she'd return and try another radial. Each time she began her return to the tree, her heart rate increased and she had to quell another wave of panic. On the seventh try, she was about to return to the tree when she saw snow thrown down the mountain. She peered intently in the direction it came from and saw Jonah pulling another arm load of snow out of the cave's opening and tossing it away from the entrance. Beth hurried to his side, dropped her bundle and threw her arms around him.

"Your last trip took a while," he yelled, briefly embracing her.

"I was lost. Scared the hell out of me."

He tried to smile but his cold face muscles were too stiff. Instead, Jonah yelled, "You're home now. Hand me the branches and come inside."

She crawled through the opening. The interior was just tall enough for the two of them to sit upright and slightly longer than needed to lie down. The two back boards were placed against either side of the entrance.

"Not much light," Beth said. "But you can barely hear the sound of the storm. Glad to be out of that vicious wind. Hope it gets warmer."

"It will."

"You've done this before?"

"My grandmother took us camping in the winter. She's an outdoorsman of the first rank. Always found a way to work with nature instead of against it. A kind and gentle woman who taught my brothers, sister and me how to make one of these plus tons of other outdoor survival skills."

"Speaking of which…"

"I hollowed a corner and dug a hole over there. Squat over the hole and cover what you've left with a good handful of snow. Whatever you leave will freeze and not smell."

"I can go outside."

"Hell no. Exposed flesh will freeze in seconds."

"Please turn away."

He did and she relieved herself.

"Any idea what time it is?"

Jonah pulled out his watch. "Six."

"The sun was short of straight up when the wreck happened," she said. This has been a grueling seven hours." Beth rubbed her thighs. "My legs and hips are killing me and I'm still freezing."

"How are your hands and feet?"

"My hands hurt like hell and I don't have much feeling in my feet."

Jonah pulled the quilt out of his bag and wrapped it around her.

"You're not shivering like me." Beth said.

"This leather coat has a shearling lining as do my pants plus I'm wearing lots of wool underneath. We should lie down and try to get some rest."

She stretched out.

"Beth, we should spoon."

Her eyes went wide. "I'm not kissing you!"

"I mean lay with your back against my chest. Like two matching spoons."

She didn't move.

"This is not romance. This is survival. It's cold enough to be the death of us. My father's a doctor and I've seen what happens to frozen body parts. We need to combine our body heat."

She hesitantly turned on her side. He positioned his body against hers. After thirty minutes she still shivered. Jonah opened his coat, wrapped as much of it as he could around her and pulled her tight against him. Beth reached for his arm and pulled it around her. Over the next half-hour, her shivering subsided and she slept.

***

The following morning, Beth woke realizing her hands no longer hurt but her feet throbbed. She heard the sound of chewing. Looking over her shoulder at Jonah, he held out a piece of pemmican.

"Grandpa's recipe. Venison, nuts and blueberries. I never met him but Grandma taught me how to make this."

"Chewy."

"Yes, but not bad when it's boiled into stew."

"I'm thirsty. I should eat some snow."

"Eat snow and your body cools off. You'll be shivering in no time. Here." He pulled a whiskey bottle out of his coat. "I found this near the caboose."

"Whiskey?"

"I poured out the whisky, continually stuffed it with snow and kept it inside my jacket. The heat leaving my body melted the snow."

She pulled out the cork and drank some.

"Still tastes a little whiskey-ish."

"Take a good drink. We'll need it climbing this mountain."

"Think the weather's cleared?"

"An hour ago it wasn't snowing but still mostly cloudy and windy. Sun, what there is of it, came up an hour ago. We should try to head for the cabin."

They strapped on the backboards and climbed the mountain toward the cabin.

"This is like continually climbing stairs," she complained. "And my feet are killing me."

Chapter Thirty-Nine: The Cabin

They stopped four times to rest before they arrived at the cabin. A pile of neatly stacked logs placed against the outside of the cabin were sheltered by the little building's extended eve.

"The door's nailed shut," Beth yelled to Jonah while he examined the wood pile..

"That's to keep bears out. Look for a hammer or nail puller around the entrance."

She brushed snow off an area next to the door and found a twelve-inch-nail-puller. Beth worked the nails loose and entered the cabin whose wood floor was roughly ten-by-twelve. A small pot-bellied stove sat in one corner with a box of kindling next to it. A table with a bench and two chairs occupied the other. A feather mattress was rolled up at the far end of the table. Jonah entered after removing the shutter from a small window. He walked to the stove and opened it.

"Ready for a fire. I better make sure the chimney's clear."

"Someone left it like that?" Beth asked.

"When we leave, we'll do the same. First thing when anyone arrives at a cabin is starting a fire. I'll do that now. Why don't you take this pot and fill it with snow? Soon as the stove's warm we'll have water. Don't go far from the cabin. There's likely wolves around."

She took the pot from his hand and stared at him.

"What?"

"I'm a city girl. Never lived anywhere else." She gave him a warm smile. "Good thing I got stranded with a country boy."

"It was your idea to use the boards to cross the trestle. I didn't think of that…and you dug me out or I'd have died." His brow furrowed as he turned back to the stove. "We're not out of this yet."

By the time she returned, he was replacing a burner plate. Beth placed the snow filled pot on the stove. He reached for an oil lamp, checked to see that it contained fuel and used the end of a burning stick to light it. Jonah hung it from a wall hook. "I'm going to chop more wood. We'll need more then this pile to get us through the night." He stopped to stare at the front corner of the cabin. Jonah pointed at three sets of snowshoes. "We'll use those to get back down the mountain."

Beth walked a few steps and grimaced. "Country Boy, my feet hurt like hell."

"Maybe they're wet. Dry them, get them warm and let me know if they still hurt."

Sharp pains shot up Beth's legs as she gingerly removed her shoes and socks. She sucked in her breath. Three toes on her right foot and four on the left were black. Walking on her heels, she pulled the quilt out of Jonah's bag, then moved both chairs near the stove; wrapped herself in the quilt, sat on one chair and placed her exposed feet on the other close to the rapidly warming stove.

The wood cracked and popped. Jonah entered with an armload of kindling. He took one look at her feet and cursed.

"What?" Beth asked.

"Black means dead tissue."

"My toes won't recover?"

"They have to be amputated."

Her eyes widened and the color left her face as she spat out, "No. You're crazy! Not going to happen!"

"If we don't, the black tissue can poison your whole body and kill you."

She slowly shook her head then wrapped the quilt tight around her. "I won't let…you won't. I saved your life and this is how I'm repaid?"

"Blood poisoning is a painful way to die."

She began trembling.

"You want to die here?"

Again, she slowly shook her head. A tear rolled down her cheek.

"Then they have to come off."

"How?"

"Quickest way would be the ax."

"What if you miss? You could chop my whole foot off."

"I'll hold the ax near its head. It won't take much motion."

More tears rolled down her cheeks. "Is there nothing else you can do?"

He shook his head. "It's going to hurt like hell and I've nothing to deaden your pain."

Beth looked at the ceiling. "Why?" she pleaded. "Am I being punished for living a life of thievery? What else could I have done?" She put her hands on her face and wept.

He put an arm around her. Beth composed herself then pushed his arm away. "If you're sure there's no alternative…"

"I'm the son of a doctor. I've seen this before and there's nothing else."

"Then do what you need to."

He went to his bag and removed the emergency medical pack William had provisioned for him. Jonah dropped it in her lap and walked outside to get the ax. Returning, he kneeled at her side. He cleaned the ax and the front of Beth's feet. "Put your feet flat on the floor. Keep your jaw closed so you don't bite your tongue."

She wiped a tear away. "Get it over with."

"Close your eyes and keep them closed. I'll tell you when to open them."

Beth screamed when the ax dropped. Jonah did some things which seemed to painfully poke at her foot. She screamed anew when the ax dropped a second time. The poking pain followed as well.

"You can open your eyes now."

Beth saw her feet neatly wrapped in bandages.

Jonah wiped tears out of his eyes.

She asked, "You in pain?"

"I know how much pain I just caused you."

She opened her arms. He held her firmly. Beth kissed his cheek.

"I'll open the mattress. You should rest." He unrolled it. "Sheepskin and an elk hide inside. You'll be warm with this over you. Still wrapped in the quilt, Beth tried to stand but moaned when putting weight on her feet. Jonah scooped her up and gently placed her on the now cushioned table. He pulled the sheep skin over her.

A few hours later Beth opened her eyes.

Jonah stood at the stove, stirring the contents of a pot. "I made us a little stew."

After they ate he told her, "I'm going to sharpen my knife and fashion some arrows. If you need anything…"

She pulled him close and kissed his cheek. "I'll be fine."

***

When Beth awoke the next day, sunlight streamed through the small window. Jonah stood at the stove, breaking pemmican into a small pan of steaming water. She sat up and greeted him.

"It's clear and sunny out but cold as can be," he said. "Way below zero I figure."

"How can you tell?"

"I spit outside. It froze with a cracking sound. That means at least twenty below."

"I don't think I can walk."

"I'll help you into a chair."

"How will we get out of here?"

"You need a couple days rest to let your feet begin healing. There's huge drifts over the train tracks. No one's coming up here anytime soon."

"We'll need more to eat."

"I spotted deer not too far from here."

***

"Jonah, when we hike out of here, I don't want to damage my feet any further. Do you think we can make boots and mittens out of the elk hide?"

"Good thinking." He began witling an elk horn. "Needle for sewing," he said, answering Beth's inquisitive look. Jonah scratched the outline of her foot onto a piece of the hide, then measured and cut pieces for the sides.

"I'll do the rest," Beth said. Jonah cut one thin strip of the hide for lacing and she assembled her new boots.

He left the cabin briefly, then returned with a four-foot- by-three-inch branch. Jonah sat on one of the chairs and worked the ends.

Beth slipped into a just completed boot which came just below her knees and secured the lacing. "These will be warm." She watched Jonah.

He held up his work. "Going to be a bow."

"Why not use the pistol?"

"I'm afraid a shot will attract wolves. I'll take it with me for protection."

A number of hours later and after braiding a bow string, he said, "I'm heading out to find us something to eat."

"Don't get lost," she said, as he strapped on the pistol and a pair of snowshoes.

***

"Match your surroundings if you want to sneak up on an animal." Grandma Kimimela's voice echoed in his head.

Jonah smiled at the memory. His tan leather pants and jacket were taking on the whiteness of his surroundings as blowing snow stuck to them. He wondered what she'd think of his current predicament.

The snowshoes weren't fast but were much less tiring than sinking into the deep snow. Trying to avoid a brutal climb back to the mountain, he tried to stay at the same level as the cabin. He took the whisky bottle out of his jacket and took a long drink then refilled it with snow. After three grueling hours he spotted a few deer. They were about-a-mile-distant and halfway down the mountain. Their front feet pawed at the ground trying to clear the snow to find vegetation

Jonah moved to put a small wooded area between himself and his prey. An hour later he proceeded to the edge of the wood and surveyed the area. The deer were gone.

"Animals like to find water at the same time every day," Grandma said. "But they're quite weary when they drink." He thought, "*The waterfall. It might have moving water above it, but I only have a few more hours of light. Do I try again tomorrow?*" He gazed at his surroundings. *"What if I can't find them?"*

Taking a deep breath, he headed for the stream above the waterfall.

Jonah bent low as he approached the area. Two deer slowly hopped through the deep snow and stopped. One looked in his direction. He froze for what seemed an interminable time. The deer looked away. He continued to edge closer at a snail's pace. A slight snowfall began. At twenty-five-yards, Jonah put his first arrow in the bow. He slowly pulled back, took careful aim then loosed the arrow. It sailed just over the back of one deer and silently embedded itself in a snow drift. One of the deer noticed the motion of the arrow as it flew by. It lifted its head. A small bird flew from a low branch near where the arrow disappeared. The deer watched it fly away then returned to pawing the ground.

Jonah loosed a second arrow. It struck the nearest deer. It took two hops. He felt joy but the emotion turned dark as he saw his kill tumble down the mountainside. It came to rest a few hundred feet below him. Jonah walked and slid to its location. He was horrified to discover it was still alive. The hunter pulled out his pistol and put one round in the deer's head. He hesitated before butchering it only long enough to apologize for not killing it humanely and thanked the deer for giving up its life so he and Beth could eat.

There was little light left as he strapped the deer meat to his backboard. The snowfall stopped and the night sky revealed a canopy of stars and a full moon. After two hours of climbing, his thighs and calves ached. He stopped to rest and observed his surroundings. In the pale moonlight, shadows distorted the shapes of the rocky outcroppings. He couldn't recognize any of the landmarks he'd tried to commit to memory as he trekked away from the cabin. When a wolf call shattered the silence, the thought of staying outside until it was light didn't seem like a good idea. He shivered remembering the stories of men being ripped apart by wolf packs. If he wandered too far in the wrong direction, he might not find the cabin. He stood and surveyed the mountain ridge above him, still thinking the cabin must be above his level. Jonah sighed and slid the straps of the backboard over his shoulders.

Chapter Forty: Survival and Rescue

Back at the cabin, Beth heard the wolf call as well. Startled, she realized she'd been sleeping most of the day.

"What if he doesn't return?" She ran her fingers through her hair. "He has the skills to survive out here. I can barely walk."

With pain in her feet shooting into her calves, Beth pulled on her new boots. Walking on her heels and grimacing with each step, she slowly moved to the small window. Peering out into the full-moon-illuminated-night, she shivered; mostly from fright. When Beth exhaled, her breath froze on the window pane.

Her head spun around. She stared wide-eyed at the stove. Beth treaded gingerly across the cabin, placing a hand on its side. It was stone cold. She felt her heart pounding as if it wanted to leap out of her chest.

"I've let the fire go out and I didn't see how he started it."

***

Jonah kept his head on a swivel, watching for danger. He glanced to his left. Out of the corner of his eye something was approaching at a rapid rate. He turned as a mountain lion lunged at the back of his neck. Jonah managed to get his left forearm up which the cat clamped on to. Jonah screamed as he felt and heard bone breaking. The force of the two-hundred-pound-cat pushed him backwards. He drew the Colt and pulled the trigger multiple times. The sounds of pistol shots echoed across the mountainside. The cat fell to the ground, unmoving. Jonah writhed in pain. He gritted his teeth, slid the backboard off his shoulders, gingerly removed his coat and examined his arm. A puncture wound bled profusely.

He shuddered as he knew there was only one way to repair the gash. Jonah sat on a felled tree and removed the medical kit from his coat pocket. Removing his gloves, he tightened a cloth bandage around his upper arm, securing a knot in the tourniquet with his teeth and good hand. He unrolled the medical kit and located the curved needle.

Jonah checked his surroundings for wolves or any other animal that might be hunting him. He thought, *"Shit! How will I get a thread in this damn needle?"*

His body began shivering from the cold. Jonah pinched a bit of his leather pant material over his thigh then ran the needle partially through it to keep it still. After numerous attempts to get the suture material through the needle's eye, his frustration reached a boil. His good hand was shaking. Jonah thought, *"I have to calm down or I'll never get this done."*

He took a deep breath and tried again. Success!

Jonah pinched the skin together over the wound with the last three fingers of his good hand then after gritting his teeth, pushed the needle through with his thumb and forefinger. He tied off the first suture and moved to begin the second. Just as the needle pierced the skin, the fingers which held the skin together lost their grip due to the slippery blood around the wound. He backed it out and carefully put the needle through his pant leg again then wiped the wound area. Each wipe put pressure on the tissue around the broken bones and caused intense pain to radiate up his arm. His whole body shuddered and he closed his eyes until the pain subsided. Jonah secured the needle and began again...and checked his surroundings once more for predators.

He tied off the last suture then removed the tourniquet from his upper arm and used the material to wrap over the sutures. The medical kit was rolled up and stuffed in his jacket pocket. His entire body shivered not just from the pain but also from the cold.

As he slid the coat sleeve up his arm, lightning-bolts-of-pain exploded in the wounded appendage. Jonah slid his good arm into the other sleeve and buttoned the front…difficult to do with one hand let alone one hand stiffened by the cold.

He glanced at the backboard and considered leaving it behind but remembered there was nothing to eat at the cabin. Jonah thought, "*Have to get back with this. Beth is depending on me.*"

All the while moaning from the motion-caused-pain, he placed the backboard against the base of a tree and sat down in front of it. Slowly and carefully working his bad arm past the shoulder strap, Jonah realized this was the most pain he'd ever experienced. With his good arm in the other strap he stood. He slowly lifted the broken forearm and cradled it with his good arm.

He felt dizzy so leaned his shoulder against a tree to steady himself.

***

Beth carefully sifted the ashes and found two glowing embers. She shaved tiny strips of wood from a piece of kindling, placed them on the embers and gently blew air over them. Nothing. She tried again. More tiny strips and more air. Beth cursed as she noted only one ember still glowed. She remembered the sheep hide. Although pain shot up her legs with each step, Beth retrieved it and, using her Bowie knife, sliced a good handful of fleece to use as tinder. She placed it on the remaining ember and blew gently. After the second try, a tiny wisp of smoke emerged. She blew again. More smoke. Continued blowing coaxed more smoke until the fleece flamed and ignited the kindling. Beth thought, "*Never thought the sound of crackling wood would be such a relief.*" She glanced at the ceiling. "Thanks for watching out for me, Lord."

Beth added wood to the fire then returned to the window. An icy scene, devoid of life greeted her. A shiver went down her spine as an overwhelming sense of loneliness enveloped her. She tightened the quilt around her and yelled at the sky. "Is this more punishment? Would you have me die here?" Beth glanced around the cabin then gingerly returned to the chair by the stove. "Where the hell is that guy?"

***

Jonah surveyed his surroundings. He wondered if he would lose consciousness from the pain. The tall man's jaws ached from gritting his teeth…as if doing so would ameliorate his pain.

A tiny thin vertical cloud, some distance away and slightly below him, attracted his attention.

"Thank you, Lord!" he shouted.

With renewed vigor and cradling his bad arm with the other, he slowly headed toward the ephemeral beacon issuing from the cabin's chimney. As each of the snow shoes crunched into the blanket of white, pain shot into his arm and shoulder.

After fifty-yards, his pulse was rapid and breathing labored. He thought, "*Getting dizzy again. Must stop.*"

A wolf's howl echoed through the woods.

Jonah shook his head to clear it. His memory replayed the sight of a man and woman's remains after they'd been torn to shreds by wolves. "*Can't lose consciousness. Have to keep moving.*"

He proceeded at a slow but steady pace.

Two hours had gone by but it seemed much longer to Jonah. He looked up to see the cabin only fifty-yards-away. His vision fixed on his goal, he didn't see the sapling which caught his right snowshoe. Jonah tumbled and screamed in pain. The cold and exhaustion numbed him. He thought, "*Maybe I should just lay here for a while.*"

"NO!" his mind yelled. He forced his tired body to a sitting position, gathered his legs under him, and stood. Jonah wobbled at bit then one slow step at a time kept moving toward the cabin.

***

As he approached the door, he heard the bolt slide open.

"Home is the hunter," Beth said, and returned to the chair by the stove. "Took you long enough."

In between heavy breaths, he said, "I was lost until I saw the smoke." He closed and bolted the door, gritted his teeth and lowered the back board to the floor. "How are your feet?"

"Uncomfortable but…"

He saw tears rolling down her cheeks. "Beth?"

She wiped her eyes, walked up to him and wrapped her arms around him. The thin girl trembled and shouted, "I was terrified something happened to you. You took so long. If you didn't come back, how the hell would I get out of here? The thought of dying alone up here..."

"I'm here now." He wrapped his good arm around her. Jonah grimaced and groaned when she bumped his broken arm.

"Wait...what's wrong?" She pushed away from him. "What happened to your arm?"

"It's broken. I sewed it but I need a splint."

"You sewed it?"

He shifted slightly and moaned. "Damn, it's painful."

"Sit down, Jonah. Let's get your coat off."

The tall man trembled and gritted his teeth, once again enduring intense pain as she slid his coat sleeve down his arm. "I'll cut flats from the kindling," Jonah said. "I need you to secure them for me and make a sling." He grimaced and moaned then began to stand.

"Stay where you are. I'll cut the wood and do the rest."

"That's better," he said, as she guided his arm into a sling. Jonah kept his eyes closed and took deep breaths. He gave her a weak smile. "Stay still. I'll cook the meat."

"No." She gripped his shoulders. "Don't move."

Jonah nodded.

Beth stripped meat from one of the deer quarters, placed it in a pot with water.

"After we eat," Jonah said, "we'll place the rest outside in the latched box."

"Won't bears come for it?"

"Not this time of year. Boiled venison without any seasoning might not be too tasty."

"Hungry as I am, you won't hear any complaints."

"Beth, I'm exhausted and my arm is throbbing like hell."

"Lay down. I'll wake you when dinner's ready."

***

They twosome awoke with a start three-days-later when a steam whistle shattered the morning's silence.

"I'll clean out the stove and ready it for the next occupants," Jonah said.

"I'll tie our gear to the backboards."

After an hour's busy work cleaning and restoring the cabin for its next visitors, they pulled on their coats and jackets.

Jonah said, "Let's fit you with snow shoes."

The moment he tightened a strap, she screamed. "Stop. It hurts too much."

"How will I get you out of here?"

Beth kept her eyes closed and remained silent until the pain subsided. "We'll combine our gear onto one backboard. I wear it and you'll have to carry me."

He stared at her.

"Can you manage that?"

"Skied down a mountainside with 100 lbs. of elk meat on my back one time. I'll unstring the bow and use it as a staff. Might be extra work with a bum arm but I'll manage."

***

A gandy dancer with incredulity written in his expression, hurriedly approached them.

"What in tarnation are you folks doing out here?"

Beth responded for Jonah who was out of breath. "We were at my hunting cabin when the storm hit."

"In a couple hours the train is heading back to Seattle. You can ride with it."

Jonah used his good arm to help Beth up the steps and into the warm passenger coach.

"Better accommodations than the first part of our journey," Beth whispered to Jonah.

He laughed and said, "A marked improvement."

That evening the conductor told them, "Another hour and we'll be in Seattle."

"Country Boy, tell me about your family."

"My grandparents on my father's side came from Ireland, my mom's side from France. They settled on the east coast at first then Independence, Missouri, followed by Portland, Oregon and finally Seattle, Washington. My grandfather built various businesses along the way."

"But your father became a doctor."

"He wasn't interested at first, but with lots of encouragement from the family, ultimately, he chose that career path."

"And you?"

"All I've ever wanted to do is run a business. I live for buying and selling. Been like that since grade school."

"What dreams did your parent's have for you?"

"Mom was hoping I'd go into Dad's medical office. Of my siblings, I was the only one with enough brain power. I think Dad wanted me to go into medicine but didn't push me about it until it was time to decide on attending college."

"Brothers and sisters?"

"Younger brother Ethan, in engineering school. Older brother Noah, a school teacher. Older sister, Shifra, teaches Physics at the University."

"Lots of people for support."

"Too many. Everyone has their own dreams for you and you feel like you let them down when you don't follow them."

Beth stared at the passing scenery.

"What were your dreams?" Jonah asked.

"No dreams."

"None?"

She folded her arms across her chest. "Unlike you, I spent my life having to hustle just to eat. No fancy warm clothes for me. Just someone else's worn throwaways." She tugged at the side of her waist overalls. "First pair of new ones I ever owned. Wear like iron. Made by some San Francisco company called Strauss or something." Beth ran her hand over the arm of his coat. "Hell…you were raised like a rich kid."

"I worked hard all my life."

"And if you didn't work hard, would you have missed a meal?"

"Well…"

Her posture stiffened. "Of course not. Your family would make sure you were fed."

"We experienced tough times."

"Not tough by my measure." She stared out the window again.

"Beth…" He put a hand on her shoulder.

She shoved it away. "You gambled away that train ticket like it was nothing. You have any idea how hard and how long I'd have to scratch to earn that much? I could've eaten for a week."

"What's the anger?"

"I'm fine." She crossed her arms and stared out the window.

"You upset with something I said?"

"No."

"You in pain?"

"Not too bad."

"Where will you live?"

Continuing to watch the scenery, she said, "I'll manage. I always have."

"You can have a room at my house."

"I've been managing a life alone since I was twelve. I don't need anyone now." Beth sighed.

"Besides, we're different. I wouldn't fit with your family."

"You don't know that."

They sat silently for many minutes.

"Beth, I've enjoyed our time together."

"Time to go our separate ways."

"I assumed we were good…partners."

"We were in a survival situation. There wasn't a choice. You go back to your big, wealthy family. That's where you belong."

He slowly shook his head. "Beth, did I do something to upset you?"

She turned to face him, her cheeks red. Beth shouted. "Stop asking stupid questions. You have your family and I'm not becoming part of your or anyone else's life."

Jonah tried to hold her hand but she pulled it away. He said, "I care."

"Your problem, not mine. I don't need some overgrown oaf in my life."

The train squeaked to a stop at the Seattle station. Jonah helped her off the train.

"You should have a doctor check your feet."

"Goodbye."

"Let me help you."

"Get the hell away from me," she screamed. In obvious pain, she gradually hobbled away.

Chapter Forty-Three: New Beginnings

Jonah's eyebrows lifted, his heart rate increased, and eyes widened when he opened his front door just before sunset, four weeks after his return to Seattle.

"Please come in."

Beth briefly glanced at the mezuzah on his door post. No longer wincing with each step, she still walked slowly. Noting the partially set table, she said, "Looks like you were in the middle of something. I didn't mean to interrupt."

"A meal for myself. It can wait. Please sit down."

She moved to a chair and gently sat. "That's better." Beth looked up at him. "Doesn't hurt so much when I sit."

"You in constant pain?"

"Mostly when I walk. Been seeing a kind doctor. He said you did an excellent job. When I saw him earlier today, he gave me your address."

"Dr. Kaplan?"

"Yes."

"My father."

Beth twisted on the chair. "How's the arm?"

"Dad said the breaks should completely heal."

After an uncomfortable silence, she said, "We need to talk about the argument."

"You decided not to become part of my or anyone else's life."

"I was scared."

"Of what?"

"You have so much family. You can depend on each other. I wouldn't fit in your world."

"You and I were dependent on each other…hell…took care of each other for a number of days. We got close to Seattle and you said some awful things."

"An indication of how frightened I was."

"Frightened of what?"

"Every person I've ever known has let me down."

"I didn't."

"You have your family."

"And you have me."

They stared at each other briefly.

Beth looked at the floor. "I said some terrible things. I apologize for them."

"Thank you."

She twisted on the chair again. "I should get going."

"If that's what you want."

Beth used the arms of the chair to push herself onto her feet and walked toward the door.

"Beth, please don't leave. I need you."

She stopped and said over her shoulder "Need me?" She partially turned toward him.

"When we were together, I was driven by thoughts and actions to take care of you. Exhausted and in absolute agony after the mountain lion attack, I was driven to return so you'd have something to eat. You recognized my suffering and despite your own pain, took care of me."

She turned to face him. "Like you said, a survival situation."

"More than that. For the first time in my life, I understand, and feel, the kind of love my father has for my mother."

Beth's face became radiant. "Lighting Sabbath candles tonight?"

Jonah's jaw slowly dropped as his eyes widened. He approached her.

She slowly wrapped her arms tightly around him, her head on his chest.

Jonah firmly wrapped his good arm around her.

Beth luxuriated in his embrace, took a deep breath, and let it out slowly. Beth looked up at him with gleaming eyes and a radiant smile. "One of my fondest childhood memories was reciting the Sabbath blessings with my mother."

"You're … ?"

"Country Boy, are you certain; I mean absolutely certain, you care for me?"

He replied with a long kiss.

She leaned away from him. "I know nothing of Judaism."

"We'll manage."

"I know nothing of being a wife."

"Not true. The way you took care of me was more than I deserve."

"I can't even cook."

"My mom will be in heaven teaching you her Irish and Northwest recipes. We'll work out the rest ourselves. You and I survived in primitive conditions; we'll get past anything down here."

They kissed a while longer.

"Beth, will you marry me?"

"We haven't been together that long."

"When I ask my Grandfather about his age, he says, It's not the years but the mileage."

Beth laughed.

"You and I may not have spent much time together but we've accumulated some incredible mileage."

"We should take more time to get to know each other but when the time's right..."

"My Uncle Nathan lives in Spokane. He's a Rabbi. I'll write him and he'll marry us."

She tightened her embrace and kissed him.

"Where are you living?"

"I have a room in town."

"I have a spare bedroom you can use. Or my folks have space. I'm sure they'd provide a place for you."

"They don't know me."

He glanced outside.

"I see the first star. Light and bless the candles for me?"

Jonah recited Kiddush, the prayer for wine, after Beth blessed the candles. He began putting food on the table.

Beth tried the soup. "This is so rich."

"Scotch Broth. Grandma Myra's recipe," Jonah said.

"This is my favorite," Jonah said as he reached for the plate holding the salmon gefilte fish. "Mother Celeste's recipe," he intoned. "Grandma Myra makes it as well but Mother smokes it with alder wood and seasons it with a combination of ten spices she learned from a neighbor who grew up near Chesapeake Bay."

"Sounds like assembling a puzzle."

"Yes but when you get the spices balanced…"

Beth tasted a piece. "A symphony of flavor."

"Let's move to the parlor," Jonah said after cleanup from their meal. Beth sat on the couch and Jonah on a chair opposite her.

"What is your work day like?" she asked.

"It varies. Generally, I leave around six and I'm home about six or seven."

"Long day. Your workers toil the same types of hours?"

"My workers are there most of that time and sometimes longer."

Beth frowned. "How do they have a family life?"

Jonah grinned. "You going to be my conscience when it comes to my workers?"

She folded her arms across her chest. "I've seen good men die in their mid-thirties from long hours at an ironworks. Seemed like their bodies just wore out."

Unsmiling Jonah stared at her.

Beth shook her head and gazed at the floor. "I remember the shriek of a mother with eight children gathered around her when she saw her young husband laid out at the undertaker's. Poor woman was devastated. No clue how she'd earn enough to feed and clothe her family. I emptied my pockets and gave her whatever coin I had."

"We're good as we can to our workers but there's immense pressure to keep wages low. Perhaps a woman in that situation can put her older children to work."

Beth's eyes widened and she put her hands on her hips. "Do you hear what you just said? Children need to work?"

"You found work at ten."

"Yes, and until I met you, I hated my very existence and everyone around me. I've entered your life with next to zero skills as a wife, let alone a mother. That's what childhood is for and I was robbed of that."

After a long silence with Jonah staring out the front window, Beth asked, "What are you thinking?"

"We lost a good man. Was only twenty-eight. Dad said his heart gave out. Poor man worked two jobs and rarely slept."

"You need to remember him. No man, woman or child should have to give their life for their job."

It was Jonah's turn to fold his arms across his chest. "It's steam power."

"What is?" Beth asked.

"Since steam engines have become common, fewer men are needed on farms. They arrive in the city by the dozens and they'll work for next to nothing. That's why there's so many women and children working. Their families need the income to survive. Also, with steam engines, factories don't need to be near water or use horses for power. My entire operation is steam powered."

"I've always thought the most honorable job was farming as it produced food to feed one's self and neighbors."

"It's the same with steam-powered ships. Don't need as many men to run them as the sailing ships. Men being Shanghaied doesn't happen anymore."

"Do you have children working for you?"

"A few." He shifted his position and avoided looking at her. "Most businesses do."

"Adults and children who work for little and lots of them. Must be a good time to be a business owner."

After many minutes of reflection, Jonah asked, "Would you like coffee or something?"

Beth patted the cushion next to her. "Come sit next me."

He joined her on his couch. Beth pulled his arm around her and intertwined her fingers in his, resting her head on his shoulder. "Please think of me when making decisions about your workers. Except for meeting you, I might have been one of them." She cuddled against him.

"My grandmother Kim lives alone. I'm sure she'd have space for you."

"She's the one who taught you outdoor skills?"

"Yes. I'll hitch up a buckboard, we'll get your things from your room, and go there. You'll love her and she'll love you."

Chapter Forty-Four: Kim and Beth

Jonah arrived at Kim's home on Sunday morning the following week. Beth sat with them in the kitchen while they ate breakfast.

"I told Beth the story of how I met my husband, Andre." Kim sighed. "It was near the Columbia River, north of a long lake called Tsi Laan. One of the most scenic locations I ever experienced. My heart warms just thinking of all that beauty."

"Perhaps Jonah will take me there one day."

"I pray he will. Jonah, get me some paper and I'll create a map."

He left the room.

"Jonah," Kim said, "hasn't mentioned work this morning. I believe this may have been our longest conversation without mentioning business."

Beth gave Kim a quizzical expression.

"He's been earning money since grade school. Last year, his grandfather David bought a new business for him to run."

"His own business?"

"Jonah needs to mature a bit more before David actually lets him run it alone…but…from getting the workers to do their best to finding ways to grow a business, Jonah is a natural."

"His outdoor skills are all I've seen and I doubt we'd have survived without them. Jonah said he learned them from you."

Kim thought for a while and laughed. "You should have seen his expression when he was eleven-years-old. I insisted he skin and gut an elk he'd shot. I'd never heard the word yuk used so many times."

***

Two months later and Kim helped Beth into her bridal gown. She stepped back and smiled, then briefly embraced her. "Getting to know you has been a joy."

"I can't thank you enough for taking a stranger into your home."

"Jonah's face shines when he looks at you. Grandmothers don't have favorites when it comes to their grandchildren but my relationship with Jonah has been special since he was a little boy."

"I hear how special the relationship is when he talks about you. I believe many of his values come from you."

"Beth, you're a strong, intelligent woman and that's what he needs in his life."

"I don't think of myself as strong or intelligent."

"It takes strength of character and intelligence for a child to survive on city streets. You surely possess both. One day Jonah will be in charge of a large business. Many workers will be depending on his decisions to maintain their livelihood."

"He doesn't need me to help with that."

"Yes he does," Kim insisted. "Jonah can be strong willed and only listens to two people. You and his grandfather David. Your words carry substantial weight with him. He needs you to temper his thoughts and actions."

***

Three weeks later, Kim was eating breakfast with Beth and Jonah per their weekly Sunday morning routine.

"Grandma Kim, Jonah mentioned you have two boys."

"Alex, the one you met and who runs the metalworking shop at David's business and Andre, who moved to Alaska."

They cleaned dishes, Jonah left for work, and the two women headed out for their three-times-a-week morning walk.

"How's the pain?" Kimimela asked.

Beth glanced at her feet. "Substantially lessened since we've taken regular walks."

"And you and Jonah?"

"Doing well but he works such long hours. He's even working today to finish an accounting task."

"These businesses which make things seem to take up huge amounts of time."

"Fortunately I have the garden. It keeps me busy. Plus I'm glad you have time to spend with me. Gives me a chance for girl talk."

"A good time for both of us."

"When I have a child, I'll be chained to the house."

"Nonsense! I was outdoors my entire childhood. I'll teach you how to bundle a child and the little one will accompany us on our…"

Kim turned to Beth whose was expression was radiant. "You're with child?"

"Yes."

"You've filled my heart with sunshine like a bright spring day!" They briefly embraced then resumed walking. Beth stared off to the side. "I'm frightened."

"More nonsense. You're strong as an ox. You'll be fine."

"If I have questions…"

"If I have the answer I'll tell you but don't forget Jonah's dad. They say he's most knowledgeable about babies and children."

"I wish I knew a lady doctor. It would be easier to ask questions."

"Jonah's Aunt Abbey is the only lady doctor I've ever met."

***

"Was Kim your Indian name?" Beth asked when her pregnancy was in its eighth month.

"It's actually Kimimela, which means butterfly."

"A lovely name. May I call you that?"

The old woman smiled. "My mother was the last person to use my actual name. It would be an honor if you did."

Jonah brought in tea and joined them as they sat in the parlor.

Beth put her hand on Kim's arm. "Grandmother Kimimela, Jonah and I have a huge favor to ask." Beth paused briefly, looked at Jonah who nodded then took a deep breath, and sat upright. "Our first child will be arriving soon. I don't have my mother to help me. We were hoping you would move in with us and assist with the baby."

"What about Jonah's mother or his grandmother?"

Beth said, "They're good to me and I love them but …"

"She feels closest to you," Jonah said.

"I don't have strength like I used to." Kimimela held up her hands. "My joints ache and my hands quickly tire. I can barely sew. I'm not sure how much help I can offer."

"Grandmother Kimimela," Beth said in a subdued voice and looking directly in the old woman's eyes, "I…we…need your counsel; not your strength."

Kimimela put a hand on each of their shoulders. "I was tired of living alone." She glanced from one to the other with a broad smile. "A new purpose in my life will be good for me."

Beth relaxed. "Thank you." She leaned over and grasped Kim's hand with both of hers. "I'm so relieved knowing you'll be here."

Kim leaned back, briefly looked at the ceiling then at smiling Jonah and Beth. "The day I took her in, my mother predicted one of my children or grandchildren would do the same for me. I'm sure it will happen for you as well."

***

The Midwife attempted the delivery but found the baby's bottom presenting.

"Bring your father," she said to Jonah.

Upon return, William asked for wine. "White if you have it."

He cleaned his hands and administered a light amount of ether to Beth. William performed a rapid caesarian section.

Kim leaned over and quietly said to Beth, "It's your daughter."

William tied the umbilical and said to Jonah. "Your child, you cut."

Still drowsy, Beth smiled as Jonah wiped off their daughter then wrapped her in a blanket. The bundled child was placed on Beth's chest. She softly put her hands around her daughter. "Monica is beautiful."

"Like her Mom." Jonah said, as he kissed Beth's forehead.

Kim gasped. "What did you say? Monica?"

"Do you mind?" Jonah asked.

She stood straight as tears welled up. "Children, you honor my daughter and me."

Jonah turned and embraced her. "You've done so much for us."

"Grandma, please hold Monica," Beth said.

Jonah took her from Beth and passed his daughter to Kim.

She moved to a rocker, swaying and singing.

"Precious Monica. She will bring joy to all who meet her."

Chapter Forty-Five: The Kaplan Family Grows

Five-year-old Mark Landau yelled for his brother. Seven-year-old Thomas came racing into the kitchen of their tiny apartment.

"Mom isn't moving," Mark said. "When I talk to her she doesn't answer me."

Thomas waved a hand in front her face.

"Mom? Can you hear me?"

"Stay here. I'll get Dr. Kaplan."

He did a quick exam and talked to the boys. "It saddens me to tell you this but your mom is quite sick."

"Will she get better?" Mark asked the doctor.

"I'm not sure. She may not."

"Where will we live?"

"I'll talk to Mrs. Blaze, your neighbor. I'm sure she and Mrs. Mendoza will take care of you until we can find a permanent arrangement."

***

"I need everyone's attention, please," Sixty-year-old Edna Blaze shouted before the Friday night service began in the synagogue. She stood behind two forlorn appearing boys, placing a hand on each of their shoulders. Edna waited for all the conversation to end before she continued.

"Our Jewish community has a crisis. Most of you know, these two boys are Tamara Landau's children. They're currently homeless. Many of us remember their father who passed away five-years-ago. Tamara suffered from melancholy since Mark was born. Now she's taken a-turn-for-the-worse. Dr. Kaplan told me she's incoherent, no longer recognizes her sons and may not recover."

William nodded, affirming her words for the benefit of those who turned to him.

Bernice Mendoza said, "The boys are staying with Edna and me but we're too old to raise them. If no family takes them in, they'll go to an orphanage."

Beth Kaplan, holding nine-month-old Monica, slowly shook her head while listening. She approached the despondent looking boys. "I'm Mrs. Kaplan. I lost my mom when I was young. It was certainly painful. What are your names and how old are you?"

"I'm Thomas. I'm seven."

"I'm Mark. I'm this many." He held up five fingers.

"This is my husband," Beth said.

"Hello boys," Jonah said, leaning down and shaking their hands.

Beth turned her back on the boys, motioned Jonah to bend forward so she could whisper to him. "We should take them home."

He straightened and stared at her without reply.

"We have room, Grandmother Kimimela knows about raising boys, and we can afford it." She poked him in the ribs and said with an impish grin, "You accepted an orphan readily enough when I entered your life. Now it's my turn."

Jonah nodded. "Home with us. That's fine."

Beth turned to the boys and shifted her daughter so she was facing them. "Monica, this is Mark and Thomas who are coming to live with us, if they like."

"We'd have a sister?" Mark asked.

"Is that okay?" Beth asked.

Thomas touched the little girl's hand then grinned when Monica's tiny hand gripped his finger. "She'll have big brothers to watch out for her."

"We have lots of room in our home. We'd love having you live with us."

The boys looked at Edna who nodded to them.

Jonah said, "I've never had boys living at my house. You'll have to tell me how to take care of two big boys."

"We can do that," Thomas said with a grin while his brother nodded.

Mark tugged on Mrs. Mendoza's skirt. He whispered something. She laughed. "He's wants me to teach you to make my honey cake. I'll write it down for you." Mark thanked her.

"So…" Jonah turned and eyed the boys. "Do you know how to fish?"

"No, sir," Mark replied.

"On Sunday, my father, grandfather and I are going salmon fishing. We get up early and head to the Sound to see what we can catch…you can join us if you'd like."

"I would," Mark said.

"Me too, Mr. Kaplan," Thomas said.

"Come on boys," Jonah said placing a scullcap on each of their heads. "The service is about to begin." He walked to the rows of benches and the boys sat on either side of him.

***

On the way to the river the Kaplan men passed a few of their employees who were also fishing.

They heard yelling from Bruce Goldman.

"Bruce, what are you cursing about," Jonah said shortly after he caught and released a fish.

"You threw it back."

"It was a bit small."

"You don't pay us enough to live on and then throw back a fish that could've provided three meals for my family."

One of the men pushed Bruce. "Shut your damn mouth or you won't have a job to complain about."

Undeterred, Bruce continued, "We break our backs ten to fifteen-hours-a-day. If one of us gets hurt and can't work anymore, how's he supposed to feed his family? I suppose when my children are old enough you'll find a place for them and…"

The same man put a hand over Bruce's mouth and a second man helped drag him out of earshot.

"What's he talking about?" Jonah asked. "We pay like everyone else."

"We'll talk to the supervisors," David said. "They'll know."

***

"Did you and your grandfather have a meeting with your supervisors?" Beth asked.

"We did."

"And?"

"My head's been spinning ever since. Had a terrible argument with my Grandfather David."

"Evening meal is ready."

Jonah sat at the kitchen table which was laden with a wide variety of food. He didn't move.

"You're not hungry?" Kimimela asked.

"Based on their pay, one of our worker's families would have to make this meal last a week."

"What are you talking about?" Beth asked.

"We pay them by the day. Ten-hours or fifteen-hours they get paid the same pitiful amount."

"Can you pay them more?" Kimimela asked.

"I think so but my grandfather doesn't. He said we'd go broke if we paid more. That started the argument."

"Over worker's pay?"

"Bruce Goldman, the man who mentioned the lousy pay when we were fishing last Sunday, his supervisor fired him first thing today for complaining about work conditions. Bruce snuck into the office when he saw me arrive, apologized and pleaded for his job." He glanced around the table. "Kids. Eat."

"Did your grandfather find out?" Kim asked.

"He did and we had one hell of an argument when I said we should give him back his job. He insisted, I let the supervisors run the production floor the way they see fit. I pointed out that I asked around and a number of men have been severely injured. He replied he didn't know. I told him either Goldman gets his job back or I'd quit."

***

"What do you mean, he quit?" Myra shouted at David.

They'd just sat down to evening meal with William and Celeste.

"He doesn't want to work for me any longer," he said without looking at her.

"What happened?"

David began eating.

Myra shouted. "Put your damn fork down and tell me what happened."

"He gave me an ultimatum. It's my company and nobody gives me an ultimatum."

"Oh heaven forbid," Myra said in a voice dripping with sarcasm. "Kaplan men butting heads like Billy goats, neither one willing to give an inch."

"No, it wasn't like that," he said, shaking his head and waving his hands.

"You, Nathan, William and Jonah," Myra said in a sarcastic tone, "You make up your mind, put on blinders and quit thinking."

"Please don't include me in that group," William said.

Now Celeste spoke in a sarcastic tone. "How many years did you talk about bad air causing cholera instead of admitting you had no idea?"

William started to reply but simply shrugged his shoulders.

"This is different," David said. "Jonah overruled a supervisor. You can't do that."

"Perhaps old age is preventing you from thinking clearly," his wife said.

"Myra…"

"For years you've been telling me how great he is, what a great head for business he has. What a great owner he'll be. Jonah makes one decision you don't like and you push him out?"

"He quit. I didn't push him out. You don't overrule supervisors. They run production for us."

"You do what it takes to get him back," Myra said.

"I've been running this company since we moved to the west coast. I know what I'm doing."

"Until a few years ago you could name all your employees. Largely because of your grandson's effort, you have over three-hundred workers now and I bet you know few, if any, of their names."

"The supervisors know them."

"It's not the same company and from what you tell me, Jonah is better at running it. It's time to let him run the whole thing."

"Myra, he's too young."

"How old were you when you started running the store in Boston?"

"That's different."

"Only in the sense that Jonah is capable of running a much larger firm. You told me...your words...he has a better head for business than you."

"Myra please, I know what you're saying." He leaned forward; momentarily rubbing his face with his hands. "I know."

"David Kaplan. You'll get him back or this will go down in family history as the biggest mistake you've ever made."

"It may be too late."

Chapter Forty-Six: Aaronson's Factory

"Work with old man Aaronson?" Beth asked. "His business is tiny."

Jonah paced up and back in the parlor. "I showed him three contracts. Each one worth more than he's made in the last few years. I explained how we could go to the bank, show the contracts and borrow money to expand."

"Does the bank know you?"

He stopped pacing and flopped into a chair. "Grandfather made sure I learned more about finance than he knows. I'm the one who dealt with the bank during all of his expansion."

"He'll be hurt when he knows you're working for someone else."

"Not working for someone else." He stared at the floor and sighed. "I own half of Aaronson's Wood and Metal Working." He ran his hands through his hair and sighed.

"Why aren't you happy? You own your own business." Beth asked.

"Eventually I'll be a direct competitor of Grandfather."

"What about Bruce Goldman?" Beth asked.

"He comes to work with me tomorrow."

"You should make him a supervisor," Kim said. "See if he listens to the workers and tells you the truth about what's going on."

"An excellent idea, Grandmother." Jonah sighed and shook his head. "I have to admit, I've seen dogs treated better than some employers treat their workers." He stood and began pacing again. "This is going to develop into a huge headache one day and I don't have any idea how to head it off."

***

A few months later on a Saturday morning, Jonah said, "I'm taking the boys to see the woodshop at Aaronson's this morning."

"You said you planned to take them to services," Beth said.

"They've been asking. I have to check on a machine that's giving us problems, so I figured today would be a good time to show them around."

"You keep them close."

"I promise."

***

"This place is loud," Thomas said, having to shout to be heard over the noise of the woodshop's numerous spinning blades which screamed at many discordant pitches as they sliced through all manner of wood.

"Mr. Kaplan," one of the supervisors yelled. "We're having trouble with the same bearings overheating. We may have to shut down to replace them."

"How hot?"

"Can't put my hand on its case and we have to continually oil them. I've got a man over there doing little else."

"Will they last the week?"

"Not sure. It may not."

"Let's take a look."

They approached a steam-powered, spinning, four-foot- diameter, flywheel which put its energy into a twelve-inch-wide belt. The stench of steam and hot oil filled the air. A worker added oil to the drip oiler.

"You boys walk carefully," the supervisor shouted. "These floors are slippery."

"Do we have a replacement?" Jonah asked.

"Yes but the bearings are lasting less than eight days."

"Why?"

"We keep increasing the load on the flywheel."

"What do we need to do?"

"Buy and install bigger and wider bearings to handle the load. We'll also have to lengthen the shaft."

The boys were bored and began poking each other.

"Let's go up to my office," Jonah said, "and get what we need on order."

The adults turned to walk away.

Mark tried to poke his brother but Thomas jumped out of the way. He slipped on the oily floor then put out his left arm to stop his fall. The spinning fly wheel trapped his arm between itself and the belt. In a fraction of a second, the young one's body flew through the air and his arm was ripped off. The injury caused massive blood loss which caused his death within a few seconds.

His younger brother screamed. A sound which was quickly drowned out by the cacophony of the wood processing machinery. Mark grabbed his brother's remaining arm and yelled, "Wake up. Wake up."

A few machine operators saw what happened, shut down their machines, and ran to the scene.

The sudden lack of noise caused Jonah and his supervisors to turn in that direction.

"Where are the kids?" he shouted.

***

Jonah arrived at the house carrying sobbing Mark. Beth sat on the end of a couch, a skein of yarn at her feet and her wood knitting needles clacking as she worked. Kim entered the room with a pot of tea which she placed on a small table between them, sat on a rocker and swayed. She put Monica on her lap.

"What's going on?" Beth asked, seeing Mark's tear streaked face. Mark ran to her, buried his face in her lap and sobbed. She embraced him then glanced up at Jonah.

"What happened?"

"There was an accident," Jonah said.

Kim stopped rocking.

Beth asked, "Where's Thomas?"

Jonah's eye's filled with tears. His jaw quivered. He opened his mouth to speak but no sound came out.

"Jonah," Beth shouted, "answer me. Where's Thomas?"

With drooped shoulders, the tall man cleared his throat and wiped his eyes. "Thomas is at the undertaker's."

"No!" she shouted. "He's your responsibility. Your son. How could you let this happen?"

"It was an accident. I looked away for a second…"

"You promised to watch them. You…"

He moved to her side.

"No!" She pushed him away then dissolved into sobs, burying her face in her hands.

Kim handed Monica to Jonah and sat next to Beth. She put one arm around her and patted Mark with the other.

***

Late that evening, Kim sat on a rocking chair in front of the fireplace wrapped in a shawl and reading a book of poetry. She thought she was the only one awake until Mark walked into the room. Kim looked at him over the tops of her glasses. "You're supposed to be asleep."

"I couldn't."

She motioned him over then pulled him onto her lap. "Why couldn't you sleep?"

"I was thinking my dad is gone, my mom is gone and now Thomas. Will I die next?"

"Not for a long time. You will have a full life, become a father, and a leader of men. And you will be a man who solves other men's problems."

"Like what?"

"I'm not sure but...there are many problems in the factories...the workers will need intelligent spokesmen...you will be one of them."

"How do you know?"

Kim smiled. "My mother told me."

"Didn't you say she was dead?"

"She is…but I still hear her voice."

"I'm afraid to be alone in my room."

"You get back in bed and I'll sit with you."

~~~ The End ~~~

If you enjoyed my novel, please leave a review on the website from which you purchased it. Reviews help Indie Authors like myself to become known to more readers, ranked with book sites, and earn an income. Thank you!

ABOUT THE AUTHOR

Richard is a 101st Airborne Division, Vietnam veteran. Having a lifelong passion for history, a creative mind, and being a mesmerizing storyteller, historical fiction was a natural career choice after a life in software engineering. His love of travel allows him to accumulate research from libraries, museums, and historical sights. Traveling the nation in his RV with his wife Carolynn, Richard is always on the lookout for interesting historical perspective, personal stories, and quirky characters.

ALSO BY RICHARD ALAN SCHWARTZ

(Previously under author's pen-name, Richard Alan)

Have you read them all?

Additional detailed blurbs and purchasing information available on villagedrummerfiction.com/books

THE AMERICAN JOURNEYS NOVELS

THE EMIGRANT
A Journey from Ireland to America

Previously titled American Journeys from Ireland to the United States (1847–1854) Author: Richard Alan

Previously titled American Journeys: From Ireland to the Pacific Northwest (1847–1900) Book 1 Author: Richard Alan

A cruel famine. A fight for survival. Can a voyage across the sea bring new life? After so much death, this young immigrant will do anything to start her new life. If you like courageous heroines, richly-detailed settings, and stories of relentless determination, then you'll love Richard Alan Schwartz's poignant tale.

~ ~ ~

THE PIONEER
A Journey to the Pacific

Previously titled American Journeys: The Pacific Northwest and Oregon Trail (1854 – 1880) Author: Richard Alan

Previously titled American Journeys: From Ireland to the Pacific Northwest (1847–1900) Book 2 Author: Richard Alan

Their dreams carried them this far, but what happens when the next generation doesn't share the same vision? A new generation. A dangerous town. Can an immigrant family make room for new traditions? If you like multi-generational sagas, beautifully-wrought settings, and stories of the human experience, then you'll love Richard Alan Schwartz's rugged tale.

~ ~ ~

THE SURGEON

A Civil War Novel

Previously titled *A Female Doctor in the Civil War*
Author: Richard Alan

Virginia Field Hospital, 1862. Abbey Kaplan will do whatever it takes to become a doctor. As a surgical assistant, her first major test is tolerating her chauvinistic male associates. But when her inaugural posting lands her smack in the middle of a Civil War field hospital, proving herself isn't about pride—it's a matter of life or death. If you like brave heroines, authentic settings, and stories that bring the past to life, then you'll love Richard Alan Schwartz's stunning saga.

Although this book is the 3rd American Journeys Novel, it can easily be read as a stand-alone.

~ ~ ~

THE SOLDIER

A Novel of the Vietnam War Era

Previously titled *Wind Chimes, War and Consequence*
Author: Richard Alan Schwartz

The Soldier is a harrowing book in An American Journeys Novels historical fiction series. If you like gripping combat scenes, exploring the horrors of heroism, and true-to-life depictions of PTSD, then you'll love Vietnam Veteran Richard Alan Schwartz's unforgettable novel.

Although this book is the 4th American Journeys Novel, it can easily be read as a stand-alone.

~ ~ ~

COMING SOON

Richard's next novel portrays Dr. Abbey Kaplan's struggles to develop America's awareness of the cruelty of the early industrial age, the American scrap heap known as mental asylums, and the inability of American women to own property and to vote. The fifth American Journeys Novel will be published Fall of 2020.

Sign up for the Village Drummer Fiction Newsletter (villagedrummerfiction.com/newsletter) to be notified when new books, discounts, and author appearances are available.